# MOSAIC

### BY M.C. RENEE

Cover Design: M.C. CREATIONS

Development Editor: Laurynn Fox

Paperback ISBN: 979-8-9998904-0-5

Published by the Author.

For information, requests, or permissions, contact:

www.authormcrenee.com

"And there she was, a MOSAIC, pieces of art."

# MOSAIC

A Debut Novel written by

## M.C. RENEE

# Author's Note

This is my heart book with a point of view from real and haunting experiences through depression, anxiety, and chronic pain. This book talks about trauma-related panic attacks, visions/nightmares, and dark thoughts; death in the family, feelings of abandonment, and mental health triggers. I want my readers to understand what they will be reading. If any of these things are triggering or upsetting, please consider them before moving forward. Writing this was cathartic through my personal experiences and Mental Health journey, and it's meant to shine a light on our broken pieces and create a masterpiece. My underlying message is that *you are worthy* even when you are carrying the weight of everything. I would encourage anyone on this journey to seek help when you need it and know you are not alone.

Take care of yourself,

With Love,
*Melissa*

*To all the cycle breakers who fought to feel safe.*
*Who worries about not being enough...*
*This book is dedicated to you. I see you.*

# PROLOGUE

I was fractured long before I knew what *whole* felt like. The past took its pound of flesh, the present left me bleeding, and the future closed its eyes. I am nothing but jagged edges and piercing points—too sharp to hold without drawing blood. Every fragment of me screams *worthless*, every shard cries *damaged*. Touching me is to risk being cut open, to be torn apart, and to bleed out alongside a fractured soul.

The casket looked to be made of pure granite, the kind you can see your reflection in. it didn't show my face as much as it fractured it—half shadow, half ghost. Not that I'd want to remind myself of the dark. Unwashed strands stuck to my head as the rain fell with no end in sight. I stared until my features blurred with tears, until I looked like someone else entirely.

Someone already sinking.

She tried. God, she tried to do right by me, by all of us. But you can't pour from an empty cup. She was empty—emptied by her own heartbreak from the present and by generational wounds passed down like heirlooms. And she gave me her fair share of them. The hope with every new generation is to do better than the last. But hope without action is just whispered promises. The cycle keeps weaving its heartache until someone faces the undeniable truth, feels every aching crack, and chooses to end the curse. The suffering.

Whether my mother knew of this or not, her strength wasn't enough, and I learned at an age too young, the heartbreaking truth of promises unfulfilled. Of death, and abandonment, and the darkness that comes as a result. Papa was one of the beautiful things in our lives, in her life. He softened the hard edges until his death stole that light. Mama's light dimmed shortly after.

My little brother Stefan was born during a brutal East Coast storm that haunts me still. A fatal car accident took Papa's life and the lives in the other vehicle that hit him, while he was rushing to the hospital to meet his son. The remaining light that had shone in my mother was forever lost after that harrowing day. I saw the deep crevices of what fear and loss created, some from her mother, and new ones that were a result of her own choices. I saw the shadows lurking around her irises, even when she tried to cover them up with picnics at the beach, playing in the sand, chasing the fleeting waves, all hiding under the perfect mask. A good mask, but one I saw fracture over and over with each punishing day that stole a little more light from her, leaving darkness in its place.

*Crack.*

Too little to know it then, I watched with innocent eyes, taking on her pain little by little so that maybe, just maybe, she could feel relief. A moment to breathe. To break the surface of pain and feel the light's warmth, kiss her face. That light was magic. I loved watching her face light up when she was able to take a full breath of life, even for a brief and fleeting moment. Those moments were bursts of gold, flickering like diamonds in the sand on days that were good. Unfortunately, as time passed, the heaviness grew, as did her pain; her shadows bled out and cut deeper each time... the coldness leaked in, and the silence grew until my own voice became distant and quiet. My body was breaking from the inside, pulling me down in a spiral toward a familiar darkness.

*Crack.*

Life was never the same for my mother, for us. After losing the love of her life, her heart never recovered. I like to believe she held on as long as she could, for me and my siblings. So the day when officials showed up at our shabby apartment—the one my younger sister, baby brother, and I shared with our Mother—I knew. I'll never forget the pity I felt from the officer, like lukewarm sympathy. She had taken her own life five years after Papa's death and was no longer with us.

Our mother's life ended just like that, her soul set free. No more pain. At least not for her. We became orphans in more ways than one.

*Crack.*

We all stood dressed in black several days later, hovering under wide umbrellas, sheltering us from the darkening storm with its endless rain, void of sunshine. Fitting weather to go with the somber mood. I wanted to feel sorry for her, but I couldn't bring myself to. She escaped her pain and was now free. She left us, and she was never coming back. I held my siblings' hands firmly through the ceremony, feeling the weight of responsibility left behind as the dark clouds closed in, dropping the temperature. The cold crept along my legs and her shadows became a heavy burden on my chest...seeping into the cracks, a formidable weight deep within.

I stepped up to the casket before me, the scent of fresh peonies clashing with the bitter taste of finality in the back of my throat. The wood looked too smooth, like it was trying to cover up all the splinters she carried in life. Funny how death makes everything look softer—when nothing about her life ever was.

We were her only shining light after Papa's death. Until that was stolen.

"Can you hear me, Mama?" I whispered, voice thin and uncertain, as they lowered her into the earth. My fingers curled tightly at my sides, aching to reach for what wasn't there. I made promises in that moment—ones I'm not sure I even understood, let alone could keep. But I said them anyway, hoping maybe she'd find a way to hold onto them from wherever she was now.

"I'll try," I choked out, barely audible, my words cracking in the wind. A single tear slipped out before I could stop it. I swore I wouldn't cry—not here. Not in front of them. But grief doesn't listen. It doesn't care how long you've been preparing for the goodbye. It thrashes inside, matching the storm like a ravenous beast.

As the casket was laid in the shadows, a deep feeling stirred within me like a warning. This wasn't just the end of her story—it was the beginning of mine. The part where I'd have to carry what she couldn't. Where her ghosts might finally start to speak, and I'd have no choice but to listen. A tremor slipped beneath my skin, tiny sparks racing down my arms before I could stop them.

"I will fight for a life they deserve. I'll make it right, with everything I have; they won't have to carry our past. I promise." I gave everything I could in that promise that day. That was my responsibility, as the oldest of three, to take the curse on, a curse I wasn't sure I could break or fully know its depth. But I had to try, so that they didn't have to suffer from an emptiness so vast, painful, and a life full of dark secrets.

I was only sixteen.

*Crack.*

I never felt like the hero of my story. I don't wear a cape that blows in the wind, helping me to fly. Instead, I wear invisible scars cloaked in sorrow as deep as the endless ocean, wearing pain as armor. Over time, those scars cracked the exterior, breaking a fragile surface and seeping venom deep within to an empty core.

My life became a haunting path from one tragic relationship to the next. The past kept clawing its way to my present, my thoughts shrouded in the mist of memory, while echoes of my mother's pain linger like ghostly whispers.

Every push to an unbreachable surface left me restless. Any time the pain became unbearable, I locked it away, not realizing that it sat there marinating. Expanding its hold. Until I was sifting through all the shattered pieces it created, and discovered how lost I had become.

Sharp, splintered edges, too cruel to cradle without internal bleeding. They echo, *worthless*. They thunder, *broken*. A warning carved into every fragment. To touch is to be *severed*, to embrace is to *suffer*, and to hold is to *hurt*.

*Crack.*

Careful, the terrain is treacherous, with pitfalls of denial and self-blame lurking around the corner. It's easy to get lost in the labyrinth of your psyche, to become entangled in the webs of self-deception that have been woven in black over the years. And I have believed in the lies for far too long.

Sometimes I wonder if it would be better to cut ties with the world and walk around with a sign saying, *Better off Alone.* That way, no one gets too close and suffers in my orbit. Seeing my mother's heart shatter after Papa's death taught me that the cost of intimacy can be hauntingly elusive and often too high a price to pay. But the flesh craves touch. The heart yearns to feel the warmth of love, so it doesn't stop beating. If only the choice were simple to live in solitude.

Year after year, watching my siblings grow up and chase dreams of their own, I became less and less needed. Those early years were a constant struggle; I gave up a deep passion for painting for parenthood. I continued forward, carrying the responsibilities a young adult shouldn't have to, so my siblings had stability. I didn't know it at the time, but the deepest parts of me suffered. I was a snuffed-out candle, constantly trying to relight and shine, only to have a fierce wind blow me out again. Leaving me in the dark.

Even after all these years, the darkness pulls at me still, calling me under. It has a hold so tight, all I can do is yield to the shadows—the nightmares. I am an empty cocoon, beckoning me deeper...until there is nowhere else to go but down in a free fall to the deep end. Perhaps that's where I belong. Maybe it's not as bad as it looks. Just maybe, I can survive the landing.

*Crack.*

# Chapter One

"You just can't help yourself, can you, Eve?"

I know he's angry. He has every right to be. This is why I should just stay away from people. I seem to inflict pain on anyone in proximity to me. It was only a matter of time before I regretted getting involved in another relationship. I watch as he pulls on his dark-washed jeans after staying over. I should have waited until breakfast to tell him it was over. Coffee, toast, the civilized way. But I didn't. I couldn't.

God, even my rock bottoms find new lows.

Conner has a way of reeling me in with pretty words and frankly ignoring my hesitant nature toward relationships. But he made it too easy, too comfortable as time went on. And I craved connection. Nikki, my best friend, set us up on a blind date after seeing me crash after what's-his-name last year.

My head blurs with the buzz of white noise. Names and faces blend together in this hazy torment of depression. The dark days keep closing in, each one heavier, more suffocating than the last. Just when I thought the bar couldn't sink any lower, it does. Pain has become the only place I belong.

Conner was so easy to talk to, even when I couldn't give him all of me, he made it easy to be with him. Too easy. A needed distraction during the inky black days.

*The candlelight flickered across the table, brushing his face in gold. He reached for my hand, warm fingers brushing over my knuckles like he'd done a hundred times before. I let him hold it, but my eyes dropped to the glass of wine in front of me. The stem twisted between my fingers until condensation dampened my skin.*

*"You're quiet tonight," he said softly. No accusation, just concern.*

*My lips curved faintly, almost a smile, almost an apology. "I'm tired, that's all."*

*It wasn't a lie, not exactly. Just not the truth he wanted. It's for the best.*

I meant to tell him last night, but my body craved his touch one last time, and I selfishly stole another moment. With his pointed stare on me, the warmth of last night is gone. An icy one takes its place. I reluctantly sit up, observing the warm glow of the early morning bathing the cream walls. My body feels heavy, and there is an ache in my chest that presses against my ribcage. I reach for my vintage nightie with the lace that makes me feel feminine, willing the buttery soft fabric to offer comfort for this conversation. I take a deep breath while my feet hover over the cold hardwood floor, then I lightly touch the rough surface. It momentarily cools the burning tension in the room. I let out a long sigh.

Is it normal to feel relief when you let someone go?

I hesitate only for a moment, peeking over my shoulder to where he fills up the doorframe—his stare heating me with shame, waiting for an explanation. I really don't want to give him the excuse, *"it's not you, it's me,"* and yet, it's exactly the speech I'm about to deliver.

"Conner, you deserve more than what I can give you." I lowered my gaze, noticing the morning sun rays peeking through the window in front of me. A beam of warm light crossed my path. A lifeline. My heart pulls and twists as I gingerly wave my fingertips through the dust.

He is one of the good ones. One who would fight for his loved ones, his friends, even me. He does not deserve this. I can see that determination in him now. The one he reserves for associates in the board room, a deal he often wins. My eyes feel too heavy all of a sudden as I take another moment before standing to face him fully. The hard lines on his face tighten as his chest rises and falls with sharp frustration.

That's good. It's easier when they hate me. The resolve I've been waiting for.

It helps them to move on. I don't blame them.

I blame myself.

"I wanted to marry you, Eve," he states, his eyes never leaving mine. I had my suspicions of his plans to take our relationship further, but hearing him say it out loud breaks my heart even more. It never gets easier letting someone go.

"I am not in a place to commit... *long-term*, Conner," I admit, looking at the specs of dust on the floor. *You're too broken, Eve.* I feel like a vessel long emptied. I used to hold light once. Now it slips through the cracks, and I don't even try to catch it.

Crack.

Conner stands firm in front of my bedroom door, his brows drawn together. There's anger in his eyes, shadowed by hurt and disappointment. But what stuns me the most is the loss, lurking around his irises. Beneath it all, I see him piecing it together, the realization of why I've been slipping away these past few weeks. A hollow ache settles in my chest as I force my trembling feet forward, closing the space between us, not to pull him back, but to let him go.

He reaches out, his thumb tracing a circle on my skin, patient. Steady. I want to lean into it, to close my eyes and let the weight of his care press against the hollow spaces inside. But that's what got me here in the first place. So, I pull back my hand and brush the nightgown down perfectly straight, feeling the tremble in my hands. I swallow, throat tight. Words crowd at the edge of my tongue, but none of them make it out.

Not the *"I'm broken,"* nor the *"I don't know how to be loved."*

I look at him. "I will always care for you , Conner. You brought the type of joy into my life when I didn't think any was left. I am thankful for that. Truly." I see fire burning in his eyes; the ferocity in them makes me look away. "But you deserve so much more. A girl who matches your wit and jumps in with both feet. I want that for you." Even if he refuses to hear me, I hope for his sake, he understands my plea.

"Don't tell me what I should want," he fires back before he turns and walks away. The smile from last night, like I was worth waiting for, is gone. I deserve that.

I watch as he pulls his soft white button-down over his arms from last night's dinner with a little wine stain on it when he spilled from laughing too hard. I really should have let him go last night, but my selfishness wanted his breath on my skin one last time. His warmth embracing my cold.

I have to stop. No more relationships for me. I refuse to drag another person through this pain and suffering again. He turns back to face me, my feet shifting while I hug my trembling body, bracing for impact.

I want to look away. His eyes, almost liquid amber, show a different kind of heat that I am not used to seeing on him, especially when they are imploring me, begging for truth. It hurts because he is hurting. I look down, afraid I might shatter in front of him if I don't.

He gestures wildly in the air between us. "I don't understand how you could throw all of this, all of us, away, just like that. Like it's nothing to keep pursuing!"

I wince, shifting my eyes toward the bay window before returning my gaze to him.

He presses further in that heated but calm, determined voice of his, the one that pulled along longer than I care to admit. As time went on, it was just easier to go through the motions instead of creating more cracks in the already fragile shell of mine.

"Eve, I need you to explain how you can go from sharing this connection and then ending what we could have continued to build together? How do you just turn that off? How can you just walk away? Seriously, what am I not seeing?"

His demand is a surprise, while his confusion stiffens my spine, but it also chips away at the carefully polished facade I cling to. Inside, my stomach twists and tightens, coiling into knots. All I can do is stare at my hands, chipping at my nails like a little girl in trouble. Frozen. No one ever comes close to exposing my deepest fear.

I don't allow them to.

Except this time, I became too comfortable in the safety of his arms. The cost of intimacy. It unveils and reveals what is really underneath the surface, and I let it go on for far too long with Conner. I let myself hope, and he is suffering because of my recklessness.

My shadows bled out once again. Those sharp jagged edges of broken pieces revealed themselves yet again. Hurting those I care about. I really need to keep them hidden better. It always comes back to me. I never seem to learn. I chase companionship like a drug, knowing it will only end in ruin. I've learned it's safer, kinder, if I walk alone.

With a deep breath, I push forward.

"Conner, I'm sorry. Please understand." I look up, meeting his fiery stare, my stomach roiling viciously now. "I...just can't. I need you to know that yes, while I care for you, I am not right for you." My voice shakes. I am not even right for me... but I don't say that. "You have to go. It may not feel like it now, but this is for the best."

*Crack.*

I held his gaze. A heaviness fills the room like a thick cloud as he fixes his eyes to the window, creating a silence that is deafening. Suffocating. So this is the Conner most people see in the courtroom. I can see why he wins most of his cases. But not this one.

It's too much. I close my eyes, feeling an unbearable weight on my chest.

*For you. I am doing this for you.*

Please, please understand. His pain cuts and slices at my resolve, but I hold firm. I have to.

I don't want to drag another person down on this sinking ship.

*Please, just go.*

I silently bet him to just walk away. With finality in my decision, I take the final steps to the front door, needing to escape this turmoil, each step heavy with the weight of my decision. I grasp the worn, splintering handle. The door groans in protest as I ease it open, revealing the dim stairwell beyond. For a moment, I linger, pressing my cheek to the cold edge, my gaze flicking over my shoulder. He needs to know there's no going back to us. No hope for a future. I want the realization to carve into me like a blade so I won't forget what this feels like and close off his admiration for me once and for all.

"Don't come looking for me, Conner." He snaps his head toward me, a deep frown etched into his forehead. I lower my gaze. "I wish you the best. Truly. I hope you can forgive me someday. But it's okay if you don't." The last words barely escape in a whisper, more for me than for him.

There's a faint shuffle before the air shifts. The hairs on the back of my neck rise as he moves past me. There's nothing for him to gather. No shared life, no pieces of me to take. I made sure of that. Another brick in the wall, carefully constructed with the words KEEP OUT carved deep.

*Crack.*

I feel the heat of his palm pressed to my lower back, my eyes close for a brief moment, relishing in his touch. I keep as still as I can, careful not to give away my trembling resolve, waiting to crumble. I force myself to stand firm against the darkness that's emerging like an abandoned ship on a tumultuous tidal wave.

My throat ached with everything I couldn't say. His faded cologne hits me a second before his lips caress my temple. He pulls me close, the warmth of his embrace seeping into the cold cracks. *No, no, no...*

"Can I convince you to reconsider? Please, Eve, don't do this to me. To us." He pleads one last time. "I am willing to give you space. I want to be here for you. We can be great together." There was a tremor in his tone, quiet but breaking. "You don't have to do this alone." Every swallow felt like sandpaper with his confession. If I inched a little closer, I could probably feel his heartbeat. Was it racing like mine? He has to know now, it's over. A choice I have robbed him of.

*Crack.*

I've spent so many years trying to stuff this pain down, to raise my siblings through every obstacle we faced, through sickness and grief. To hide the pain from them. I felt like I did good, tried to be. But you can only lock away so much before it splits deeper, giving these cracks depth. They are cutting deeper every day, and I don't know how to stop them. No like before. But the weight is too much. I fear one day, they will consume me whole. Cast me down into an unyielding abyss.

*Crack. I'll never reach whatever "enough" is supposed to be.*

*Crack. I'm sinking under it.*

*Crack. The ache runs deep—too deep.*

"I'm sorry," I whisper, the words barely scraping past my lips. They feel hollow, meaningless against the weight pressing down on my chest. My shoulders sag, drained of whatever fight was left in me. He was one of the good ones—maybe the last—and now he's just another ghost I'll carry.

With a final, silent goodbye, I watch the sway of his white shirt as he moves toward the stairs, his steps slow, heavy with the weight of unspoken words. He glances back once, and in his eyes I see it, the quiet collapse, the resignation. Then he's gone. I drop the door's handle, feeling its weight drag shut, closing out another person from my life like it has become second nature.

*Crack.*

# Chapter Two

After rotting in bed and letting most of the day slip by, I try to quiet the racing thoughts that send my heart into a frenzy, pounding in my ears. When that proves impossible, I get up and brew a pot of coffee. A small act of self-care before facing what comes next. It doesn't matter what time of the day it is; coffee should always come first, a steady ritual in the ever-unfolding journey of adulthood.

Ignoring my phone's messages as well as reality, I make my way into the living area and turn toward the bay window of the old Brownstone building I'm in. Not the fancy ones Boston is known for, but one that hasn't been upgraded yet. With rent climbing year after year, I'm sure it's only a matter of time. I pull the fuzzy green sweater over my medium-sized frame and turn the heat up a little. Not too much, that electric bill likes to hike up as my bank account drops.

I wonder if my boss would allow me to work overtime for a few months over winter to help recover the cost after my trip to Italy for my sister's wedding. I'll ask her on Monday at the gallery.

Suddenly, Arlo, my Siamese cat, makes himself known, purring around my legs and swishing his tail back and forth. A quiet comfort, solidarity after the heartbreak I just experienced. That, or he just wants food. Either way, I'd better get used to him being the only man in my life.

"Hey buddy, what are you up to?" I reach down, scratching his favorite spot behind his ears. Not too much, though. His independence demands that he not be touched unless he requests it. A meowed response is all the confirmation I need.

After feeding him, he turns away, opting for an old antique chair with a lovely textured sage cushion. A great find from a flea market, methodically placed in front of the bay window, of course. I can't help but smile at his comfort.

"At least one of us is living life with ease," I smirk as he twirls in place several times before settling on the perfect spot with that High Lord attitude of his.

I look out the window where deep, rich golden rays replace the soft glow from this morning, casting beams over the carpet and cutting through the shadows in the room. I reach out to the sliver of sunlight, the last warmth of the day a welcome caress. I imagine what sunlight would sound like as my fingers move gingerly through the dust motes in the air, playing with the strings of light that shine through despite the interruption. What tune would light dance to? A light-hearted soft percussion perhaps, or possibly a beautifully carved harp flitting in perfect harmony?

My eyes drift from one beam to the next in wonder.

My fingers itch to paint this scene. To mix yellow, golds, and oranges to create the perfect hue. I'd also have to use blacks to capture the shadows. Without black, there would be no depth. But those paints and canvases sit locked away with the rest of the painful memories. For now, observing will have to do.

Waking up with the light soothes parts of me, chasing some of the dark shadows that beckon and whisper, lulling me into a false sense of security. Making false promises and holding dark secrets. More times than I can count, those shadows are starting to make sense. A cold shiver prickles up my spine as I shake my head in an attempt to clear the dark thoughts. I wrap my sweater tighter around me.

The coffee machine dings in the small kitchen, bringing my mind out of the dark haze. The deep, rich, and nutty aroma tickles my nose, moving my feet and my soul to begin the day, even though it's the evening now. I mix hazelnut creamer with the rich coffee in my favorite ceramic cup and take a sip. So good. A smile plays on my face as I sink into the vintage hunter-green velvet wingback chair across from Arlo.

Simple. Elegant. Peaceful.

This beauty caught my eye at a rare flea market event, where I purchased most of my household items. They have the best selection and quality for the price. I was invited to attend a private showcase and saw her amongst several pieces of vintage furniture throughout the centuries, making it impossible to choose just one. Especially when it was cozied up next to an 1800s Century Green Velvet Parlor American-styled chair. I left it behind because I simply couldn't afford it. I dream about it, though.

A small smile lifts my face as I gaze around my apartment, feeling nostalgic, my thoughts drift to the first day I moved in four years ago. Running around with my younger sister Gi to the best flea markets and shops scattered around the city of Boston. So many markets to choose from make for a unique shopping experience. Antique Markets are my personal favorite, so many options to drool over. Getting there early is a must for the best deals. With my love for antiques and furniture, I could have been an interior designer, but art and art history won me over in the end.

I could have pursued a Master's degree in Art History, but my siblings needed me and I wanted to put them first. Then, as time passed, it just became harder to try and manage my responsibilities with low finances. I let that dream go. It was for the best. I love my job now and my one-bedroom apartment may feel small at times, but its historic charm and calming atmosphere make it special. Securing it was a battle. With rent climbing, I worry about being able to stay here in Boston.

I take another sip of coffee, curling my fingers around the warmth of the mug. Evenings are where the magic happens—the sunset painting on the buildings, leaving deep golden-red hues over the brick. A splash of rich color before it all fades to black and the city's nightlife shines. I peek out over the street below, watching tenants and visitors alike, roaming about, hurriedly checking off their task lists for the weekend.

One more week until I fly out to meet my sister and her fiancé, Josh, in Italy. It's the place of our heritage and somewhere I have always dreamed of exploring. Ever since Papa shared his stories and landscapes of his birth, I've been transfixed.

As a little girl, Papa talked about our Italian history and culture. We would visit the Museum of Fine Art, spending the day exploring every open wing. I marveled at dozens of stunning portraits by Italian masters and stood in awe before carefully crafted sculptures, leaving me breathless. Every piece told a story, pulling me deeper into the magic of Italian art.

I begged him to take us back to Italy someday. He always expressed his excitement about showing us kids and Mama the place of our ancestors. The last time he was able to visit was a funeral for his Uncle Dario after a rock climbing accident. Makes me nervous for my younger brother Stefan when he is out on his expeditions and adventures.

In those early years of wonder, I would imagine exploring Italian museums while playing tour guide through each of the historic land-marks that sparked the Italian Renaissance. Of course, I had no idea the significance of that time period. Not until college, when I dove deeper into my studies, wild with the urge to learn more. It unraveled a yearning to learn from the best.

I wish I'd said yes when it still meant something—before the silence between then and now grew into a canyon I could no longer cross. Each year stretched the distance a little farther, until the thing I once reached for with both hands became a void I could only remember in fragments. Dreams have a way of rotting quietly. You don't notice the decay until you try to hold them, and they crumble in your hands.

My home is my safe haven. I value the oddity of foreign objects but need the comfort of minimalism to keep a balance. Everything has a special place of uniformity and complexity that art brings. Multi-sized vintage frames painted off-white with splashes of muted gold decorate the dark green walls, each holding a different portrait of historical women with their own stories. Their unique secrets.

I take another sip of my coffee—the nutty hazelnut flavor and sweet vanilla making a perfect combo—before setting it down on a table full of unopened envelopes. I'll open them tomorrow. I don't have the energy to see another bill. I glance at a sleeping Arlo, my fluffy cuddle bug and companion. I'm so glad I let my sister convince me to adopt him. She was concerned for me being mostly alone after she moved in with Josh, the love of her life.

She worries for me far too much.

Naturally, as an introvert, I don't see the problem with being alone. Mostly. While some people have a hard time being stuck alone, the silence in the room never bothered me. It settles the parts in me that long for peace in the chaos caused by the world around me. Here in my home, I don't have to fake a smile or be in my head rethinking what I said or dwelling on why conversations didn't turn out the way I wanted, keeping me restless and agitated. The noise of everyday life is loud, and I find myself programming my responses to other people's comfort levels.

When alone, I am free to be me.

I drift toward the narrow doorway of my bedroom, lit up by golden hues. My gaze settles on the framed portrait of Ophelia on the wall—an eerie, surreal rendition I'd acquired at an art show months ago. The colors bleed like a fevered dream, her wide, glassy eyes eternally suspended between serenity and despair.

Ophelia's story was one of pain and turmoil, so naturally, I was drawn into the tragedy. I can't help but wonder what haunted Shakespeare's mind as he breathed life into her tragic fate. If Ophelia had been real, what ghostly thoughts would have flickered through her mind in those final moments, as the cold water crept over her porcelain skin?

Did she watch the world blur above her, her lips barely breaking the surface before surrendering to the depths below?

Did the weight of life press heavily on her as mine does? Did it cause a relentless storm that battered her fragile heart, too? Did she ache to be cherished, or did she wish love never found her at all? Love. Cruel and fleeting. Or when it slipped through her fingers like water, leaving only the sting of abandonment, did she regret it?

Or are we all just fated for tragedy? The burdens of adulthood are enough to drive anyone to the brink. Add love to the mix, and it becomes a tangled web of expectations and heartbreak. I wish it could be a sanctuary. But that's only in fairytales.

I love my brother and sister and care about them deeply, but trying to protect them and shield their innocence cost me my own. I was faced with the obligations that belonged to my parents. It felt suffocating and cruel at times. A childhood I can never get back. Through the years,

I have learned to hold others at arm's length while keeping the silent promise to my mother.

Now that my siblings have grown up and have lives of their own, they don't need me as often. I did what I needed to do. I prefer people not to need me. I've collected too many shadows along the way; it's exhausting.

Was it love that finally unraveled Ophelia, or was it just madness? Perhaps they are one and the same. No wonder she sank beneath the weight of it all. But did she choose death, or did death choose her?

Turning away from the painting, I step into the small bathroom. The claw-foot tub looks inviting and adds to the charm of this place, but I opt for a quick shower to wash away the day's rot and the many questions I ask myself. They unravel in my mind, becoming the daily white noise I can't get away from. Mostly, I shove them into a box marked 'for later', fearing the day when "later" becomes "present."

The lingering agony of past choices makes way for the sorrow of tomorrow's consequences. It's easy to blame myself. For the silences. For the endings. For the way I've drifted from one person to the next like tides pulling back from shore.

Maybe I was never meant to settle.

Maybe I was only meant to be haunted.

# Chapter Three

Sitting up against the soft headboard of my bed, I cradle my phone in unsteady hands, mentally preparing to face a flood of messages from Nikki over the hours since Conner left. I wrap the towel tighter around my body, securing the soft fabric. I can't believe he only left this morning, when it feels like days. I glance at the clock and wince, it's already eight o'clock at night. The day bled out in front of me, and I did nothing but sit with the ache.

The first text comes through from my best friend, Nikki, followed by several others from her—fired ten minutes apart. I tilt my head back, exhaling through my nose. Nikki has known me the longest; she is as close to a close friend as I will allow. Not that she's given me much choice. She loves pushing herself into my life and thinks she has power over me, and maybe she does. But I will never tell her that. That ego of hers would explode.

*Nikki: Damn girl, I really thought Conner could've been "the one," seeing as he's been pining for you for months. It took him all of one hour to message me. Want to talk?*

*Nikki: Okay, I should have known better than for you to have your phone on or in another dimension entirely from where you are. I get it. Call me if you need me.*

*Nikki: Blink three times if you have been abducted. Once, if you need me.*

A strangled laugh leaves me. Her humor is infectious and has a way of neutralizing tension. Okay, maybe she does have a little power over me after all. I give a small shake of my head. I love her for not judging me about Conner or anything else, really. She understands me and my solitary ways, but she also likes to challenge me.

Thankfully, now is not one of those times.

*Nikki: If I don't hear from you, I WILL be abducting YOU. Text me if you are alive.*

I swipe out of her messages and open the unread one from my sister Gianna. I take a deep breath again, because I love her, but Gi in wedding mode is a LOT to handle.

*Gi: Josh and I just landed here in Florence. I can't believe this is happening. ITALY Eve! Ahhhhh!"* Her voice is lound in my ear. *"I can't wait for you to see this place and be here with me! Also, have you heard from Stefan? I know he was still somewhere out of cell range a few days ago, but I wasn't sure if he was stateside yet. Let me know if you hear from him first.*

Stefan is on another one of his adventures, living his dream job. He works for an outdoor magazine, focusing on most recreational sports. He is sponsored for everything. I am so proud. He comes back from Canada the same day we fly out to Italy; it's a time crunch, but he's used to having a tight schedule. I wouldn't be surprised if he had on his wedding attire underneath his outdoor gear. The plan is to meet at the airport if he is running behind.

I swipe away a water droplet from my collarbone as Arlo jumps on the bed, decidedly getting comfortable on my legs. Great, now I'm immobile. I look at my phone to finish Gi's message so I can get dressed.

*Gi: I will be calling you tomorrow to check in, and you better answer my call this time, sis! Don't ignore me. I love you. Talk soon! Ciao! Xo.*

A small smile spreads over my face. I am truly happy for my sister; she deserves her happily ever after. I glance down at her message once more, just as it suddenly buzzes in my hand, making me jump. Arlo too. He moves to the other side, sulking from the disruption. My smile falters when Nikki's name flashes across the screen. Air slips from my lips in surrender.

"Finally! I thought I was going to have to send in the Search and Rescue team, Eve! A text would have been enough, girl!" Nikki's voice bursts against my ear, too close.

"I wasn't sure I had to check in with you every day. Would you believe me if I said I was just about to text you?" I resist the urge to roll my eyes, not fully prepared for this conversation. If it weren't for Nikki, I would likely live the hermit lifestyle.

"I love that you think that, but I know better. Are you covered in cat hair yet? Add any more cats lately? Because that is your future, if you don't stop convincing yourself you're better off alone."

I drop my head back with a low groan, too drained to admit she's probably right. "Can I at least have a few days of self-loathing? And Arlo is awesome, but I doubt he'd enjoy sharing his kingdom with roommates. He's a dictator with fur."

"Haha, very funny. Besides, that's something he and I have in common. Without the fur part. Now that I have you on the phone, get ready. We are going out tonight."

"No. I am not going anywhere tonight," I say with as much certainty as I can muster.

"Yes, you are," Nikki demands, leaving no room for arguing.

"Nikki, I can't. I'm in no mood to even try to be a functional human being right now. I won't survive the night." Is it a bit dramatic? Probably.

But she won't leave me be otherwise. It's my best shot at staying home and watching reruns of Grey's Anatomy.

"You would be surprised at how well Mr. Jack and Coke can motivate and uplift in your time of need."

I chuckle at her bluntness, silently wishing I had just ignored her damn call. But her determination knows no bounds. I know there's no escaping this, no matter how hard I try. That's Nikki for you; she never lets me sink too deep into sorrow. Even though right now, I wouldn't mind being swallowed whole.

"It's late, and I just want to go back to bed and forget about everything for one more day. You should have seen his face, Nikki. I am the worst person." The thought of his reaction drags at me, the ground giving way down a hole I can't seem to stop falling through.

Nikki's heavy sigh is a weight I am often confronted with. "Girl, I know you cared about Conner. You'd be crazy not to. Well, maybe you are, but that's beside the point. You can't keep blaming yourself for everything that goes wrong. You need to get out of this funk. I'm coming to get you, whether you like it or not. There's a music pop-up for a new artist I'm managing their socials for. You could use the distraction, and I could use a plus one. Let me sweep you away from your misery before you leave me for some Italian hunk when you leave next week. PLEASE?!" She gives her famous, dramatic, almost childlike plea, layering on the desperation until it's impossible to say no.

Damn. She is relentless. Why am I friends with her again? I suppress a laugh.

"Oh, Nikki. I can't shake the feeling that something bad is coming. Something I won't be able to recover from. And as for love? Not a chance. I'm officially banning guys from my life and focusing on what actually matters."

"Like making your bestie happy and dancing with me tonight? I'll buy all the drinks."

"You really won't leave me alone tonight, will you?" I ask in defeat.

"Aw, you know me too well. I'll pick you up in an hour. Be ready. Okay byyye!"

I end the call and reluctantly get up to pull off some kind of miracle so I don't look like an extra from *The Walking Dead*. Thirty agonizing minutes later, a pair of skinny jeans and one of my fancier black loose-fitting blouses later, I feel less likely to fall into the *pits of despair*. Another great movie.

I'm pulling on my ankle boots when I hear the doorbell ring. Leaving my naturally loose chestnut curls flowing down my back, I head to the door for tonight's death sentence.

Help me now.

# Chapter Four

True to Nikki fashion, she arrives exactly fifty-nine minutes later, looking one hundred percent like the redheaded spitfire she is. She is such a heartbreaker, welcoming drama into her life and owning it. Her family comes from old money, but she is determined to support herself fully with her career as a "Social Media Countess," as I like to call her. Her success is astounding and matches her tenacious spirit.

She loves being in the spotlight—the very opposite of me.

Perhaps that's why I am drawn to her. Truly fascinated by her. While I wear simple, comfortable styles, she shines and sparkles in a black mini skirt paired with a deep green sequined top and thigh boots. Her tight red curls bounce around as she gestures wildly at me through the window to hurry up. I reach for my purse, pausing halfway like maybe if I wait long enough, she might just give up on me. Then I remember who the fuck she is and head out the door to the whirlwind that awaits me.

I can't believe I let her persuade me so easily.

I briefly take a deep breath of the cool night air before Nikki's knowing eyes flicker at me like it took half an hour instead of four minutes to get outside. As if I would try to delay her any more than I already have. Mostly, she consumes anything nearby like a hurricane when she's on a quest to have fun and get work done simultaneously. One of the greatest multitaskers I have witnessed.

"Let's go, girl! The party doesn't start unless I'm there to get things moving! The Twins have been extra cranky this week about opening night. Honestly, D.J.s are the biggest Divas. We have to arrive at the venue early to make sure the catering delivers top-notch goods in all their glorious aphrodisiac display. Oh, and you look AMAZING, Eve! Proud of you for making the effort."

I swear she doesn't even breathe between sentences.

I run a few fingers through my loose curls, only to get them tangled in the mass. Maybe I should have worn it up. "What club is this again?" I ask as we head out of the building to a town car.

Even though Nikki hates using her parents' money, she hates driving in the city even more. She gladly calls for a town car to avoid any "unnecessary conflicts" or "distractions," leaving more time to check things off her list. She constantly works on several social media accounts whenever she has the opportunity and needs the extra time in between locations to maximize her efficiency.

I bite down a groan. My socials have been silent for months—Arlo, food, bits of art, the same landscapes cycling through the seasons. A quiet archive of everything that stayed still. Maybe Italy will stir a fresh outlook. Maybe I'll remember what it feels like to share beauty again.

We climb into the car and set off toward whatever crazy club Nikki is into at the moment. She still hasn't responded, so I ask again.

"Nikki, what club are we heading to tonight?" I don't want to stay out too late."

She doesn't even look up from her phone. I roll my eyes. I know it's her job, but damn, it's annoying sometimes. I wave my hands in front of her. "Nikki," I repeat a little more forcefully and continue to stare at her.

"Oh, it's a vacant venue called *Ephemera* that allows pop-up shows for up-and-coming artists. A showcase, if you will. The Twins wanted an intimate space with a touch of mystery to play their new Melodic Techno album. The club specializes in creating intimate settings with just enough people to make a great crowd without being too much. It's brilliant, actually. A place that's always evolving to stay relevant."

I arch a brow at her. "You say 'The Twins' like I'm supposed to know who they are."

She looks up fast, her brows drawing together. "Seriously? What rock have you been hiding under? Wait, don't answer that. I already know." She barely holds in a smirk.

"What? I'm just not familiar with the music scene like you."

"Or any current scene for that matter," she mumbles to herself. "You really need to get out of those musty museums and ancient artwork and join people your own age once in a while."

Well, they're my sanctuary, so I won't be giving them up. Not if I ever want a future as an Art Curator." A muted dream I'd considered and then shoved into the "unknown folder."

Nikki's face lights up as she remembers what I told her a few months ago. "Oh, have you finally sent in your application letter for the Master's program of Fine Arts?" she asks, with a glint in her eyes.

"No," I say, shooting myself in the foot for saying something. I won't hear the end of it now. "I said I was thinking about it, not that I was actually going to do it. It's fine. Really. Just drop it."

"You're impossible," she says, her voice soft but sharp. "What's holding you back?"

I hesitate. Not sure I want her to know the truth or the dark thoughts that haunt me daily. "Registering for the program is only the first step to even being considered. The second part is submitting an original art piece that represents my artistic style."

Nikki shrugs her shoulders. "So? I still don't see a problem."

"Nikki, I haven't touched a paintbrush in over five years. Working long hours, I haven't felt the urge to create anything or have the energy to start anew. I feel like a black hole," I stare her down until she laughs. "That's not funny."

"It kind of is. That's quite the imagery you've got going on," Nikki states like the true friend she is.

I plaster on the cheesiest smile. "That's my specialty."

We both burst out laughing. She really is a bright spotlight on a stormy day. I'm thankful she hasn't dropped me as a friend. Even after long periods of time, we can pick up our friendship wherever we left off without worry of being too absent. Me more than her.

"And besides, the program is in Italy. I would have to move my life over there and I'm not sure I am ready for that. It'd be a huge change." I toy with the edge of my sleeve, and my eyes turned away.

"Italy would be a great place to study. You should at least consider it," Nikki says, already shifting her focus to her phone. She is always trying to get me to try new things.

I met Nikki at a fundraiser event for a unique museum here in Boston, a few years back. It was designed by a woman, and her love for Italian art after her husband's death in the late 1800s. Nikki was there for the marketing, I was there for the art. The widow played a very active role in its construction until it matched her creative vision. Together, they traveled all over Europe, falling in love with Italy most of all. They bought decorated art pieces, collecting a variety of artifacts and tapestries that adorn the halls today, and their Italian-inspired Museum features a beautiful open courtyard.

Combining her love of botany and art.

My two favorite things.

While she passed long ago, wealthy in many ways that had nothing to do with money, her museum still lives on today. It reflects her passion while inspiring many artists and tourists alike. A little piece of the Italian Renaissance is expressed in the building and a carefully cultivated garden in the courtyard itself.

A smile lifts my face as I watch tiny water droplets catch multicolored lights as we pass the city skyscrapers. Wouldn't that be something? Building a lasting legacy full of artistry and positive impact.

"We're here!" Nikki sings-songs as the car slows to a stop in front of an imposing building that feels more business like than an exclusive club. I straighten my spine out of habit, as if good posture could disguise my unease. We walk through the revolving doors of a grand lobby before climbing up a large set of stairs. I follow Nikki into the elevator, taking us up to the top floor.

I rub my thumb and index finger together, bracing for what's on the other side of the doors. This should be fun. I fight the urge to stay in the elevator as Nikki pushes through the glass doors, opening to the thumping of deep bass and flashing lights.

I look longingly at the elevator button, then back at Nikki. "Don't even think about it, Eve. It's not going to be that bad. Trust me," she says as she grabs my wrist, pulling me into the fray of bodies and endless chatter. Already exhausted, I'm regretting answering Nikki's call. I should have just let it go to voicemail.

"Let's get this party started!" Nikki shouts, swaying her hips and fighting through a throng of people. I look back at the elevator doors just as they shut behind me, closing my escape route. I let out a frustrated breath and pushed forward.

Here goes nothing.

After mingling with random people and countless introductions, I spot a free booth in a darkened corner with a table and slip away. Hopefully, I can go unnoticed for a while as Nikki does her thing. Now that I'm not dodging bodies, I can finally breathe.

I sit on the plush cushion and take in the vivid blue lights swirling over blurred bodies with indigo hues throughout the venue. White running lights above and below weave around the dance floor, all leading lines drawing your eyes to the raised platform where the DJ is bound to perform. The "Twins," I imagine. All the booths are off to the side and up against the wall, creating intimate spaces for personal conversations.

Large vertical screens grace every other wall, showcasing moving abstract art with wired figures. It's mesmerizing but not the art I'm usually drawn to. It moves with the music track, which I suppose is entertaining for the crowd here tonight.

I gaze across the sea of people, some moving to the music's rhythm, others singing and laughing. I glance toward the elevator doors, counting the minutes down until I can go home. As if summoned, Nikki sways her hips toward me with what looks like shots of regret for the next few days. So much for going unnoticed.

"Bottoms up!" She places four shots of clear liquid with a little pink swirl of something fruity, I'm sure, in front of us and sits next to me. That could only mean one thing: it's one of her "special" shots that will most likely give me a massive headache tomorrow. I swallow a groan as I down the sugary drink after clinking cheers, and the next hour becomes a bit of a blur.

A small reprieve.

The bass thrummed through the floor, vibrating up my legs like a heartbeat. Lights strobed across the room—violet, crimson, gold—painting strangers in halos. For a brief moment, I lose myself in it and let the music drown everything else. I lost Nikki in the throng of bodies after she handed me another shot. Her larger-than-life laughter carries in the air, making it feel like she's right next to me. I love her for that.

The music changes into a more sultry and slow rhythm, the energy shifting like the ocean's tide. Two hands come around my hips, squeezing gently, while a warm body moves me in tune with the music. My heart skips a beat, surprised by hands that aren't Conner's. My mind is hazy, but it feels good to be pressed against him. Whoever he is.

"You feel so good, beautiful," he says, his voice deep and rough in my ear. The sound jarring me out of my haze. He presses into me more. I sway with him, not responding. I don't know how to feel right now, so I just keep moving. But something doesn't feel right.

*Pretend harder.*

My stomach tightens as he moves a hand across my middle. I flinch and step away.

"I need air," I say to him, and walk away. A brush of fingers grazes my arm, making me jump. I jerk my arm to myself—just someone passing by. The floor seems to tilt.

*You don't belong here.*

I stumble toward the bar, blinking through the haze of motion and blinding lights, trying to breathe through the noise. The crowd pulses around me, and the bodies look like ghosts.

"Water," I whisper to the bartender, barely letting him set it in front of me before I grab it with both hands and gulp it down in one go.

"You okay?" he asks, concern written on his face.

"I'm fine, just needed hydration. Thanks."

*They're watching.*

My hands tremble against the countertop, nails digging into the varnish. Then someone laughs—too close to my ear. I whip my head to the sound, but no one is there, the movement making my head spin while flashes of light shine in my eyes. I close my eyes, look down, and count. Sweat beading at my forehead.

One, two, three—breathe. But even that rhythm seems to betray me.

I look up into the crowd only to see everyone looking at me through a distorted lens, shattering my fragile hold. My pulse races as I shut my eyes once again.

*They see you falling apart.*

The heaviness of sweat and alcohol fills the room to a suffocating point. I need to leave. My clothes feel too much, clinging to my damp skin. The laughter around me fractures into sharp edges, too loud.

My pulse quickens, too fast against my ribs. With wide, frantic eyes, I search for Nikki in the chaos. I try to find her fiery hair and green sequins, but my eyes blur against the mass of bodies and blinding lights. Together, creating a distorted painting.

Just then, the song changes.

A softer and slower beat, almost tender. The air thickens, suffocating in its sweetness. Peonies. I turn to find the direction of the elevator when I see *her.*

The girl from my nightmares.

The crowd moves like a tide around her, swaying bodies blurring into color and light.

I press a hand to my chest, chanting over and over.

*You're fine. You're fine.*

Trying to convince myself I'm not going crazy. I close and open my eyes only to find her still in the middle of the dance floor, beneath the strobing lights.

Barefoot. Soaked to the bone.

Water pooled beneath her feet, rippling outward, though no one seemed to notice. Her white dress clung to her thin frame, translucent and trembling.

The music warped and muffled—as if I was underwater.

The girl lifts her head. Pale skin, hollowed eyes. Her lips were moving, but no sound came out. Only the faint drip of water hitting the floor.

Drip.

Drip.

Drip.

My breath hitches. "No," I whisper to no one. "You're not real."

But the girl only tilts her head, the way a reflection bends in rippling water. There's an ominous feeling about her, a terrifying familiarity. That tilt. That look of apology. Like she was the one who had done something wrong.

A flash of memory slices through me: the smell of rain on asphalt. The sound of my mother crying behind a locked door. My own voice, small and shaking, asking if it was my fault—pleading with my mother to hold me.

But she didn't.

She couldn't.

I blinked hard, but the image stayed.

Now the girl was closer, dipping puddles as she walked forward. The crowd danced through her, unaware, like she was only fog and shadow. The lights flickered with every step.

"Go away," I hissed, backing into the edge of the crowd. My throat burned. My heart ached with a pain I couldn't name but felt a lot like grief. Fear. Recognizing this feeling all too well.

The girl stops an arm's length away while I stay frozen in place. The tightness in my chest intensifies. I feel trapped in a nightmare of my own making. I can't escape it.

She looks at me with such sadness. Her eyes—gray and endless—meet mine. And for a moment, everything else falls silent.

The music. The lights. The crowd.

Just me and the girl.

And in the silence, the child whispers one word—soft, broken, and soaked in sorrow.

"Why?"

# Chapter Five

I stagger backward, my pulse roaring in my ears. The little girl's question echoes through my head—*Why?* It splinters deep inside me.

My shoe catches on a man's foot. "Sorry," I say as I claw my way to an exit. White spots dance in my vision as the beat of the music intensifies alongside the frantic beating of my heart, sounding close and yet far away. Shoulder against shoulder, through the crush of dancers and the bass, every brush of skin feels like fire. Every burst of laughter is like a knife slicing through my mind.

The floor tilts beneath me as I push through the crowd, the smell of sweat and perfume curdling in my stomach.

*Why?*

It follows me, that small, trembling voice. The one I'd spent years burying under caring for my siblings, trying to be strong for them. The one I'd stopped painting for because it brought up too many painful memories.

My vision fractures—flashes of my mother's face, mascara streaking like ink down her cheeks after my father's death.

*Why couldn't you have stayed?*

I stumble out into the hallway, finding the elevator door. I push the down button and painfully wait for them to open. My breaths come in pants now, rising, growing more frantic and uneven. When the elevator dings, I rush inside, the bass fading to a dull heartbeat behind the walls.

As soon as the doors open, I abruptly push through a waiting couple and leap out into the night air.

Outside, the air is wet and cold, brutal rain pouring from the storm.

I look up at the dark sky, letting the rain wash over my shaking body and ground me. People pass me by in slow motion, but I don't move. It feels like the world is spinning and I can't do anything to stop it. The storm inside unleashes, matching the storm swirling around me. It feels like my heart might just implode while visions flood my mind.

I press my back to the brick wall of the building, sliding down until the pavement catches me. Streaks of color and memory make me feel lightheaded. My hair clings to my damp face as I try to breathe, but every inhale brings more of the past rushing in.

My father's death—quick, crushing the air from that hospital room. My mother's heartbreak—slow, relentless, like a wound that refuses to close. We lost both of them that night. When Stefan was taking his first breath, Papa was taking his last.

I wrap my arms around myself as the tears fall down my face. The same way I used to as a child, hiding under the covers, so my sister didn't hear me. Pretending that if I held still enough, quiet enough, I could feel my parents' arms around me.

But they never did.

Somewhere deep inside, beneath the noise and panic, the little girl's voice whispers again. Not accusing this time. Just... pleading.

*Don't leave me here.*

And I realized with a hollow ache that I already had.

I barely make it home before full-body chills take over, the rain making my clothes stick against my sensitive skin as pools of water collect at my feet. I leave my coat and shoes by the door and text Nikki to let her know I made it home. Then I silence it and drop it on the table with the forgotten envelopes.

I didn't bother turning on the lights. The city's glow slips through the blinds, painting the room in blue shadow. I moved quietly through the darkness, peeling away the layers from my body, the fabric cold, like the ghost of that little girl's touch.

Haunting images flood my mind of how pale her skin looked, dark shadows swirling around her, life-like and yet fake at the same time. The claw-foot tub fills slowly, the water running against the porcelain. I watch the steam rise, ghostlike, dipping my fingers in.

Warm. Too warm. It stung, but I didn't flinch.

I sank into the water, inch by inch, until the heat enveloped me. I pray the panic goes away, hoping I can break free of these thoughts. But prayers don't shatter chains. Not ones laced with heavy shadows consuming anything in its path. A malevolent specter hides in the recesses of my mind. My head falls back against the edge, eyes fluttering shut.

The water wraps around me like a shroud.

For a moment, I pretend I can wash it all away—the whispers, the panic, the memories seared behind my eyelids. The music still pulses faintly in my ears, slower now, like a dying heartbeat.

Then I hear it.

A drip.

Another.

Then dozens.

My eyes open as the ceiling blurs. The sound wasn't from the faucet. It's coming from above, around, *inside*. I look down. The water is still, yet I swear I saw ripples, spreading from nowhere.

My reflection shifted.

And there she was again—the little girl, submerged beneath the surface, eyes open and empty. Her hair, floating like seaweed, while her pale lips moved soundlessly in the water.

*Why did you leave me?*

I jerk upright, water splashing over the sides, heart pounding against my ribs. The vision dissolved into ripples, but the words remained, clinging to my skin.

"Don't do this," I cry into the empty room, shadows dancing at the edges of my mind. "Please..let me just breathe. Leave me alone." I take a shallow breath in as I press my palms to my face, but all I saw were flashes of my mother at the kitchen sink, staring out the window with tears that never fell. The sound of my own crying was swallowed by the hum of running water.

The same sound I hear now.

I slide deeper into the bath until the water touches my chin. The water ripples around me as I try to slow my breathing. To quiet my mind.

But the silence whispers back.

*You can't outrun water.*

It fills my ears, my lungs, my memory. A flood of grief drowning not in fear, but in the unbearable pull of recognition. And beneath it all—a soft, mournful humming. A lullaby I hadn't heard since before my world broke.

I release the wall that separates me from the world. I weep with shaking hands until the rawness splits like an open wound that never truly heals. I let go and sink further down, the water slowly covering my face, until I surrender under the weightlessness, the silence, of the emptiness within.

Forever drowning.

*Crack.*

# Chapter Six

After feeling Arlo and gulping down burnt coffee because I'm too lazy to go buy a new one, I rush out of the house. I pull my coat over my arms in a frenzy to get to the bakery down the road before I have to catch the train to the gallery for work.

Yesterday, I was a mess. I didn't get out of bed for anything other than feeding Arlo and going to the bathroom. Sleep eluded me all day Sunday. I just couldn't shake off the feeling I had Saturday night, keeping me restless. Every time I closed my eyes, I saw her haunting face.

A face, I will never forget.

As I step into the early September air, my phone buzzes in my bag. I finally charged it after leaving it out and forgetting its existence while I crashed out. The sound of "Here comes the bride" rings, my sister's ringtone reminding me that she is going to be a 'Mrs.' I knew she would be the first one, perhaps the only one of us, to get married. With me swearing off marriage, and Stefan isn't in a place long enough to hold any kind of relationship.

Probably for the best.

Gi, has a big heart. She's always trying to make the world a better place by volunteering in the community and helping people in need. I'm not surprised Josh saw that sparkle in her, the very first time he laid eyes on her. It's sweet and endearing the way he looks at her, cherishes her. He showers her with his adoration every chance he can. She looks at him in the same way.

I smile, thinking of the wonderful life they will share. One full of life and love, and with lots of babies. Gi, only twenty-three, always said she wanted to have several children. I'm not surprised, as a little girl, she would tend to all her baby dolls. She'd arrange them like triplets and make sure they were fed, warm, and soothed. She mimicked what I did for her after Mom died. That fills my heart with joy, knowing I did what I could, and it was enough for her.

My siblings have a worldly view and big personalities despite our rough upbringing. They have embraced life and are chasing after their dreams. I knew Boston was just too small for them. Stefan has grown into his own this last year at only twenty years of age, rock climbing, surfing, backpacking, anything that gets him outside and not a stuffy office. Pretty sure his rise to fame is one adventure away.

It suits him.

They have flourished into amazing people, and I admire their courage to go after what they want. I'm twenty-eight, and I don't know if what I am doing will sustain me forever. I'd like to think it will. But every time I reach the edge of something bigger, something real, I freeze. The weight of it locks me in place, making it impossible to move forward.

I have moments of clarity, where I feel like I am capable of more. Giving me hope that the paralysis isn't my truth. But my mind keeps me stuck, suspended in a place I can't escape. It pulls me back into the shadows that never leave me alone.

With shaky hands, I reach for my phone to answer my sister, "Hello Gi."

"Good morning, sister dearest!" She exclaims, too vibrant for this early morning. Or maybe that's the hangover and panic attack talking still.

"It's alright, same as always, just grabbing a bite to eat from the bakery before I catch the "T" to work," I reply, while buttoning my coat all the way. I turn down the old block that has my favorite lobster tail pastry.

"Oh, are you going to Florentine's Bakery?" She asks.

"Yes, the one and only."

Gi groans, "I love that place! But you are going to die when you get here! There are so many bakeries and pastries, you are going to have a hard time choosing one. Eve, I love it here! And I can't wait to have you by my side already."

"Are you loving the villa you booked then? Is it everything you've dreamed of?" I ask, knowing that she was afraid to book without seeing it first.

"Oh my gosh, yes!" She screeches into the phone. I'm going to need new eardrums after this wedding. But her excitement is infectious, and I could use some good energy right now. "This place is perfect, not too big and not too small. It only has six bedrooms, so Josh's family booked another Villa closer to town, giving us the extra rooms to get ready in. My to-do list is growing, but today Josh planned a winery tour with a travel guide to taste only the best wines. Then we'll finish with a romantic dinner, testing out main course dishes for the reception."

"Wow, that sounds dreamy and perfect, Gi. I'm so happy for you."

"In two short weeks, I am going to be MARRIED in the most beautiful country in the world! I feel so lucky. It's all happening just like we talked about. You are still leaving on Friday, right? You better not back down at the last minute, I need you."

There's no denying her. And she is relentless in pulling me into her orbit for a long overdue vacation. "Nothing would keep me away from being there with you. How is the countryside?" I'm itching to know if the landscapes are as beautiful in person as they are in the paintings I've seen. I look down a side street, watching the fall leaves gather around the fence line.

"Eve! It's more than you could have imagined. It's magical and poetic. Even the flaws somehow add to the Italian charm. I'm in awe of everything. Josh says we can come back anytime I want. Oh, Eve, you are going to love it. The citrus aroma in the air, the whole place feels like one massive painting."

I stop in front of the bakery, my heart beating a little faster, knowing I get to experience it with her and Stefan. Heat pricked the corners of my eyes as my throat tightened. "I can't wait to see all that in person. Listen, I gotta go, I'm here at the bakery and need to order. I love you, Gi, be safe and have fun with your fiancé. Bye for now." I swipe at my eyes, pulling back the emotion that slipped through the cracks.

"*Ciao, mia bella sorella*. Bye, my beautiful sister," she says in perfect Italian. She and Josh took a language class in preparation for their honeymoon. Gi is prepared for anything.

Ending the call, I take a deep breath before going in, steadying myself. After only a short waiting period, I step onto the train with a lobster tail pastry in one hand and a much better-tasting hazelnut latte in the other. I let myself indulge in deep thought for a little longer while I sit on the train, also known as the "T," to work.

I take a bite of the flaky crust, letting the orange and cinnamon cream dance beautifully on my tongue. The texture is absolutely divine paired with my hazelnut lattè. I could eat pastries every day for the rest of my life and not get tired of them.

Morning light filters through the train windows, catching the edges of open books and crinkled newspapers. A woman in a navy coat sways gently with the rhythm of the tracks, eyes closed, earbuds in—lips barely moving with the lyrics to a song.

It could also be a spicy audiobook. And now I'm curious. I look again, her foot isn't tapping, and there's a serene smile decorating her face.

Definitely a spicy audiobook. I smile at that.

I watch in silence, the hum of the city mingling with the soft rustle of pages and the occasional clink of a coffee thermos. My thoughts wander, as they do, imagining their destinations, their worries, their routines, their spicy book choices. Outside, Boston unfurls in amber and gold this early Autumn day, the leaves falling on the pavement.

I can almost hear my parents' laughter echo down the brick-lined streets, back when the world felt wide and uncomplicated, before I understood how tangled life would become.

Does every year just keep getting harder? Will there be a time of peace, when I'm not feeling like I'm fighting so hard to stay afloat in a world pushing me under? I would love to be able to paint again one day without it triggering some warring emotion in me, spiraling my thoughts out of control.

Some days, I'll get a phantom smell of turpentine or the smell of a fresh new canvas. Freedom. Not feeling shackled and chained by my own thoughts.

Dark and intrusive thoughts that take and take and take.

Will I ever be free from it?

I would like to dream again. To blossom under a creative warmth and watch it take shape with possibility. I imagine if I had started college with both of my parents alive, cheering me on, how much I would have grown and learned. What choices I would have made back then, or how hard I would have pushed myself with those art classes. Becoming a parent at a young age was hard, but I would do it again in a heartbeat to ensure my family's safety.

The gallery is great where I work, but something is missing. I can't quite pinpoint it. But it's felt flat over the last year. And I feel like I want to fill it with something different. Something new. I love helping my boss create the best atmosphere for our clients, even hosting fun events over the holidays to draw attention to and inspire new artists.

With the holidays right around the corner, I'm surprised my boss hasn't booked anything substantial yet. I make a mental note to remind her. I'm not too worried; she can be somewhat of a last-minute person.

The train rattles along its worn tracks, a dull hum rising and falling beneath the chatter of strangers. I watch the blur of buildings streak past the window in a hypnotic rhythm when I notice a flick of movement across from me.

A man in a tailored suit—his tie loose, hair still damp from a rushed morning shower. A small sketchbook balanced on his knee. Not the kind of thing I expect to see in the hands of someone like him. A commuter who looks born for ledgers and meetings, not graphite smudging the pages. Yet his pencil moves with ease, quick strokes shaping into something alive on the page. I lean in just enough to see the lines taking form: the curve of an old woman's face, eyes turned downward, lips pressed into silence.

My chest tightens. For a moment, I can almost feel the phantom weight of a paintbrush in my hand, the familiar gut of bristles against canvas.

My fingers twitch at the thought, desperate to reach, to create, to *be*.

Instead, I curl them into fists on my lap, until the knuckles blanch. Creation is not mine to touch. Not anymore. What was once a beautiful haven, became dangerous shadows that burned away its beauty. I sit still, nails digging crescent moons into my palm, watching this stranger bring life to paper while my hands tremble with the memory of what they used to be.

The train jolts to a stop, lurching us forward. He doesn't look up. He doesn't react to the invisible turmoil within me. I clench harder, holding myself together, ignoring the ache forming in my chest.

I check my phone one more time before putting it away. I just need to get through this week, and then I am off on a plane to Italy on Friday. Vacation awaits. Well, sort of. It will be filled with wedding stuff, and I will constantly reassure my sister that the venue is great and that all her wedding choices are perfect.

And her. Always.

Everything is going to be fine. It's the last thing going through my mind as I step off the "T" and shuffle my way to the gallery.

I pause at the gallery door, my hand hovering over the handle. One steady breath in, then I push it open, the city's breath follows me inside—the hum of traffic and the wet smell of coffee in the distance.

The scent of fresh paint and old wood greets me. I settle my nerves and get ready for another work day, making people happy with beautiful art pieces that will decorate their homes.

Today is going to be a good day.

# Chapter Seven

Just inside, by the entrance wall, a cluster of frames leans against each other, wrapped in parchment, corners labeled in marker. Not one or two. At least ten. My steps slow to a stop in front of them. We haven't moved this many pieces since the gallery opened years ago. That's exciting. There's hope for the gallery's longevity. I bet Clara, my boss, is over the moon. I wonder where she's hiding.

The mornings always start the same way: Clara opens the gallery, and I close it. It's just the two of us, unless we have an event. I finish turning the lights on in stages, each one peeling away a layer of darkness until the paintings reappear like old friends. I take my time walking through the rooms, making sure everything is exactly where it should be.

No fingerprints on glass. No tilted frames. Just stillness, perfect.

I pause in front of a landscape like I do every morning—oil on canvas, thick strokes of color that swoop and swirl. I trace the motion of the brush with my eyes, trying to remember what it felt like to move like that.

To create with intention.

But my hands stay in my pockets, safe. Useless.

I walk by the office to find the door closed. That means Clara is with a client. I leave the hallway to start greeting visitors trickling in. By ten, the city is awake, and so is the gallery. Students with sketchbooks are my favorite, whispering about color and form. I smile and answer their questions. Older couples ask if we sell postcards, and I guide others to the pieces I think they'll love most.

It's easy to talk about art when it isn't mine.

I handle sales, catalog inventory and answer emails that all sound the same. Between tasks, I find myself drifting toward the corner near the window of the lobby, where the light hits the marble just right. Sometimes I pretend I'm studying the way it falls across the floor—the geometry of shadow and glass. But really, I'm just avoiding the ache that starts whenever someone mentions their studio.

Across the room, my boss stands, angled toward a woman in a tailored navy pantsuit, heels planted as if she owns the floor. Odd. Not your typical client. She must be a buyer for high-end clients who usually send others to fetch pieces for their large estates. I know it's common, but I feel like they are missing the best part of letting the art speak to them personally. Takes the magic out of it.

She's the type of woman whose lipstick doesn't smudge when she talks. I know the type of shopper, one who only a client sends to make an expensive deal. Her eyes flick briefly in my direction, sharp. I pretend to make myself look busy, arranging a plant to catch the natural light better. But, something about this woman's posture, it's official, I think.

My boss looks at me with a tight smile as I pass them to the office.

I file away leftover catalogs and receipts from last week when my boss enters the small space. I put on my best smile, but I instantly feel uneasy with the look she's giving me.

"Eve, it's nice to see you. How was your weekend?" She asks, only glancing at me briefly, before she grabs a stack of papers and puts them in a drawer.

"It was... good," I kept it short. "What's with all the wrapped canvases? Looks like a big haul for the gallery." The words leave my mouth, but I already feel something's off. Her eyes meet mine, too slow, when normally I am met with warmth. A knot forms low in my stomach, coiling tighter with every second of silence.

Her lips press into a line before she speaks, and that's all it takes. My pulse stutters. The air between us thickens, heavy like before a storm.

Not again.

"I'm selling the gallery," she says, looking away. Not even sugar coating it. Right to the point. I prefer it that way anyway. I close my eyes as I process the punch of words and what that means for me now.

This can't be happening.

"Say something, Eve," Clara pleads.

"I honestly don't have any words," I look up at her, trying not to sound harsh, but damn. This is an unexpected change I was not prepared for. And today was supposed to be a good day.

Releasing a resigned sigh, she explains. "You know business hasn't been the best lately, and I want to visit my grandkids more as I am getting older. I am truly sorry, Eve. I thought I could hold out a bit longer. At least through the holidays, but this offer gives me an opportunity to pay off debt and have enough money for retirement."

"What does this mean for me, then? Can I keep my job?"

"Unfortunately, no. She mentioned this type of gallery being irrelevant and hard for marketing. She is turning it into a high-end event venue because of its location. But, she's offered to buy all the artwork, too. I couldn't pass it up."

While I am happy for my boss, I feel cold. Numb. Motionless.

She takes a step toward me. "The gallery's last day will be in two weeks."

"But I will be in Italy at my sister's wedding?!"

"I know, I am so sorry. There was no other way. Please know that I have been so thankful for your help these past few years. She's giving us all a nice parting bonus, and you will be paid through the end of the month. It's very generous, even though it's so sudden."

Her words blur into static. I let the air slip from my lungs, trying to steady myself. My mind reels, spinning out like a car on black ice. I'm still standing, but everything inside me is skidding, unmoored. I move past her, heading out of the office to help relieve the tension in my body.

I move through the day like a ghost. Watching Clara play up the space to the viper in the navy suit, taking away a creative space that brought so much joy to the community. It feels like I am saying goodbye to a family member, a steadiness I took for granted, and now it's too late.

By afternoon, the air grows heavy with the quiet shuffle of visitors and the faint hum of the climate control system. I love that sound—steady, constant, like the heartbeat of the building itself. Sometimes I imagine the art is listening too.

When the last guests leave, I lock the door and do a final walk-through. The gallery settles into silence, its stillness wrapping around me like a breath held too long. I will miss the structure this place has given me, something to look forward to. I stand in front of a small abstract piece—smears of blue dissolving into white. I wonder if the artist ever felt what I do now.

That strange distance between who you are and what you want to make.

The answer never comes.

I switch off the lights, one by one, until only the glow from the streetlights outside spills across the floor. The paintings fade back into shadow, and I tell myself I'll bring my sketchbook tomorrow.

I tell myself that every day.

Then I leave, the echo of my footsteps following me out into the night.

Another chapter slams shut—loud and final. The door doesn't just close. It locks and seals.

Darkness presses in, thick and airless, no sliver of light sneaking through the cracks.

When I get home and behind the door of my sacred space. My home. I reach for a soft landing, anything. The walls are getting closer. My lungs tighten, greedy for air that won't come. Emotion quells within me, my eyes sting with unshed tears and hidden truths, desperate to be seen.

I can't take much more of doors slamming in my face with no open windows.

I decided right then, taking my phone out, pulling up the registration letter I filled out but hadn't sent for the Master's Art Institute program—I've been keeping it at a distance for far too long—and pressing send.

Whether I get in or not, I have to move forward with a plan.

Hope for the future.

Anything.

What have I got to lose?

# Chapter Eight

I had always believed that "new beginnings" were just Pinterest lies wrapped in faux-inspirational fonts, that is, until I watched my whole life packed in one truck, ready to be shoved into storage until I could figure out my next steps.

Disaster comes in threes after all, so I had to laugh out loud—way too loud—when I got a final notice in the mail that our building was being sold and we had thirty days to move out. Funny, I don't remember getting the first notice.

It's probably at the bottom of the unopened pile of envelopes.

Now I am sweaty, breathless, and completely out of shape from scrambling to clear out my apartment before I leave for Italy. Miraculously, I'm not crying.

Progress.

It could be that I am in utter and total shock, numb to everything.

This last week has been a week of endings. Saying goodbye to clients at the gallery and the students who frequent the place. It all feels heartbreaking to let go. I will never forget the many gatherings we've had and the connections we've made.

Their goodbyes still echo in my ears.

Tight hugs, hesitant smiles, and too many versions of *Keep in touch.*

Back at the apartment, cardboard boxes litter my living room like a maze of what used to be. Mismatched mugs, a photo strip from two summers ago of Nikki and me at a posh party, and the green sweater I always wear on rainy days. It all went into the same boxes, as if maybe, if I packed carefully enough, the memories would stay intact.

My bank account still reads the same depressing number—at least until the nice little severance package gets deposited. I should be spiraling, gasping for air, or bracing for the familiar rush of panic. But it doesn't come.

Instead, I sit cross-legged on the floor, clutching a half-wrapped picture frame and listening to the quiet. Stillness. Not peace, exactly. But an acceptance. Change is happening whether I like it or not, and normally, I would be freaking out. Except, I'm glad it happened. A change to actually look forward to.

"Hello?!" Nikki screeches from the front door, breaking the calming silence.

Well, that quiet didn't last long.

"In here!" I call out from the closed bedroom, regretting saying yes to staying with her tonight before my early flight tomorrow to Italy. But also thankful I have her.

She opens the door and closes it behind her. "I thought you would be done by now. The hot moving guys are almost done with the last load." She sits cross-legged, matching me with leggings and a big sweater, gently holding a frame in her hands.

"I just have this last box of fragile frames I wanted to spend a little more time packing," I wrap the newspaper around the frame and put in the box marked *fragile*.

Arlo comes out of hiding to sniff at Nikki, unsure of her presence. "Oh, hey, little man," she reaches out a hand to pet him, but he walks back to my open closet. "How has he been with all the commotion?" Nikki asks.

"I can tell he's been nervous since I took away the first load of boxes. Honestly, he might be more mad that there isn't any left for him to play with." I chuckle, the sound hollow.

"He does love a good cardboard box. Anything I can help with?"

"Yeah, can you hand me that stack of frames over there on the chair?"

"Sure thing," Nikki gets up and carefully grabs the frames and sets them in front of me.

I pull from the top, a faded black-and-white photo of my parents in a field with long grass, smiling in a way I've tried to imitate on hard days. They were so good together.

I miss them. Even now.

You never get over grief; somehow, you just fill the hole with other stuff as the years go by. The next frame I grab is a watercolor I created after a challenging day, but it changed when I saw the sunset the day my siblings moved out on their own. The crayon drawing from my sister, crooked, wild, and perfect, was taped into a frame far too elegant for it.

A professional photo in a solid black frame sits at the bottom, taken of Stefan on his first wild adventure for a local website. Each is a piece of fond memory I hold dear. Each watching over me.

"The way you look at things sometimes makes me feel like I am seeing only a fragment of what you see. It's kind of unnerving, Eve." Nikki looks at me with a mix of curiosity, confusion, and a little bit of awe. We finish wrapping the frames and tape up the box.

It pulls an unexpected laugh, "Gosh, I don't know if that's a good thing or a bad one, Nikki." Half the time, it feels like I feel too much or don't see enough, and I can't get past the insecurity of it all.

"I think it's a brilliant one. You are truly a marvel, Eve, and I hope one day you will allow yourself to see how special you are. And when you do, please let me be a witness. Because that is going to be an explosive day."

Nikki never gets choked up, so to see water in her eyes unravels the water in mine. For a moment, I'm speechless.

Nikki breaks the short silence first with a cough and stands up, holding out a hand to help me off the floor. "Let's go, bestie. We gotta give these hotties a reason to sweat more."

I laugh. We pack up the rest of the small items and boxes, the quiet between us now filled with the rustle of packing paper and the soft thud of memories being sealed away. I catch her eye once as she gently places the frame with my sister's drawing into the last box, and for a second, I feel the weight of everything I'm leaving behind. My safe haven for an unknown future.

I have to remind myself that I don't have to have it figured out right now.

Just take a step forward.

Get through my sister's wedding next week, and then I will worry about what comes next.

The room feels hollow when the final strip of tape is pressed down. Like it's holding its breath, waiting for me to say goodbye. Nikki pulls me into a tight hug that says everything neither of us wants to speak aloud.

Last week, I had a job I was proud of, my own space I felt comfortable in, and a man who loved me deeply before I ultimately screwed that up. Now, I have to face my family with absolutely nothing going for me in a different country.

I am beginning to think that all these events are leading me somewhere I'm not sure I am ready for. Decisions I'm not ready to explore. It feels too close to walking out into the deep end of a pool, treading water for an unknown length of time, feeling exhausted and frantic. That kind of unknown is pulling me out of my comfort zone, my bubble of bliss. I know what happens in my own bubble.

I am safe here. Lonely, but safe. I can't help but feel that the bubble is about to burst, and I am not prepared for what happens next.

I turn away from what I called home for the last three years, turn off the lights, and close the door.

Closing a chapter that felt too short.

The next morning, I sit by the window seat on a plane bound for Italy, the early sun spilling golden light across my lap. My fingers are still slightly sticky from the cheap airport croissant, and my passport peeks out of the seat pocket in front of me, creased but full of empty pages waiting for worldly memories.

Turns out Stefan was able to catch an earlier flight yesterday, so I'm on my own for this trip. Which is fine by me.

Maybe I can sleep the whole way there.

My last night in Boston was perfect. After seeing all my stuff in a small ten-by-twenty storage unit, Nikki brought me back to her parents' hotel suite and ordered all the junk food and wine to host a party, even though it was just us. Even Arlo was spoiled with a dish of sardines that cost more than my rent, I'm sure. When she placed the salty snack in front of Arlo's carrier—on a gold dish—I gave her a withering look.

"What? I need the dude to like me. I am taking care of him for a couple of weeks after all," Nikki shrugs her shoulders, smiling like she's the bestest friend in the world. Which she is. I feel better knowing Arlo will be living his best life with her while I'm gone, even if he will be insufferable when I get back.

We ended up watching the classics—*Breakfast Club*, *Sixteen Candles*, *Girls Just Want to Have Fun*—on the big screen in a fluffy king-sized bed. It was perfect. It was what I needed to get on the plane, leave a part of me behind, and look to the future.

"I'm going to miss you," Nikki says, with a slight sheen to her eyes, which she one hundred percent claims were due to her allergies. I know better, but I nod anyway. She gives a big hug, squeezing like it's the last time she will see me.

"Ompf, Nikki. I'll be back in two weeks." I force air from my lungs with her hug, trying to calm the jitter beneath my skin. "Thank you," I whisper.

"Don't forget to call me when you land," she gives me the kind of look that says *I will hunt you down if you don't.*

"I will, I promise."

As the plane lifts off, I don't cry. I thought I would. But instead, I rest my head against the cold window and let the hum of the engines settle me. Below, the city I knew becomes smaller and smaller until it's just a blur of color and memory.

Ahead of me, a new chapter waits—unwritten, unpredictable, and terrifying in all the right ways. And for the first time in weeks, I smile a genuine smile.

# Chapter Nine

The plane touches down in Florence, with a jolt that rattles my nerves back into my chest. I clutch the armrest and let out a slow breath as the engines roar to a halt, like the plane itself was just as unsure about landing as I was. I'll never get used to that, no matter how often I fly, which hasn't been a lot.

The customs line crawled, filled with jet-lagged travelers, and the muffled rustle of passports being flipped open. My bag thuds on the carousel, somehow looking dirtier than when I'd checked it in. I sling my backpack over my shoulder, bones aching and my heart feeling somewhere between dread and anticipation.

Outside the terminal, the air smelled different—warmer, scented with something sweet and fruity and car exhaust, making my nose twitch. A breeze picks up, carrying that sweet scent again, along with something else—something unfamiliar. I'm looking forward to visiting as many different places and smelling all the aromas of Italy. I scan the crowd, heart hammering now, not from anxiety but from something deeper.

Hope, maybe.

That's when I see them.

A flash of blonde hair—my sister Gi, waving like she'd been standing there for hours, her eyes already glassy with tears. Beside her, Stefan, our younger brother, leans against a tiny Fiat with his usual smug grin and a coffee in hand. I know that look, the look of a bet having been made and Gi losing because she cried first.

He loves being right.

Gianna reaches me before I can take a full breath. She throws her arms around me, squeezing so tightly it knocks the wind out of me, and maybe, just maybe, it squeezes some of the grief out too. "You're here," she whispers into my hair, her voice full of the type of warmth and love only Gi could give.

It could melt ice caps.

I nod against her shoulder. "I'm here."

Stefan comes in with a one-arm hug and a mock salute. "Welcome to the land of carbs and questionable driving habits. We saved you one of the good bedrooms. And by 'good' I mean it has a window that opens." Gi slaps at his chest with a healthy dose of side-eye glare. "Just kidding, the villa is top tier. Josh would have had us all moved to some five-star hotel if it wasn't."

Gi slaps his arm, "He absolutely would not!"

"Stop being so violent," Stefan defends, rubbing at his chest.

I laugh. It feels good to have them around, even though they fight like cats and dogs. "Now, now, no fighting until after the wedding," I say in a light, teasing tone. This is actually mild in comparison to when they were in their early teenage years. It was impossible to come in between them, so I often just let them hash it out.

Gi turns to me with mischief in her eyes, the kind of tell that always says she would get her way eventually, just like when she was little. "I wanted to have the ultimate Italian Villa experience. I just knew this one was a hidden gem when we saw it online, but it doesn't even compare to what it looks like in real life. The old couple who owns it are just the sweetest people." She's the kind of person who throws her heart behind the quiet fighters and champions the overlooked.

It's who she is at her core.

I give her a squeeze one more time before turning to the red toy car in front of us. I laugh. A real one this time, short and startled and full of the kind of relief I hadn't let out in weeks. Stefan grabs my luggage and shoves it into the smallest trunk ever.

"That's our car?" I question my eyes darting between the car and Stefan.

"Oh, what have you got against her?" He looks at me with fake shock, putting a hand to his chest.

"Is it... sturdy? Maybe we should get something bigger," I say. It doesn't look like we all would fit at all.

"We do have a bigger car, but Stefan rented this one for himself, to blend into the Italian culture." Gi rolls her eyes and crosses her arms. A common look when she actually doesn't get her way. It makes me smile.

"Shhhh.. you might hurt her feelings." Stefan leans down to the hood. "Don't listen to the mean old ladies, they know nothing about classic cars." I join Gi, matching her stance and eye rolls.

Turns out, we all fit. We crammed into the tiny Fiat, my knees pressed against a box of fresh lemons, a couple rolling around the floor. After miles of city, we pulled onto a winding road toward the countryside estate that would house the Wedding and the wedding party. Rolling hills blur past, dotted with vineyards and sun-drenched villas—the kind of scenery that looks like it had been filtered through a dream. The kind of glow you get from a photo filter.

And for the first time since my world shifted, I didn't feel like I was running away.

I felt like I was arriving.

The shutters creaked open with a groan that felt theatrical enough to match the golden light spilling into the room. I blink against the sun, my body wrapped in crisp sheets that smelled faintly of lavender and sun-dried cotton. It was quiet. The kind of quiet that lets you hear birds arguing in the olive trees and the distant hum of a Vespa winding along a country road.

I expected to feel different, waking up in a new place, but surprisingly, I feel the same as I did yesterday when I got on that plane. Still torn between what I should do about my future. Still feeling the loss of losing my life in Boston, and at some point, I have to tell my family I've lost it all. So many changes in a short amount of time —I haven't processed what that means for me right now. For now, I stuff down the pain of the past and focus on Gi's wedding to help make it the day of her dreams.

I roll out of bed, putting on a fuzzy green robe, trapping the warmth. I pull my curly locks into a messy bun and wash my face in the adjoining bathroom. The floral wallpaper is charming with the warm wood trim. The queen-sized bed sits on an ivory iron frame, with a soft sage-green comforter. Now I know why Gi gave me this room. It has all the green and cream accents she knew I would love, and it makes me feel at peace here.

I love her. I smile at that knowledge and pull on slippers to chase the cold from the tiled floor.

Last night was a chill evening of open conversation, two bottles of wine, and wedding details. We all agreed to go to bed early in preparation for the multitude of wedding tasks ahead of us for the week. I can already feel it slipping by, with my baby sister being married by the end of it.

As if summoned, a soft knock comes from the door. Gianna pokes her head in with that mischievous grin again. "Get dressed. We're heading to the market." And then she shuts the door.

No further explanation. No lead-up.

And so it begins.

Twenty minutes later, I was crammed into the back seat again, after Josh said he was staying behind to take care of some work and make a few calls. Stefan instantly claimed he was driving. This time, a woven basket lay on my lap, my hair still damp from a rushed shower. Stefan drove like a rival espresso dealer was chasing him. Somehow, we made it to the quaint village without incident—or whiplash.

Here we are, together again after so many months of separate schedules on different continents. We have found ourselves in the land of our ancestors. Our Papa's dream was to have all of us together someday, visiting the Italian coast from coast to coast. From the mountains to the sea.

Tears well up in my eyes, one of many before my time here is done, I'm sure.

The market spread out before us was like a living painting—stalls bursting with color, voices rising and falling in rapid Italian, and the mingled scent of tomatoes, basil, and aged cheese wafting through the warm air.

It's utterly perfect.

I take another deep breath and let out a long-awaited sigh. The sun warms my face as I listen to the hustle of the morning.

"Isn't it great?" Gi says from beside me, watching the scene with the biggest smile.

"Yeah, it's amazing." I can't help but match her smile and instantly feel grateful I'm here with her. "I can't wait to explore."

"I'll be right back, I want to check out the food," Stefan informs us as he walks away.

"Follow me," Gi says, already walking through the crowd. I watch her greet vendors like old friends. Of course, she's a natural. Already knowing who's who.

She has no *stranger danger* bone in her body, even from a young age. A fact that gave me one too many scares trying to find her in large crowds. Gi meets everyone with a warm smile and a helping hand, ready and willing to give what she can. Even if it was a small act or nothing at all, she found a way to make an impact. She's a beautiful soul that I admire.

A spry man with a crooked smile hands her a bundle of fresh rosemary, slipping it into her back with a wink. *"Per tua sorella,"* he says, gesturing to me. *For your sister.*

Gi beams. "Word travels fast."

"How often do you come to the market?" I ask.

Gi shrugs her shoulders. "Oh, just about every day. We only buy what we need for the day and the following morning. Everything is so fresh here, and I love to try something new each time." She has that whimsical light in her eyes when she gets excited.

A dreamy wedding glow.

I wander a little down the street from Gi, my fingers brushing over sun-warmed peaches and purple-hued figs. My notice stacks of glossy eggplants and strings of garlic braided like jewelry. Italian floats around me—full of warmth—accompanied by wild hand gestures. I don't understand most of it, only catching bits and pieces that are familiar. But I feel welcome.

An old woman behind a small stand with a yellow sunshade smiles, her eyes lit. Her hands are stained red from tomatoes, her apron dusted with flour. She catches me looking at her, calls out "cara," and hands me a wedge of what looks like cheese without asking.

I take it. "Grazie." A little unsure, but curious. I look for a sign to help me with what I'm eating, but I don't see anything obvious. It's sharper and creamier than I expected. Definitely a type of cheese, though. I look for a way to pay her, but she waves her hands and shakes her head no. I thank her again.

Passing more tables that overflow with produce that look like they've been pulled from the soil or plucked from a tree this morning, I can't keep my eyes off the people, the arrangements, and structures.

This place holds an old Italian charm, rich with history.

For a moment, I let everything go. The gallery. The apartment. Conner. I push it all far behind me, like a chapter that had ended in another book entirely. As I venture through the crafted stalls, I notice that no one rushes. The vendors take their time, talk to each other, flirt, argue, laugh.

Food here isn't just food—it's an identity.

It's a memory. It's love.

Time slips away, and I fall into this beautiful Tuscan scene I could see myself painting. Each brushstroke invites slowness. It strips away the noise. And before I realize, I'm sitting on a bench, watching more closely, breathing more deeply. The air changes often, smelling like earth and sunlight and food cooking I can't quite place. Chatter rises and falls like birdsong—fast, musical, and full of warmth.

People walk unhurriedly, some with backpacks, others in fancy suits and dresses. Some tourists, most of them locals, as far as I could tell, work diligently from one task to the next and with a lot of expression. Hands often flail in front of them to make their point. It makes me smile on the outside and inside.

My phone buzzes from my handbag in rapid succession like an alert on steroids, pulling me from my reverie. I scramble to end the incessant buzzing. Pulling my phone out, I see Nikki's name flash, message after message, and several missed calls.

I palm a hand to my forehead and let out a groan. Oops. I forgot to text her about my safe arrival. I am the worst friend. She's never going to let me hear the end of it. I wince as I read her messages one after the other.

*ARE YOU ALIVE?*

*Did you fall from the sky?*

*Why are you ignoring me?!*

*Seriously, call or text me back!*

*Okay, I am convinced you were abducted.*

*Pretty please, let me know that you are, in fact, ALIVE and well, and whether you have met the love of your life and are currently being swept away in the Tuscan sunset.*

*I NEED DETAILS! -Yours truly.*

"Try this," Stefan says, suddenly taking a seat beside me with a paper cone of fried zucchini blossoms. Startled but also hungry, I took one. It's still warm and crisp. I nearly groan at the first bite. "Nikki is still obsessed with you as ever, huh?" Stefan teases with a smile in his eyes as he looks at my phone.

I look down at my phone, avoiding direct eye contact. "She just wants to know I'm okay. It's been a rough few days." I type an apologetic response to halt the search party she will most likely send.

He raises an eyebrow. "Seems like there's more to that statement, sis. Can I help with anything?"

I shake my head, trying to downplay it. I still haven't told my family everything. Just that Conner and I broke up. "I appreciate the gesture, but I'm good. Being here with you guys is all the therapy I need." I let my silence do the talking, hoping he doesn't push it further. I give a tight smile and get up to find a distraction.

Stuffing my phone back in my bag, I start walking away, "Let's find Gi and get some gelato. I've been dying to get my hands on a genuine pistachio flavor."

"Hmm. Good call." Stefan jumps up and leads the way down a small alley toward the town square. He's always in the mood for food or sweets. The corners of my mouth lift, remembering having to constantly have snacks available to Stefan when he was in a massive growing stage. A stage he's never grown out of.

After locating Gi with a group of local kids huddling around a pile of bikes, she looks up with a radiant smile and gestures us toward an ice cream shop. Clearly, we all had the same idea. We each grab a different flavor of gelato, share a bite, and giggle, our joy matching.

"Not bad for day one, huh?" Stefan says while Gi and I finish our last bites.

"Technically, it's day two for you guys." Gi corrects, with a glint in her eyes.

I look around at the terracotta rooftops, watching old men play cards beneath a linden tree, and admiring the culture, with small hidden gems on every street.

"Not bad at all," I say softly, tucking a strand of hair behind my ear.

And just like that, the heaviness I'd been carrying feels a little lighter. Not gone—but light enough to make room for a new adventure.

# Chapter Ten

Later that evening, after the dishes had been washed and the wine opened, the three of us sat on the open terrace beneath a canopy of stars. The warm breeze tugged lazily at the candle flames on the low table, and cicadas buzzed in the distance like a lullaby for the hills. We cooked a simple meal—roast chicken, crusty bread dipped in garlic butter, and grilled vegetables from this morning's adventure to the market.

Josh excused himself after helping put stuff away to give us a moment together. He really is a selfless man. I tilt my head, fondness pulling at my mouth as I watch Gianna get comfortable on the outdoor couch. Her legs are curled up beneath her as she sips her wine, cheeks still flushed from a very heated kiss from Josh as he left. My heart is so happy for her. Stefan leans back in his chair, arms crossed behind his head, eyes half-lidded in the kind of contentment I used to think only existed in magazine ads.

Here we are, the three of us reunited again. I look at them both, really look as they bicker about random facts. They do this a lot, ever since they were adolescents. Both smart and stubborn in their own way. And the ache came quietly, not like a stab, but like a soft press against my chest.

I pull my sweater closer around my body as I shift in the love seat.

"You know," I say, surprising myself with how my voice catches, "I still remember tying both of your shoes before school—every morning, like a ritual." I look at her. "Gi, you'd cry if the bows weren't exactly the same size. And Stefan, you never wanted to wear socks, even in winter. I would have to chase you non-stop and force them on your feet. You always complained they were cutting off the air supply to the rest of your body."

They both look at me, startled by my randomness.

Then, they both laughed, Gi covering her mouth, Stefan rolling his eyes.

"Oh, my God, I remember that! You SO did too!" Gi continues to laugh and point at Stefan.

"I'll have you know, I wear them now. Obviously," he mutters. "Proper gear is the most important thing to prepare yourself with when doing any kind of outdoor activity. Or else, you could wind up dead, injured, or packing up early." Stefan takes another sip of his wine, making a disgusted look before setting the glass on the table. "Gross, that tastes like perfume. How can you guys drink that stuff?"

"Hey," Gi throws a pillow at him, which he easily dodges. Throwing isn't Gi's strong suit. "This wine is some of the best in the area. And I need to taste several different bottles to help me decide what to serve at the wedding." She takes another sip. As do I. It's good, but I can taste hints of rose petals. I'm assuming that's why Stefan doesn't care for it. He's not much of a drinker. He is only twenty-two after all.

It's quiet for a few minutes, not awkward, just *us*.

"You practically raised us," Gi says, her eyes meeting mine with a love and understanding only she could give. "You were more of a parent than a sister some days." She says, in thanks for the sacrifices I've made.

"I didn't know what I was doing," I admit, blinking back the sting behind my eyes. I look at the overhead lights bouncing in the breeze. "I just... knew I had to keep you both okay. That was the only thing that made sense back then." I fight off the urge to hide the emotion in the back of my throat, slowly tightening and becoming uncomfortable.

Like it always does when I think about the past.

I don't even know why I brought up the stupid memory in the first place. I never do that. This place is already starting to unravel the parts I've kept hidden. I blow out a breath and take another sip of wine—the tobacco notes coming through now.

"You did more than that." Stefan's voice is softer than I'd ever heard it before. "You gave us normal when everything around us was falling apart. All I really knew was what you provided. You, Eve, were my parents, my only one. For that, I'm incredibly thankful."

What he says strikes me hard. He's right, I've been the only parent he's ever known. And while I've always known that, it's never hit me as hard as it does right now. I look at them—their faces older, wiser, full of lives I hadn't always been around to witness in full bloom. But I realize I'm not responsible for them anymore. They have grown into themselves —beautiful, complicated, whole— without needing me to hold everything together.

"You guys have really grown into amazing adults. I hope you know that." I say, as a tear slipped down my cheek, and I let it.

I. Let. It.

"You don't need me anymore," I whisper, not with bitterness, but with wonder and appreciation. And I am in awe of my siblings and their ability and strength to pursue what they want and succeed in their lives.

Gianna reaches over the table, grabbing my hand and squeezing. "No. Not in the way you're thinking, but we still *want* you." I nod and then look at Stefan. He nods my way in agreement. And just like that, a warmth bloomed where fear used to live. The old guilt, the constant need to be strong, to be useful, to be essential. It floats off into the night like a paper lantern, and I let it drift.

We sit in silence for a long time, the kind of silence that comes only with love and a long shared history. Too much to say, and one we don't make a habit of dredging up or talking about often. It was painful enough the first time we experienced it.

I remember taking care of my siblings and day-dreaming of what choices they would make as they grew year after year.

Never did I imagine we would be in Italy one day, together.

The stars blinked above us, perhaps Mama and Papa were looking down, smiling, and for once, it didn't hurt to think of them. It felt like just being her—just *being*—was enough.

After a few more minutes of light conversation, Gianna and Stefan decided to head to bed. I lingered beneath the stars, surrounded by the rhythmic sounds of cicadas, wrapped in a thin sweater and my thoughts. The terrace had fallen quiet, and my wine glass was empty, but I cradled it anyway. Something to hold on to while everything else shifted inside me.

Their words still echo in my ears. *But we still want you.*

That difference mattered more than I realized.

For so long, I'd defined myself by what I *had* to do—protect, provide, plan. There had never been room for what I wanted—only painting in the quiet moments I had growing up, before that became too painful. Lately, I wasn't sure what I wanted.

Can I really start completely new? Am I capable? How can I possibly start anew from nothing? I guess that's exactly how you start every new chapter.

From a blank page. Or a new painting, with a blank canvas.

Being let go at the gallery and having to pack my apartment up felt like a slammed door in my face, and there's an open window with wind howling through it. I still haven't told my family. Maybe after the wedding. Just before they all go off on their new adventures, perhaps.

A chill runs down my spine as the temperature drops a bit. I stand up and go inside, turning off the lights as I head to my bedroom, when I see a faint light coming from a small room off to the side of the kitchen. Gianna had mentioned there was a studio here in passing, saying it was used now for storage. I hadn't noticed it there before, though.

I push the door all the way open, noticing the light from the window —moonlight.

I bet this room catches the light right in the early mornings before the house awakes. I step in and look around more closely. There are a few boxes in the far left corner, away from the window, stacked on top of each other, as well as extra folding chairs propped up against the wall. But what catches my eye is the bare easel in the opposite corner, dusty and well-used. A stack of blank canvases leans against the wall, as if waiting for someone to claim them.

I wonder who the artist is and what they created while in this space?

What was their inspiration?

What medium was their favorite?

I walk over and drag the stool into the light of the moon, brushing off the top with my sleeve, revealing paint splatters along the edges. My fingers tingled, not for a phone or planner or a to-do list, but for charcoal, for paint—for the soft, smudged edges of creation.

It hit me like a breath I didn't know I was holding.

*I wanted to paint.*

Not just for submission. Not just to escape.

But to *begin*.

To pick up a brush I hadn't touched in years and give myself permission to create. Not for clients, not for a paycheck, not even for recognition.

Just for me.

The thought was exciting and terrifying. And yet, it felt *right*.

*Finally,* it felt right.

My eyes stung with unshed truths, desperate to be seen. The emotion burned its way free, gentle but unstoppable. Papa would have loved being here with us. That part hurts more than I'd like. The things he missed, Mama missed.

It should be all of us here, as a family, right now. This was his dream, too. To experience Italy and all the "firsts."

Our family's first wedding. Our first trip together. Watching Gi marry the love of her life and Stefan make a name for himself. Papa would have been here, front row, and perhaps Mama watching with admiration. Mama was Papa's lily, and Papa was Mama's sun, and without the sun, flowers wither and die. I miss them, even still. I've dreamed of walking through the museums with him, gawking at the statues, watching his eyes light up as we explore the landscape.

I trace the edge of the canvas with my fingertips, with tears in my eyes. A single blink and everything shimmered. I breathe out, setting my doubt free, and I smile. Tomorrow, I will go back to the market, not for food this time, but to buy art supplies.

I could paint the bushels of lavender thoughtfully tied, the old men playing cards with sunburned necks, or the view from the vineyard behind the villa, especially at sunset.

I could paint the ache, the joy, and everything in between.

Because for the first time in my life, I'm not turning away. Hiding.

I am becoming.

# Chapter Eleven

Three days before the wedding, Gi has us all doing several small tasks and running errands. We've been all over, from flower shops to wine tastings, and many, many trips to the market. I'm beginning to understand the importance of fresh food and ingredients here in Italy, unlike the stores we have in the U.S. Meal planning and prep were a staple each week because of busy schedules and limited time at home.

Not here, in these nostalgic homes and villas. The locals take the time to greet you, to get to know you. In this unfamiliar place, I feel seen. I feel remembered and special. Like I would be missed if I stopped showing up in town.

There's a slowness that feels decadent and rich, no amount of money can touch.

I've been secretly drawing and sketching in my worn-out leather journal the last few days. Baby steps. The one where dozens of ideas lie dormant and many secrets are written in its pages... ready and waiting. Daring me to say my dreams outloud. The journal had haunted me in the past, but I could never bring myself to burn it. It held too many sacred memories, as hard as they are to keep.

It was my beating heart.

The market buzzed with late-morning energy, tourists bartering poorly made me shake my head as I walked by. The locals slipped in and out of stalls with woven baskets and practiced ease. My reusable bag hangs on one shoulder as I walk up to a small booth shaded by a striped awning, eyeing a tin of watercolor pans and a bundle of natural brushes tied with twine.

My fingertips hovered over the paper—thick, textured—waiting.

It's been years since I let myself bloom with possibility like this again. My hands trembled as I picked up a brush, running the bristles along my palm. I imagined stroke after stroke, shadows, and beginnings. An old feeling stirred, unsure of itself but alive. The little girl I used to be. *Before.* Before shadows snuffed out my desire because of painful memories.

The hairs on the back of my neck stood on end, making me pause. I set the brush down gently, not out of alarm, but instinct—a feeling like I am being watched. My eyes lift, scanning the market around me. Tourists amble from stall to stall, kids weave through the crowd on bikes, and a couple are tangled in a kiss by the fountain.

Everything looks perfectly normal.

There's nothing obvious, nothing I can point to, and yet...a presence lingers.

Just beyond my grasp. Watching. Waiting.

For a second, I think of the girl in the club, and my heart starts racing. Something is off. And it knows I know.

"BOO!"

I jump, nearly knocking over a stack of watercolors. I whip around to find my sister grinning behind me, a pastry in one hand and zero remorse in her eyes. "God, Gi," I exhale, placing a hand over my chest. "You're going to kill me one of these days."

She just laughs, completely unbothered and clearly in play-mode. She doesn't know the storm whirling in me and I can't blame her for what I keep hidden.

"Oh, please. If a little sneak attack like that rattles you, you need to get out more." She takes a big bite of her croissant, already talking through chewing. "Anyway, did you get the text I sent about the centerpieces? The florist said peonies might be hard to get in time, but I told her we are not doing roses, *no matter what.*"

And just like that, the strange heaviness falls away, replaced by the whirlwind that is my little sister in full wedding-planning mode. I glance once more over my shoulder, the sensation already fading. Whatever it was, it'll have to wait.

"Okay, okay," I say, shaking my head with a smile. "No roses. Got it. What's next on the crisis list?"

She beams. "Glad you asked. You won't believe what Stacey said about the dress fitting...why did I invite her again?"

"Perhaps it's because she's your best friend?" I chuckle at her, shaking my head.

She just rolls her eyes, eating her way through the buttery croissant like a starving person.

We Morettis sure like our pastries.

"I have one more place to go," Gi says, walking into the crowd like she's a local.

And we're off.

After several other places Gi dragged me to, we are finally back at the villa, unloading boxes of food and fabrics to be stored until the wedding day. I get up to my room and plop right on the bed, letting out a long-held sigh. My eyes droop shut, just my phone buzzes from my bag on the end of the bed, yanking me out of my peaceful state.

I groan and grab it before it explodes.

It's a text from Gi.

*Hey, Josh and I are meeting with the priest for a marriage counseling session. Apparently, all couples married at this place get one. But I forgot I was supposed to pick up the wine from the vineyard in an hour. Could you go pick them up, please? Just stop by, grab the bottles, and thank Enzo for me. Thank you, sis! Oh, and maybe put on something nice, it's a fancy place. XO.*

I was really looking forward to playing couch potato tonight. Ugh. I pinch my nose between my fingers, letting out another heavy sigh. It's only a few more days, I keep telling myself. Reluctantly, I get up, wet my hair to freshen up the dark curls, and add a layer of mascara. I grab a light pink cotton linen dress with buttons down the front, left undone from just above the knees. It's a gorgeous vintage-inspired dress with pockets, a lace-up back, and wide straps.

Perfect for a walk through a fancy vineyard. I might as well explore while I'm there, right? I gather my things, select a white lace shawl to cover my arms when it gets cooler, and head out.

"Oh, shit, what am I supposed to drive?" I say out loud to no one. I send a text to Gi, hoping she sees it before she turns it off. "Stefan?!" I call for my brother, but no one seems to be here at the moment. I look to see if his car is out front, but it's not. I see Marco, the villa's caretaker, pulling up in his small truck. Why are the vehicles so small here? I'll have to ask later. I wave at him as he parks, rolling down the window.

"*Salve*! Hello! Can I get a ride?" He looks at me and just smiles. I don't think he speaks English. "Um, *posso avere un passaggio*? I point to the brochure my sister left for me, which thankfully includes the address.

I would be lost otherwise.

He takes the brochure and nods. "Sí. *Entrare*." He gestures to the passenger side, so I get in. It's a bumpy ride, but surprisingly it wasn't as far as I thought. Still, it took twenty minutes to arrive because I'm pretty sure we didn't reach a speed over thirty.

"*Grazie signore*," I say as I exit the truck. He hands me the brochure and drives off.

The winery's courtyard smells like crushed grapes with terracotta pots overflowing with rosemary, and a lazy string of lights sways overhead. It was all very wedding aesthetic and romantic vibes. Which should have been my first clue that my sister had her hand in this.

I checked the text again and then looked around for someone to help me find my way. A man stood by the tasting counter, sleeves rolled up, dark hair curling just enough to look deliberate. He smiles when he sees me—too easily, like he'd been waiting.

Maybe that's Enzo. I approach the counter.

"*Ciao*, are you Enzo?" I ask, hoping not to make a fool of myself in front of this very attractive man.

"Let me guess," he says, voice smooth as the Cabernet in his hand. "You're the emergency sommelier."

"Not quite. I'm Eve. I'm just here to pick up wine for my sister who is getting married and apparently has zero time management skills."

"Ah." He nods with a smile that reaches his eyes. "Then I'm your—pickup?"

I blink. Confused. "Are you Enzo?" Repeating my question.

His grin widened. "No, I'm Adrian. Though I was told you might be the one who needs rescuing."

My stomach did that inconvenient flutter thing. "Rescuing from what, exactly?" I tilt my head to the man in question.

"Awkward small talk. A lifetime of explaining the difference between a Merlot and a Malbec." He shrugs his shoulders while taking a sip of his wine, never taking his eyes off mine. Who is this guy?

I set my purse on the counter, breaking eye contact. "You seem very confident for a man who just met me," I say, taking a seat on the wooden chair and looking back up at his chiseled jaw and bright blue eyes.

"I find confidence pairs nicely with denial," he replies, offering me a glass. "Try this before you decide whether you're staying."

I take it, more out of curiosity than agreement, his warm fingers lightly graze my cold ones, eliciting a shock of awareness up my arm. I try to keep my face blank, not giving away what his touch did to me. The wine is warm, berry-rich, and far too easy to enjoy.

I hum in response. "I'll give it a seven," I say. "Out of ten."

"Seven?" He leans closer. "You wound me." A mischievous grin curls his lips, making me look away. *Don't stare at his lips, Eve.*

"Well, I'm not here to inflate egos. Just here to pick up wine bottles." I take another sip, adjusting in my seat when my dress falls open slightly—exposing my knee and thigh a little more than I would like. But I don't react to it. The cool air is a comfort right now.

Adrian briefly looks down, the movement drawing his attention, and coughs before bringing his eyes back to eye level. I smile into my glass.

"Pick them up, sure. But your sister said you might need a tasting assistant."

My eyes narrow. "Did she now?"

"She did," he turns his body toward me and raises his glass in mock solemnity. "So I'm officially on duty."

I'm not sure what that means, but I have a feeling.

And if I'm right. I'm going to kill my sister before her wedding.

# Chapter Twelve

Half an hour later, my shoes were off, and the empty glasses in front of us had blurred into a spark that felt a lot like trouble. But I didn't mind. Adrian and I moved to a patio set in the corner, its soft cushions feeling like pillows. I could fall asleep here. The patio nestled up against the vineyard and looked over Adrian's shoulder at the horizon beyond. The sun is setting, matching the warmth of the string of lights overhead.

Romantic.

Adrian watches me with interest. "Admit it," he says, his voice coating my skin like a blanket. "This is better than running errands."

I roll the stem of my glass between my fingers. "Depends. Do you come with a return policy?" I can tell he's amused by my antics instead of deterred by them. I have no plans to see this man again, but I sure like the way he looks at me.

The way he rises to my banter.

There's a light in his eyes I can't ignore and a devilish smile plays on his lips. I really need to stop looking at his lips. "Only if you keep the receipt."

We stare at each other for a moment before my phone buzzes across the table, lighting up with my sister's name. I ignore it.

It buzzes again. And again.

Adrian raises an eyebrow. "Popular woman."

"Persistent sister," I correct, unlocking it and looking at the message she just sent.

*So? Isn't he cute?? Don't kill me. You're welcome.*

My stomach drops. "Oh, you have got to be kidding me," I mutter. *I knew* it.

Adrian swirls his wine, amused. "Bad news?"

I take a gulp of my wine this time, realizing just how evil my sister is. "She..." I wave my phone toward him. "She set me up. This whole thing. The wine pickup..." I hesitate. "You. *All* of it."

He winces in mock offense. "You make it sound like a trap."

I sit up taller, my heart speeding up. "It was a trap!" I point my glass at him. "You're the bait." I think for a second, realizing this was definitely a set-up. "Oh my god, there is no Enzo, is there?" A breathy laugh escapes me, setting my glass down and looking around to find if the real Enzo is lurking somewhere.

"Enzo is very much a real person and is my friend and owner of this vineyard," Adrian says, chuckling while leaning back on the couch. "In my defense, I thought you knew. She said you were looking forward to it." He brings up an ankle and crosses it over his other knee, relaxed and unaffected.

"She lied. And so did your friend. Not a very good friend now, is he?" My cheeks warm as well as my stomach, the wine hitting me hard right now.

Adrian shrugs, "I got to meet a beautiful woman, I can hardly be disappointed."

"My sister also said bangs would change my life. She's not exactly a trustworthy source."

"Bangs or blind dates—she has a theme, doesn't she?"

I try to hold my glare, but his grin is infectious, lazy, and disarming. "You're taking this pretty well," my voice gave away my mind, inquisitive with a little sass.

He lifts his glass with a twinkle in his eye. Again with the eyes. "Free wine, beautiful company, mild emotional peril. That's a solid evening."

"You're impossible."

"And you're still here," he says as a challenge in what feels like it is lit with a hundred fires all burning at once. He pours me another glass of wine, I forget what we are drinking at this point, and clinks his glass against mine before I can argue.

The air between us hummed—soft music, laughter from nearby tables. The faint citrus of his cologne tickles my senses. The vineyard is growing busier and beautiful as the afternoon shifts into night, the sky a lovely lavender. I should've stood up, made a show of leaving. But the way he looks at me—curious but patient, like he wasn't trying to win me over, but to understand. It kept me anchored to my seat.

I'm curious.

"You're enjoying this, aren't you?" I ask, finally finding my voice.

"Immensely," he answers. "Though I'll admit, you're a tougher audience than your sister promised."

My jaw drops. "She said that?" I shift in my seat, waiting for his answer.

He smiles, slowly. "She said you don't do this sort of thing. Which, of course, made me want to see why."

I bite back a laugh. "And have you figured it out?"

"Not yet," he says, meeting my eyes. "But I'm willing to keep researching."

The waiter arrived with another tasting flight and a charcuterie board with a bread loaf that had me salivating before I could come up with a retort to Adrian.

"Compliments of the house," the waiter says, as he sets them down and walks away.

Adrian leans in, voice low. "Or maybe compliments of your sister."

I groan, covering my face with one hand. "I'm never forgiving her for this."

"Good," he says, smiling into his glass. "Then maybe I'll owe her one instead."

And here I thought I was going to have a quick tour of the vineyard, a glass of wine, and be on my way. Not in a million years did I think this was going to happen, but I am glad I at least changed into a dress. Thinking about showing up in what I wore earlier mortifies me.

This night isn't what I had planned. But I don't hate it either. I chanced a look at Adrian, noticing how relaxed he is—the very opposite of me. Where he's suave and alluring, I feel awkward and unsure. He's not like any other man I've been around before. Dress pants made for him, paired with an open baby-blue button-up shirt, reveal his tanned skin and dark hair. My mouth waters even though I'm drinking wine.

I need to get out of here before I do something I'll regret.

By the time the last tasting glass was cleared, the courtyard glowed brighter and the air had cooled just enough to make me regret wearing sandals. Then again, I didn't anticipate being out this late. I put on my shawl and pull out my phone, sending a text to my very guilty sister to ask for a ride.

It buzzes shortly after with a message.

*Sorry, running late! Everyone's swamped with wedding prep. Can you Uber?*

I sigh, shoving the phone into my bag. "Well. Looks like my ride ditched me for centerpieces."

Adrian lifts an eyebrow. "That sounds like a tragic sentence."

"It's fine. I'll just—" I take my phone out again, opening the app, and watch the little spinning wheel mock me. "—wait forty minutes for a driver who'll cancel halfway here." I let out a frustrating breath, cursing my sister.

This is her doing.

"Or," Adrian says, casually swirling the last of his wine, "you could let me drive you."

I hesitate. "You could be a serial killer."

He smiles, slow and maddening. "If I were, I'd at least have offered you the good pinot first."

"That's not comforting."

"Wasn't meant to be. It's leverage."

I try not to smile, and fail spectacularly. "You're seriously offering me a ride?"

He stands, collecting his jacket from the back of the patio set. "Call it moral responsibility. Your sister would never forgive me if I let her favorite bridesmaid wander into traffic."

"I'm not a bridesmaid," I say, standing too.

He tilts his head. "Ah, so you're a reluctant one."

"Not even that. I'm the designated emotional support sibling. But also, the maid of honor."

"Sounds like hard work. You deserve hazard pay."

"Or blind dates, apparently. But I'll take my payment in wine for now." I gather my things and put my sandals back on my feet—before standing, facing Adrian.

He gestures toward the parking lot. "Then it's settled. Come on, Emotional Support Sibling." He touches my lower back just slightly, but it's enough to feel the heat from his palm. I take a step forward and sway briefly before he catches me with both hands, pressing my body to his. My head spins as I feel his breath on my cheek. I look up into his eyes, flames swirling around his irises from the nearby heating lamp.

Neither of us moves for what feels like an eternity. Adrian clears his throat and settles me on my feet, taking a step away. My cheeks feel warm as I look down to smooth out my dress.

"Right this way," he says, his voice rough. I follow him to his car, the only sound of gravel crunching under our shoes. The entrance smelled faintly of rosemary and rain.

He unlocks a dark blue car that doesn't really look like it suits him and opens the passenger side door for me.

A gentleman. "You strike me as the type who alphabetizes playlists," I say as I climb in, trying to distract him from how much he unravels me.

"Only the break ones," he replies. "Helps me heal in order."

I laugh—a real one this time, not the polite version I'd been offering the world for months.

As we pulled onto the winding road, silence settled between us, warm and easy. The kind that didn't need to be filled.

He glances over, headlights catching the curve of his grin. "So, where am I taking you, mystery woman who hates setups?"

I tell him the address, and when he repeats it, his voice wraps around the words like a promise. For the first time in a long while, I didn't feel like I was running errands for someone else's story.

It felt like I was living mine, and I like that feeling. A lot.

The ride back was quiet, humming with everything unsaid. Streetlights slid over the dashboard, painting fleeting gold lines across Adrian's jaw, the steering wheel, and my hands folded in my lap. I kept rubbing the fabric of my dress between my fingers to settle the buzzing in my body.

Pretty sure it's the wine.

I wanted to take in the scenery outside, but it was too dark to see, and also, the man next to me is so beautiful, he's a distraction I can't take my eyes off of. It's unnerving how he makes me feel. When he pulls up in front of the villa, neither of us moves right away.

"Well," I finally say, unbuckling slowly, "thanks for not murdering me." Because, of course, that's what comes out of my mouth. I'm not good at this.

He glances over, mouth curving into a ruthless smile. "You make it sound like that was a genuine risk."

"It was a calculated risk." I smile, happy my comment didn't make him feel weird. Or maybe it did—I wouldn't know, because everything he does looks easy for him.

"And was it worth it?"

I look at him, the way his eyes linger just long enough to make my pulse tick faster. "I'm still deciding."

He chuckles under his breath—low and genuine. "You're a tough critic, you know that?"

"So I've been told."

"Then I'll take that as a maybe." He gets out of the car, but before I reach for the handle, he opens the door and offers his hand. I take it —his hand is so warm and inviting. I hold back a groan as he wraps it around mine, pulling me out easily.

I collect my bag and realize I forgot the wine bottles for the wedding. "Shit," I say, with wide eyes, "I forgot the wine!" I look at him and he laughs.

"I'll have them delivered, not to worry." He slides his hand in his pocket and pulls out a small cork—the one from the first bottle we'd shared. He holds it out to me between two fingers, groomed and perfect. "A souvenir. In case you ever doubt my credentials."

I take it, brushing his hand. "You keep props for your blind dates?" I tease, finding this a bit too romantic and not enough room to put all the feelings he's making me feel.

"Only the successful ones." He winks at me, sending a warm sensation to my stomach and chest. I gave him a look—the kind that should've been a warning but probably wasn't.

"Goodnight, Adrian." I turn to walk away, but he grabs my hand and places a soft kiss on my knuckles. It surprises me and has me searching his eyes for anything not genuine.

I can't find anything.

"Goodnight, Not-a-Bridesmaid."

He releases my hand and I pause, smiling despite myself. "You're never letting that go, are you?"

"Not a chance."

When I walked away and opened the door to the villa, I didn't have to look back to know he was still watching. I could feel it—that electric charge that settles somewhere between curiosity and trouble.

And as I turned the cork over in my palm, I realized my sister might've been right about something for once. Even though I was definitely going to murder her, I was also thankful she thought of me needing to let loose tonight.

She cares for me like I do her.

How could I be mad at that?

# Chapter Thirteen

The next day, the villa is a madhouse. There are way more staff on the grounds primping and preparing for the Wedding the day after tomorrow. I'm more than overwhelmed.

There was a knock at the front door just as I was walking by, trying to convince myself that coffee was a valid breakfast. I opened the door expecting someone to just need help through. Instead, a man in a crisp delivery uniform stood there, holding a crate of wine bottles and a bouquet so obnoxiously beautiful it looked stolen from a movie set.

"Deliver for... Not-a-Bridesmaid?" He says, squinting at the card.

I freeze. "Excuse me?"

He points to a tag tied to the flowers. "That's what it says."

Of course it did.

He hands everything over before I could explain that my life wasn't actually a rom-com, then walks away out of sight.

The bouquet was stunning—deep burgundy roses and soft white lisianthus. It looked expensive and annoyingly thoughtful. Tucked between the stems was a small card.

*For the reluctant wine critic. —A*

My stomach did that traitorous flutter again.

Perfect timing, because my sister chose that moment to appear in my doorway, latte in hand, still in her yoga outfit and entirely too chipper.

"Who died?" She asks, eyeing the flowers.

"No one." I try to sound casual, but I fail miserably. "They're from the winery."

"Oh?" She set her coffee down, already grinning. "Does the winery usually send personalized bouquets?"

"They're probably a promotional thing."

She grabs the card from my fingers before I could stop her. "'For the reluctant wine critic.' Oh, this is rich." She looks up, eyes glinting. I'm going to strangle her. "So how was your *errand* last night?"

"It wasn't an errand." I set the crate on the counter, then immediately realized that it sounded defensive. "I mean, it was, but also—can you not look at me like that?"

"I'm just observing," Gi says, smirking. "And enjoying the fact that you clearly had fun last night."

"I did not have fun."

She raises an eyebrow, not convinced. "Uh-huh. You're blushing."

"I'm *hydrated*."

"Right. And the flowers are for your hydration, too?"

I blow out a deep breath, pinching the bridge of my nose. "You set me up."

"You're welcome." She takes a long sip of her coffee, utterly unbothered. "He's cute, isn't he?" No, he's gorgeous, but I'm not revealing that to her.

I glare in response. "He's insufferable, just like you." I sip my coffee, refusing to take her bait.

"Cute and insufferable. Excellent balance."

I drop onto a nearby stool propped up against the counter. "You're impossible."

"Oh, insufferable and impossible. I'm collecting quite a list of attributes." She smirks, and I want to wipe it off her face. "You know, I didn't even realize he was going to be there when I booked the tasting. Total coincidence."

"Uh-huh."

"Though," she adds casually, "it might be convenient he's helping out with the wedding now."

My head snaps up. "He's *what*?'

"Yeah, didn't I mention it? He's helping Enzo handle the custom wine for the reception. The vineyard is sponsoring the menu. He's also our travel agent while we are here in Italy. He owns a luxury travel agency specializing in romantic getaways.

I stare at her, speechless.

Her smile widens like she just won a bet. "Guess you'll need to keep that bouquet somewhere special now."

I hate you," I mutter, finishing off my coffee to go search for more. I already feel the pressure between my eyes building, and we still have so much to get done today.

"No, you don't." Gi kisses my cheek and snags one of the bottles from the crate, inspecting the label. "You just hate that I'm right."

She winks, and before I can throw a cork at her, she disappears—leaving me alone with six bottles of wine, a bouquet that smells like trouble, and a card signed with one maddening initial.

The wedding madness blurs around me while I take a moment to breathe. Then I get up and take the flowers up to my room, placing them on the dresser by the window. I admire his thoughtfulness, even though it feels too soon after Connor to feel this rush with someone else. A low churning sensation coils low in my stomach, making me feel like what I'm doing is wrong. Like enjoying a moment that wasn't mine to have.

Not when Connor is probably still hurting.

I shake off the pain, grabbing my laptop to check my email for the hundredth time since I've been here. *Nothing.* No email saying I got in for the Master's program. I drop my shoulders and put away the laptop, trying to tell myself that no response is still good, it's not a no.

I walk out to the balcony facing the olive tree grove, admiring the way they move in the soft breeze. The colors are bright but soft —greens, yellows, blues, and purples—making for a pleasant contrast to the shadows that still coil within. But I try not to dwell on that right now. I fold my arms around my torso as I watch the groundskeepers trim bushes and trees with precision and care. Stefan is swimming in the pool, while Josh's family lies around in lounge chairs. Women in white maids' clothes wipe down tables and arrange flowers around the ground-level terrace that wraps around to the front gate.

What a beautiful scene. Josh and Gi chose the perfect place.

I wonder what Stefan's wedding would look like. Honestly, it will probably be a mountainside wedding while they're summiting. I smile. Yeah, that sounds right.

I get lost in my thoughts; I don't hear the knock or the tap on my right shoulder that makes me jump back, hitting the intruder.

I hear a grunt, just as I turn around. The wind gets knocked out of me again.

It's Adrian. "What are you doing here?" I say, my voice, a pitch higher than it needs to be.

"Wow, you really pack a punch," Adrian says, holding his ribs with one arm. I almost feel bad. But then I see the glimmer in his eyes and think better of feeling sorry for him. He's the intruder, not me. "And here I was thinking you already missed me."

"What are you doing in my bedroom?" I glance at the flowers, hoping he won't see them. He follows my direction and gives me a big smile. *Shit.*

"You kept them," he says, putting a hand to his heart. "You do like me."

"I do not. Now, answer the question. Why are you here?" I tap my foot and fold my arms in front of me.

"Josh sent me."

I blinked at him. "Josh? Gi's Josh? He's in on it, too?!" I question, confused and a little annoyed.

"Is there another Josh I am not aware of? The groom, yes?" He shoots me a puzzled look, making two lines appear between his eyes. "And, in what?"

I roll my eyes, huffing out a long sigh. "Yes, the only groom around here is named Josh. You confuse me. Why did he send you up here?"

"He needs your help, and apparently mine." That mischievous look is back, and I don't like the look he's giving me. Like he's in on a secret and I have to guess.

I don't have time for this. There's too much to do. I stare and tap my foot, waiting. "Well? What is it?"

"Sí, sorry, you look cute when you're mad."

"I'm not mad." And before he can respond, I give him a withering look that says, *Be careful what you say next.*

"Okay. Can we sit?" Adrian asks, pointing to the iron table and chairs on the balcony.

"Sure." He takes a seat across from me, as I cross my bare legs. It's a warm day, so I opted for loose navy shorts that will most likely stick to the bars and a yellow daisy blouse with ties on the shoulders that reminds me of the Tuscan fields. Adrian is wearing dark green dress pants with a black shirt, which feels too hot for this warmth.

"There is an Italian tradition that happens on the eve of the wedding. It's called *La Serenata.* A night of Serenade. Josh sought out my knowledge out of respect for the tradition and love for his beloved. He wants to do it right." Adrian's accent, paired with the joy in his eyes, is a dangerous combination. I want to hear him talk all day, and at the same time, I don't.

"Sounds like a beautiful tradition," I say, trying not to get emotional. I could see Papa doing something like this for Mama. He was such a romantic too. "What do we need to prepare for?"

"I have everything covered, I just need you to keep Gianna in her and Josh's bedroom at Sunset, just after the rehearsal dinner with the doors to the balcony open," he smiles, giving away his playfulness, and I can't help but smile with him.

"Is this some Romeo and Juliet scenario?" I question, curiosity getting the better of me. I love a good tragedy, but I don't want to put Gi through any misfortune.

Adrian shrugs his shoulders. "Maybe, you will just have to wait and see." I want to push for more, but I don't, wanting to be surprised along with Gi. I already know she's going to love what happens. She's a hopeless romantic and getting married in Italy after all.

"Okay, I will help. But if anything goes wrong, I'm blaming you." I point at his face and give him a stern look.

"I wouldn't have it any other way." His eyes light up again, making it impossible to look away.

But I have to, I could easily get lost in those eyes. And I'm not ready for that.

The rest of the day consists of running around and last-minute trips to town. By the time we all have a moment together, we are exhausted, so we return to our rooms to get some much-needed sleep. Even though my eyes are tired, my mind is reeling.

I haven't had much time to think about life back in Boston, and to be honest, I've avoided the details. But in the quiet of my room, there are no distractions. Nothing to put my mind at ease.

Here in the dark, I feel everything.

My steps are light as I walk over to the desk in the room and pull out my journal. I lay the book open and find an empty page as I reach for the colored pastels in the drawer. With only a candle lighting the room, I start adding color to the page. A vineyard takes form, lush with greens and soft textures, and a sunset on the horizon, colored in pinks, oranges, yellows, and lavender.

A hint of blue for twilight.

I get lost in the landscape in my head and the sound of the night beyond the window. Baby blue eyes and dark hair often take shape when I close my eyes, but I try to push them out. They are stubborn, just like their owner. And as much as I would like to banish him from my thoughts, I would be lying to myself if I said I didn't want them. Him. But I have to say no. It isn't safe around me, especially when emotions are involved.

After the wedding, I will never have to see him again. And he won't ever be hurt because of me.

I look out the window and see a shadow in the distance. I can't tell if it's a man, a woman, or a child. But it reminds me that they're watching. Waiting.

And this story of mine is still being written.

It's only the beginning.

# Chapter Fourteen

The night smelled like citrus blossoms and candle wax. Lanterns swung from the olive trees, their light catching on champagne glasses and the soft shimmer of silk dresses. Somewhere beyond the courtyard, the distant sound of the chapel bell ringing—a low, romantic heartbeat echoing through the hills.

Gi wore a beautiful green silk dress that hugged her hips and flowed like water around her. It was traditional for the Italian bride-to-be to wear green as a sign of good luck and good fortune for a long life ahead.

She looks perfect.

She glows like she'd been born for this—the laughter, the adoration, the love story everyone could see coming from a mile away.

The rehearsal dinner went smoothly; Josh's parents were delighted with how everything turned out, and so far, the other bridesmaids have been behaving themselves. For now. There are only three of them, me being the fourth 'Not-a-Bridemaid', making me smile into my champagne glass. I've avoided Adrian all day, thankfully, but now I wonder where he ran off to.

But we are coming up to the moment of the evening.

*La Serenata.*

The band tunes their guitars, a few soft chords floating through the air like a promise. The hushed whispers around me chatter in excitement, waiting for the moment the groom sings to his bride-to-be.

I need to find Gi and take her upstairs for whatever Josh has planned. Not finding her right away, I weave through the small crowd. I round the corner by the pool when I see a couple making out on the bench and look away. But then I take a second look and see that it's Stefan with one of the bridesmaids. Go figure.

"Hey," I hiss at him, trying to get his attention. "Have you seen Gi?" I feel like that is a stupid question to be asking him right now.

He looks up. "Nope," he says, popping the "P" before diving back in. Great.

I look around the courtyard once more before heading inside, hoping she's already in her room. I ease around the line cooks in the kitchen and the waitstaff, carrying trays. I'll have to remember to try some of the mini crème brûlées going out—my mouth is watering. It's my favorite dessert.

I gather my green pleated satin dress and walk up the stairs to my room. I want to check my messages one more time before I find Gi. When I get to my room, I pull my phone out to find an unread email.

It was brief.

Too brief, considering how it had rearranged everything inside of me.

*We are pleased to invite you to submit a final piece for consideration in the Master's program at Accademia delle Belle Arti in Florence. Deadline: four weeks.*

That was it. Four weeks to create something that wasn't just technically strong—but soul-strong. A masterpiece that could speak for me before I ever stepped into a room, that proved I wasn't a fluke or a girl who used to be talented until the world cracked her open.

An opportunity to make me believe in myself again.

Which also meant I needed to stay in Italy—for four long weeks of swallowing failure and trying to remember that I'm capable of doing hard things.

It's happening.

Whether I am ready for it or not. There's no going back.

My body feels frozen. I'm staring at my phone when Gi walks in, and I cannot keep the shock off my face; tears are cascading down my face. She's there, in front of me on the bed, cupping my hands with hers.

Her face falls. "Eve, what's wrong?" She asks, trying to comfort me. I look up at her, not knowing how much I should say, but I can't hold anything back right now.

The air slipped from my lips in a quiet surrender.

"Oh, Gi. I don't know what to do." The weight of this moment feels too heavy to carry alone. I'm tired of carrying it alone. I hang my head, trying to shield my sister from the emotions pouring out of me right now. The fight in me before is gone.

"Shhh... It's okay." Gi soothes, brushing my hair with her hand. "Just tell me."

"I... I lost my apartment. And..." I hesitate, still looking down. I can't believe I'm doing this right now, on a night of celebration. "...and my job." I can't breathe. The air is tight in my chest, and I feel like I'm going to throw up. I look up and around my room, trying to find an escape.

Anything.

"It's okay, we'll figure it out." Gi's kindness spreads through me like rain on a hot summer day. Soothing the panic that's building.

I take a deep breath.

"You don't understand, I submitted an application for a Master's program here in Italy, but I have to submit an original art piece first," I explained, while trying to calm my racing heart.

"Okay, well, that sounds good. Right?"

"Gi, I haven't even picked up a paintbrush in over five years!" I know my voice is louder than it should be, but I can't help the helpless feeling of what this submission actually represents. I actually have to paint. To open up scar tissue that's been ignored for far too long. It's going to hurt. The truth of it is hitting me in more ways than one at this very moment. "It means going to a place I haven't been since I shut that door long ago. I thought I could be ready for it, but I don't know now."

Gi wastes no time in supporting me. "What do you need?"

"What?" I ask, not because I don't understand, but because I've never taken anything from Gi before. Or Stefan. I've always given.

"What do you need?" She repeats, looking me straight in the eye. "If you need a place to stay, stay here at the Villa. Josh and I will pay for the rest of the month or longer."

"I can't ask you to do that," I shake my head, "it's too much."

"Not for my sister," she looks at me in that way again, like she's not taking no for an answer, and I'm way too tired to argue with her.

"Okay, but just until the end of the month. I have four weeks to submit this art piece. Then we will see what happens after that."

Gi's eyes glimmer with excitement, and she pulls me in for a hug. A long one. "I'd do anything for you, sis. And I can't wait to see what you create. I call first dibs to see it when you finish."

I can't help but let out a quiet laugh. "Okay." I pull back and look at her with tears in my eyes. "I love you. You really are going to be the most beautiful bride."

"Enough crying, let's go freshen up so Josh can surprise me with whatever he's got planned." Gi takes my hand in hers, with one last look of understanding, we head to her room to fix the mess we've made with our makeup. I watch her in the vanity mirror and smile. She really is the most beautiful human being on the planet. I can't wait to watch her say "I do" to the man of her dreams and live happily ever after.

Fifteen minutes later, we hear a familiar tune outside her balcony window that faces the courtyard, and I can't help but laugh.

"He didn't!" Gi looks at me with mock horror as the music plays 'This I Promise You' by *NSYNC and she rushes to the balcony to see Josh with a microphone and singing to the song, out of sync and horribly. But it's the cutest thing to watch, because the smile on my sister's face cannot be contained. She's over the moon in love and equally joyful, swaying to the love song.

The crowd is enamored of the display, and I find myself singing along, remembering it as a favorite of Gi's as a teenager. I love that Josh is willing to make a fool of himself just to make my sister happy. That's a win for today.

After the song was done, we made our way back downstairs to the festivities. Everything was going smoothly, and the waitstaff handled everything. I'd like to express my gratitude to the owners after the wedding. They did an amazing job coordinating and executing every detail for this week.

Josh greets Gi with open arms and a boyish grin. They will become husband and wife tomorrow and start a long, happy life together. What more could a big sister ask for?

I'm walking around the courtyard and notice a shift in the air, accompanied by low whispers, when I hear it.

A low, steady voice—not the groom's.

Deeper. Smoother.

A note that seems to stop my heartbeat and glue my feet to the ground.

Adrian.

I whip my head around the courtyard, trying to find his location. Just as the waitstaff part, I see him. He's standing near the corner by the olive trees, framed by candlelight and grinning like he knows exactly what kind of chaos he's starting. His white shirt is rolled at the sleeves, a guitar slung casually across his chest.

"This one," he announces in accented English, "is for someone who is Not-a-Bridesmaid, but loves Italian traditions."

A ripple of soft laughter moves through the crowd as I freeze, heat rising to my cheeks. I shook my head in warning, pleading with him to stop—but it was useless. He'd already begun to play.

The first notes were soft, teasing—not a love song so much as a dare. The kind of melody that puts a smile on your face and makes your heart beat faster. I tried to hold my composure, but my traitorous pulse has other plans. People turned toward me, whispering, smiling. I could see my sister now off to the side with Josh, looking delighted, mouthing *You're welcome.*

She's gonna be a zombie bride tomorrow, because I'm murdering her right after this.

Adrian's voice hits the chorus singing in Italian—like there is no one else here, but me. Like the night, the candles—all of it existed just to witness this. And somewhere between the strum of the guitar and the tilt of his smile, a weight buried deep unfurls.

Not control.

Not resistance.

Just the warm, dizziness of being seen.

It stirs a desire I've kept hidden. A possibility I haven't spoken aloud to anyone, let alone to myself. I don't dare say it now. But I am made aware it's not going away soon. When the last note of his guitar fades, the crowd bursts into applause. Adrian gives a dramatic bow, then walks straight over to me, his grin all sunlight and mischief.

I straighten my spine and roll my shoulders.

"You didn't throw anything," he says softly. "I take that as a good sign."

I roll my eyes, but my mouth betrays me—curving despite itself. "You're ridiculous."

"Maybe," he says, his voice lowering just enough for me to hear. "But you smiled."

I open my mouth to argue, but the words get tangled somewhere between my chest and my throat. Because he's right. Even though I feel unraveled and a bit vulnerable. The world hadn't fallen apart or crashed around me.

But that doesn't mean I can trust it.

Because eventually, it will happen.

And I'm not sure if I will have the strength to stop it.

# Chapter Fifteen

The vineyard had been transformed into a scene straight out of a fairytale. Long wooden tables with white linen were set up in a U-shape, with the bride and groom's table in the center and strings of lights zig-zagged above. Laughter floated on the breeze, matching the soft music playing in the background. This place was absolutely perfect. Charming and romantic, just how Gianna dreamed of it being. I remember the wedding journal she started at age ten, religiously cutting out magazines and marking them up with all the flourishes and sparkles of a girl's future.

The wedding at the chapel went smoothly. Gi had Stefan and me walk her down the aisle—just the three of us. Like it always has been. Stefan and I both fought valiantly to keep the tears at bay, but when she looked at us with joy, love, and a little nervousness, we relented and let them fall. In that bittersweet moment, we hugged each other—a lifeline for years, now moving toward change. And as we handed her off to Joshua, we had every faith our sister was in the best of hands.

I breathed a little easier knowing she would be protected and cared for.

Now, I stood off to the side—wine in hand—a little overwhelmed by the beauty of Tuscany, the joy of community here, and the *completeness* of it all. Gianna looks radiant as she greets everyone, her happiness so bright it makes my chest ache in the best way. The way Josh stares at her says it all. They have both come a long way in their relationship.

I can't wait to see the adventures they grow.

Stefan is giving a toast near the fountain, hamming it up as usual. I laugh along quietly, having already given my toast.

I let my eyes wander around the courtyard and vineyard beyond. Over the guests that flew over to support them—family, friends from Boston, and even some of the locals. They both make quick friends wherever they go. A magnetic energy they can't help but share. I can already see their honeymoon surrounded by a beloved circle of friendly conversations and meals shared with strangers who feel like family by dessert.

I look around, slowly walking around the edge of the crowd, pretending I'm just admiring the lights strung between the olive trees. I tell myself I'm not looking for him—that I'm above that kind of cliché. But my eyes betray me, scanning faces, shadows, the spaces where his voice might slip through.

The man who somehow wedged himself into this wedding like he belonged here.

For four days now, he's been everywhere—lifting crates of wine, charming the guests, blending into the rhythm of the chaos he'd been invited into. Each time I spot him, my curiosity grows and beneath it, there's something else—a restless hum I keep mistaking for anger. Because the truth is, I can't decide if I want to shove him away or find an excuse to talk to him again.

And that confusion. That loss of control—infuriates me more than his smile ever could.

Just when I decided to try and move on from this insanity, that's when I see him.

Across the courtyard terrace, by another set of olive trees wrapped in fairy lights, he stood tall, Sun-kissed, wearing a tailored navy suit and a soft pink satin tie that matched my dress. And a smile like it came with its own soundtrack. Dark hair curled slightly at the ends, like it had given up on being tamed long ago. He leans in to whisper to an old woman, making her laugh so hard she has to clutch her wine glass.

His eyes meet mine.

And for a heartbeat, the world tilted.

He raises his glass in a casual salute, like we're old friends sharing an inside joke. I blink, caught off guard once again by the warmth in his expression. No pressure, no charm-for-hire smile.

Just a spark. Real and unafraid.

He continues to smile at me with unabashed confidence, and my heart does that silly little dance that I couldn't contain if I wanted to.

I look away and try to distract myself by rearranging the centerpieces. They're already perfect—flawless, symmetrical—and I'm probably just ruining them, but I need to keep my hands busy. Anything to keep them from trembling. My fingers brush over petals and glass, the scent of peonies strong and sweet. I get through three of them before the air shifts behind me—before warmth slides across my back like sunlight breaking through the clouds.

It's subtle at first, then unmistakable—his presence reaches me before his words do. Heat rolls down my spine, and goosebumps scatter like wildfire beneath my skin. My breath catches. I close my eyes, trying to steady the pulse that's already tripping over itself. For a heartbeat, I tell myself to stay focused, to keep pretending I don't feel it—but then his shadow joins mine on the tablecloth, close enough to make my body forget every rational thought.

When I finally stand on shaky legs, I know it's him. The man who makes the ground tilt just by existing. I turn slowly, bracing for impact. His eyes glimmer in the light, mouth curved in that infuriating almost-smile that has a way of making the world slip sideways.

And just like that, my carefully stacked composure wavers; one look from him is enough to send it all crashing down.

"Careful," his voice a low ripple in a pond. "If you move one more flower, they'll start charging extra for perfection."

I turn toward him fully, pretending his voice doesn't slide down my spine like honey. "Didn't realize you were an expert in floral arrangements."

"I'm not." His mouth curves upward a little more. "But I know when something looks better untouched."

His words land somewhere between a tease and a promise, and for a moment, I forget to breathe. He takes a step closer, not enough to touch, but close enough that I can feel the heat radiating from him, the faint scent of wine and cedar clinging to his shirt.

"You shouldn't sneak up on people like that," I manage to say, though it sounds more like a whisper than a reprimand.

He lifts a shoulder, while putting a hand in his pocket. "You looked... distracted."

"I was working."

"On centerpieces?" His grin tilts. "Or avoiding me?"

My pulse stumbles. "You have an inflated sense of importance."

"Maybe." He leans in just slightly, voice dropping to a softness that makes me want to lean in close. "Or maybe I just notice the way you stop breathing when I'm around."

The air crackles between us, a quiet standoff of nerves and want. I should say something clever, to deflect, but my thoughts dissolve the moment his eyes meet mine—steady and searching. Unguarded.

He studies me for a heartbeat, then smiles. Not the teasing one this time, gentler, like it could ruin me if I let it.

"You look beautiful, Not-a-Bridesmaid," he says, breaking the tension, and I am glad for it. I crack a smile and look down at my dress.

"Thank you." My cheeks heat, and I fiddle with the ruching of the bodice. This misty rose silk slip dress was a pretty detail Gi picked out. All the girls have the same color and fabric, but each is unique to the bridesmaid, all floor-length and flowy. Mine has an open back with long sleeves that tie at the neck; the silky ribbon tickles between my shoulders when I move. I feel feminine, and the fabric is luxurious on my skin.

"I wanted to make sure I said that tonight and that everything looks stunning." Adrian looks around and then back at me.

I hum in response, feeling awkward. "The staff really outdid themselves." I took a sip of my wine, thankful I had grabbed another glass before he came over.

Just when he was about to open his mouth again, an older Italian couple approached, greeting him in Italian. But what catches my attention is the name they used, *Romeo.*

"*Romeo, che bello vederti,*" the woman says as she kisses both of his cheeks, and the gentleman shakes his hand and says, "*Vogliamo ringraziarti per la raccomandazione dell'hotel.*"

"*È stato un piacere.*" Adrian greets the couple, and they continue their short conversation. I can't help but admire the language. It's transfixing.

I've also just learned that when Adrian speaks Italian, I have no comprehension whatsoever. I hear something about a hotel, and that's it. Oh, and *Romeo.*

I have so many questions.

My body shifts from side to side as I talk myself out of arranging more centerpieces. In what feels more than five minutes, the couple says bye to Adrian, and then he turns toward me. I only have one question.

"*Romeo?*" I say, trying to hide my smile with my hand. I press my lips together and wait for his answer.

"Heard that, did you?" He sighs with a slight curve to his lips. His full lips. He leads me to a cushioned bench next to a bush with a blend of earth and mint. "Romeo is a nickname given to me when I was younger and for the lack of a better word... wild." He looks away, pink spreading across his cheeks.

A blushing Romeo might be my favorite thing to see. It's nice to see him squirm for once. "I mean, how could you not be? This place has charm even for the most depressed person. Believe me, I know." Instead of laughing, he just looks at me with furrowed brows, but he doesn't ask for further clarification.

I'm thankful.

We take a sip of wine and stare out onto the dance floor, watching couples dance with the band to an upbeat song. It's lively. I sway my legs to the beat, enjoying the moment. I catch Gianna's eye, as they widen when they see Adrian and me sitting together. She gives a little fist pump in the air, then is swept away by Josh.

Adrian chuckles, no doubt seeing my sister's display. "Your sister is a charming woman."

"She's something. But she wants to see me happy, and I can't fault her for that."

"Can I ask you a question?" Adrian asks, waiting, watching.

"Sure? I suppose it wouldn't hurt." I cross my legs, smoothing out my dress.

"That day in the market," his eyes met mine, inquisitive, "why didn't you buy the watercolors you were admiring?"

"You saw me at the market?" I ask, my eyes narrow.

"Yes, you were studying a paintbrush like it had just confessed its feelings for you, but I wasn't one hundred percent sure it was you until Gianna scared you. Then I knew." He looks at me with the most curious eyes, like I am a puzzle he's trying to solve.

I laughed before I meant to. It bubbled out of me, real and sudden.

Had he been watching me? Was that why it felt weird that day?

"I didn't notice you," I say, averting my eyes so as not to look so much into his.

"Well, I noticed *you*," he states simply, no trace of ego, just truth.

I gulp the rest of my wine and stand. "I need another drink," I announce, because Adrian's eyes are doing that deep soul-searching thing, and it feels too close to truths I'm not ready for. Not that I'd be sipping sangria and spilling secrets tonight anyway.

I walk away, not saying goodbye.

# Chapter Sixteen

The wedding had begun to dissolve into soft music and flickering candles. The crowd had thinned, laughter giving way to murmured conversations and the sound of clinking glasses as the staff cleared empty dishes. Everything finished smoothly, and Gi and Josh slow-danced to the beat of their own song.

Their own rhythm. It's beautiful to watch.

I took that moment to slip away from the patio to catch my breath, barefoot now, heels dangling from my fingers as I wandered past the grapevines heavy with fruit and the stone path dappled in moonlight. I wanted to stay present in the moment for as long as my mind would let me, but I find it difficult to fully let go of my thoughts. They seem to follow me everywhere I go, even across miles of ocean.

"Running away already?" a deep voice calls out behind me, warm and teasing.

I turn to see Adrian stepping out from the shadows beneath a fig tree, hands tucked into his pockets, that same disarming smile curving his lips. I really should avoid him. There is an energy about him I can't quite figure out. He's alarmingly magnetic, drawing me to him like a moth to a flame.

Damn him. I need to distance myself.

"Just stretching my legs," I say. "Too much wine. Too many people."

"Too many speeches from Stefan?" he guessed, catching up with me easily.

"That too." When Stefan got enough drink in him, he was a force to be reckoned with.

"Your family is great, by the way. Easy to converse with. Funny too." Adrian's voice skates along my skin, a bit of a smile playing on his lips.

"Yeah, my siblings are the extroverts out of the three of us," I say, as if it were important he needed to know that.

"No, you? *Perche*?" he asks, not pushing, but curious.

"Um.. well, I honestly prefer to keep to myself most of the time."

"Sounds like there might be more of a reason. But I won't ask until you're ready to tell me." He says that, like I will eventually tell him, but I won't. Especially because we are still practically strangers. I don't answer him. I just keep walking.

We fall into step together without needing to agree to it, walking in silence past the low stone wall that borders the vineyard. The villa Gianna and Josh booked is stunning. I'm still in awe of the several rooms scattered around three stories of this Tuscan haven. I'm going to miss it when I eventually have to leave. For now, I'm going to have to get acquainted with the studio space and eventually open up a new canvas.

I'm overwhelmed by that, so I stuff it down and look up at the night sky. The moon hangs low, casting silver over the fields. Truly a magical evening. I can finally breathe now. Knowing it all went so well means more than I can say.

"You don't like crowds," he says gently, an observation. He seems to be doing that a lot in the short time I've known him.

I take a glance at him. "Not when I don't know who I am in them." The revelation comes easily, still unsure why I am even sharing something so personal. I really should keep my mouth shut.

He looks at me then, not like most people do, with expectation or politeness, but with this stillness, like he's content just to listen.

"That's the thing about Italy," he says. "People don't expect you to be anyone but yourself. Even if you're still figuring out who that is." Or reinventing a whole new wheel?

I smile faintly. "And have *you* figured that out?"

Adrian's laugh is low and easy. "Not even close. But I know what I love. I know what makes me feel alive. And I try to follow that. Sometimes it leads me to strange places. Sometimes... to art markets or blind dates." His smile is small, with just a hint of a dimple on the right. I bet he has dimples on both sides when his smile is really big.

I glance sideways, catching the curve of his jaw in the low light. "So you were following the feeling when you spotted me?" I know I'm digging, but I am curious about his intentions.

He grins. "Well, that, and you looked like someone who needed reminding she still has a spark." His words catch me off guard.

They aren't flirtatious. They're kind. Disarmingly kind.

I stop walking and close my eyes, letting the breeze tangle my hair, letting his words settle in my bones. I take a large, deep breath. My heart is battling with my mind. Adding to the war I am quite familiar with. If I'm not careful, one dark thought will lead to another.

"Your sister may have spilled on you losing your job and home." He winces, knowing that revelation could have ended his chance to get to know me—and yet—no hesitation to let me know the truth. Dammit, Gi, that girl is going to get a piece of my mind.

"It's hard," I say, quieter now. "Starting over. I keep thinking I should feel excited, grateful even. But I mostly just feel... untethered." Like stepping into a black hole, not knowing if anything will catch me, or if I will just keep flailing and falling to a darker place.

Adrian steps in front of me, not too close, just enough. "Maybe untethered isn't a bad thing. Maybe it's just freedom dressed up like fear."

The world pauses for a second, long enough for me to see the depth behind his lightness, the steadiness behind his stance. He wasn't just cheerful. He's deeply rooted in passion, maybe. Or joy. Or simply nosy for his own good. There's an undercurrent that sweeps away all rationality, that I should be careful of.

I quirk a smile at the jab that never makes it past my lips. I don't get a chance to. I take a few steps back, falling into a small hole I couldn't see. Too much wine. Adrian reaches out like lightning, catching me easily. "Whoa, I've got you, *cara*." Adrian is dangerous all by himself, but Adrian speaking Italian while holding me in his arms is a double-edged sword too much for my brain and my body to handle in this state.

The slight hint of citrus and masculine scent sends my nerves over the edge.

*Focus.*

He helps me back to standing, tucking my arm into his like a gentleman, playful and sure. "Come on. I know a shortcut through the vines. And there's a fig tree at the edge of the property that grows the sweetest fruit from the warmth of the day."

I hesitate—just for a moment—before nodding. Curiosity gets to me once more. And maybe to match his playfulness a bit. Or to find out what else he has hidden in that head of his.

I'm tired. Tired of holding everything in, of carrying the weight of what I've been through like it's stitched to my skin. Maybe it's a weakness, or maybe it's just human, but right now I don't have the energy to push it all away. The warmth of connection, even if it's just friendship, feels like a quiet kind of relief.

A place to rest.

Still, a voice in the back of my mind whispers that I'm lying to myself—that I can pretend this is harmless, that I'm not craving more than I can afford to feel. Emotionally bankrupt, and yet here I am—spending pieces of myself I swore I didn't have left.

And the worst part? It feels good.

Too good.

"Lead the way."

And as we disappear into the moonlit vines, the path uncertain and the night full of possibility, I feel an awareness inside me stir again. Not the girl who had lost everything. But the woman who was starting to find *something else*. But that's crazy, because nothing can happen.

I can't be in a relationship, especially not with some Italian stranger.

It's just a walk, nothing else.

The tall grass brushes against my ankles as we veer off path, Adrian guiding me by starlight and instinct. At least I hope so, I have no idea where we are. The vineyard feels like another world at night, wild with the wind, alive, breathing in time with the crickets. His movements are confident, with the kind of ease that invites you to trust him, even though my mind whispers caution.

"You always steal figs at weddings?" I ask, trying to keep things light.

"Only when the moon is this perfect," he says, looking up with a twinkle dancing in his eyes. "And when I'm trying to impress someone." I roll my eyes and look away to hide my smile. He's good. And I find myself leaning into that goodness with each step.

We reach the edge of the property, where a twisted fig tree hides behind overgrown bushes and prickly vines. To the left is a well-hidden pathway that Adrian leads us through. He reaches up easily and plucks one, then another, offering one to me without fanfare. I hesitate, watching him take a bite first. Juice runs down his chin and wrist, and he laughs, wiping it away with the back of his hand. That act alone is so sexy, and I internally slap myself for delighting in the fantasy.

I bite into mine—the white sap bleeds onto my hands, and the fig splits open, soft, sweet, with a honeyed flavor. I savor the unique flavor from the warmth of the sun that hits my tongue perfectly. "Hmmm... that is so good." Without even thinking about the company I am with, I recall a fun Italian fact. "Did you know that Italian Renaissance poets used the image of the fig as an erotic metaphor for female genitalia? Who knew eating a fig could be so provocative?"

He chokes and coughs, but recovers quickly and then smiles back at me. I caught him off guard. *Good.* Just like he has me since meeting him. I give myself a mental pat on the back.

"Well, Eve... you're full of surprises, aren't you? I wasn't expecting mystery *and* wit. Now I'm intrigued. What else are you hiding?"

"Wouldn't you like to know?! *O Romeo, Romeo! Wherefore art thou Romeo??!*" I elaborately display in my best Juliet voice.

"Careful—I might start thinking you've been hiding this wicked sense of humor on purpose. What else have you been keeping under wraps?"

"Hmmm, guess you will have to wait and see. But don't let my wine-infused brain fool you. I'm usually boring."

We stand facing each other, laughing and chewing. It should feel awkward. But it doesn't. It's fun. Too enjoyable. I hardly know this guy. I take a look around the area we are in and then up at the stars.

"So," he says after a moment. "Why does someone with eyes like that, eyes that see the world like it's made to be painted, look like she's constantly bracing for impact?"

My fingers freeze around the fig.

I look down, away, anywhere but at him. "You don't know me."

"No, I suppose not," he says quietly. "But I see fragments. Even when you think you hide them well. We are all fragments, Eve, shards of color, experiences, memories, and feelings.

I swallow hard, throat tight. A thousand things press against my ribs, none of them easy to say. The truth scratches at the surface. But I keep my mouth shut. No need to tell a complete stranger what festers. What darkness lingers, even though I am tired of keeping it to myself.

"Do you ever wonder what would happen if you lost everything?" I say, finally, voice barely above a whisper. "Not all at once. Like watching a boat drift away, and realizing too late you're not on it anymore?"

Adrian doesn't say anything. He doesn't try to fill the silence. He just lets it be.

His silence makes me want to fill it, so I keep going. Here in the dark with wine loosened lips, I feel like I can say anything. The way Adrian stands a little closer, waiting, gives me the boldness to trust the space he's created. To lean on, even if as only a friend.

"My job, my relationships. The life I thought I wanted. All gone. And the worst part?" I laugh, but it feels hollow. "I'm still not sure who I was in all of it." I'm stunned, I said that out loud. That particular insecurity usually stays hidden within my mind. Locked. Sealed.

Adrian steps closer, not touching, just *there*. "Sounds like you're finding out now?"

I look up at him, into those maddening, open crystal blue eyes. "But what if I'm too tired to start again? What if I've forgotten how?" *Too close, Eve. Don't forget how the last one ended.*

Adrian's smile fades into something softer, quieter. "Then let someone remind you. Not to fix it. Not to take it from you. Just—stand next to you while you try." He touches a loose curl by my cheek, giving it a light graze with his finger, and then tucks it behind my ear. I want to lean into his hand, but I don't dare.

I draw in a quiet breath, my chest fluttering with a mix of wonder and curiosity, wrapped up in fear and shadow. It undid the knot in me a little more.

And that was a problem.

Because I can already feel the pull, warm and dangerous. Like standing too close to the edge of a dream I might actually want. Falling for a completely different reason. "I'm not ready," I say in a rushed voice, stepping back slightly. "For anything. For *someone*."

"I didn't ask you to be," he replies, voice steady like I didn't just deliver a blow to his face. He smiles, but it doesn't quite reach his crystal eyes. "I just asked you to walk with me. That's all."

I nod, the sting behind my eyes threatening to spill. "Just a walk?"

"Just a walk," he echoes.

With that revelation from both of us, we wander a little longer through the vineyard, saying less, but somehow *feeling* more. And when we finally turn back toward the lights of the villa, quiet and close. Not touching. My heart beats a little louder than it has in a long, long time.

Not because I had fallen.

But because I knew now that I *could*.

And that terrifies me more than anything.

# Chapter Seventeen

I sip my coffee—strong and bitter, no sugar. The way I like it when I'm trying to shake off regret—and mentally scold myself for the wine and the weakness I let show. I said too much. Now, I am stewing over all the interactions from last night as I sit on one of the oversized cushion chairs, placed aesthetically on the terrace, in one of my oversized linen shirts, brushing sleep from my eyes. I cradle the warm ceramic mug in both hands, steadying it more than warming. My mouth is dry, my head feels thick, but it wasn't the wine that was gnawing at me.

*God, what did I say last night?*

Bits of the night flickered back like lightning in fog. Moments of laughing too loudly, leaning in too close, and talking too freely. Adrian's eyes—light in the dark, unguarded. The tense moment near the fig tree was honest and sincere. But the way he looked at me, like he was hearing my soul instead of just listening to my words, was the problem.

I never meant to let anyone see me like that.

Most men don't even notice when I deflect with a joke or let my silence answer for me. But Addrian watched me like he was trying to read a language he almost knew.

Or was curious to know more.

And I let him.

I blow out a breath and take a sip of coffee. The coffee scalds my tongue—just how I like it when I need to burn the sleep and softness away. I shouldn't have had that much wine.

The wind blows dried leaves across the ground, pulling a wild curl from behind my ear.

I let it.

I let myself feel undone, for a minute longer. My thoughts played like a movie of me disappearing into the vineyard with *the very charming Romeo*.

Oh Adrian. I sigh. What an intriguing man he's turning out to be.

"Good morning, sister dearest." Gi strides into the sunlight with Josh in tow. Freshly showered and full of newlywed energy. She is the epitome of light, and I love watching her shine. Even if it's a little too early.

"Morning," I grumble into my cup, not mentally ready for the day.

"Did Stefan leave already?" Gi looks at me like I should know the answer to our brother's disappearing act. He's probably already onto his next adventure. The Dolomites have been calling his name for years, and he has requested time off to climb them for his upcoming birthday. "I thought I saw him with a girl last night." She wiggles her eyebrows and starts on the breakfast buffet laid out by the owners.

"He is quite the ladies' man, no doubt. But no, I haven't seen him." I cut the questions about Stefan with a girl short; I do not need that image in my head. I already need to burn my brain from seeing him making out by the pool. Oh, the pool. "Did you check the pool? Maybe he's working out again."

"Good point." Gi pops a grape in her mouth, continuing to fill her plate, Josh mirroring her movements. "Do we know when he's leaving for northern Italy?"

"I think the day after tomorrow. He and his team wanted to get to the base of the mountains to settle before the hefty climb." Josh replies, having actually talked through the details with Stefan. We are all excited for him, but a little nervous too. The Dolomites are a beast, and it's been on Stefan's list for so long, him wanting to connect with Papa on Italian soil in his own way.

"Are you guys heading out on your Italian Honeymoon?" I smile, knowing they'll have the best time. While Stefan was heading north, Gi and Josh were heading south to the Amalfi Coastline.

"Yes, we're so excited to tour the tiny villages and cities that I've read about and soak up the beauty of the coast," Gi says, her eyes glowing as they meet Josh's. There's a softness in her gaze, the kind that only comes from trust. Josh looks back at her with a warmth so full and steady, it's clear—his love doesn't just match hers, it magnifies it.

"Well, I hope you lovebirds have the best time together. I'm so happy for you." I truly love that my sister has this next chapter in her own life to look forward to. I respect Josh for giving her the best gift of all, security.

They both take a seat on the loveseat, setting their plates down in the center of the table. Their laughter fills the space while they eat. I take another sip of coffee.

"So, Eve," Josh starts, "Gi tells me you need the villa for a bit longer? I wanted to let you know that it's yours for the next six weeks. I already talked with Giuseppe and Anna to confirm it." Josh smiles and then kisses his wife's temple. His wife.

I smile, tears filling my eyes. "You guys are so generous, and I can't thank you enough for this gift. I'm so nervous to start this artistic process again." I blow out a breath through pursed lips.

"You deserve this, Eve." My sister looks at me like she did when she was little. So full of hope and light. "And who knows, maybe you'll have time for... other things." She wiggles her eyebrows and shimmies her shoulders, in an attempt to deflect from me taking a favor. I can't deny her.

She is my absolute weak spot, and she knows it.

I still have to stand my ground somehow. "No, don't even," I say, arching a brow at her and giving a look that says *don't push it.*

Just when I thought I'd avoid talking about Adrian, she looks at me with a wicked smile. "Oh, I forgot to ask you, how did your evening stroll go with *Romeo*?" She bats her lashes, trying to look innocent. She's not. Far from it, actually. I still haven't had a chat about *La Serenata.*

Or the blind date.

I pinch the bridge of my nose and let out another deep sigh. "Don't call him that. And mind your own business," I quip, toying with my ceramic mug and looking out toward the vineyard where we walked.

She shrugs her shoulders with a wink, "Just curious." Oh hell no. Not happening.

"Gi, no. Don't get any more ideas. I am not here for that long, and it would be very wrong to lead him on." Not that I would lead him on intentionally anyway. That man already has me ensnared in his decadent smile and luscious lips.

*No, Eve. Stop those thoughts right now.*

"A lot can happen in six weeks. It's okay to live a little, sis," she says, her voice gentle but laced with a deep—quiet hope, maybe even concern. Like she's been waiting for me to stop holding my breath and finally allow myself land somewhere that feels like home. Just like she's found a home with Josh. Even if I wanted to, I can't. I promised myself I wouldn't put anyone else through that torture. Especially with Connor's distraught face still haunting my dreams.

"And for the record, don't go around telling random strangers my life story. Not everyone needs to know how pathetic my life is." I really look at her, driving my point home.

"Sorry, he's just such a genuine person and honestly perfect for you. He's been so helpful with the wine and all of our travels here. We got so many deals that I'm sure would have cost a fortune, if it were not for his expertise."

I get up to make a plate of fruit, secretly wishing there were pastries. I make a mental note to get more later. "Last night was lovely, but there will be nothing else between us. Not now, not ever. I need to focus on getting this art submission turned in and then figure out the next steps.

I can't have a future without some sort of direction—and definitely not with someone like Adrian. He's too..." I don't even know what I'm trying to say. I don't have a straight answer. I don't even have one for myself.

"Too perfect?" She provides, trying to get me out of my head.

I laugh, "Too cheerful," and she and Josh join me. She gets up and hugs me, hanging on like it's our last goodbye. We should be used to these long time periods where we don't see each other often, but we still feel the weight of it. We hold on for a second longer when a shout comes from the iron gate to the left of the terrace.

Our heads spin toward the intruder. I wasn't expecting anyone. Certainly not *him*.

I narrow my eyes at Gi, but she just shrugs and looks at me like she doesn't have a clue as to why Adrian is shouting by the iron gate.

"Eve!"

I turn to lean over the stone railing.

There he is. Adrian, Romeo—or whatever he's calling himself. Dressed in a white buttoned shirt that clings in all the right places, aviators perched on his head, and a tote bag slung over one shoulder—like a man who absolutely has a plan.

"What are you doing here? The wedding's over, nothing more for you to do." I'm instantly aware of my messy bun and lack of anything resembling real pants. And he notices, his eyes slowly raking up my bare legs.

Why do I feel naked all of a sudden?

"Kidnapping you!" He shouts, grinning from ear to ear. "I've come prepared."

I raise an eyebrow. "You're too cheerful for this early."

He holds up a paper bag with a simple reply. "Pastries."

Damn him.

I turn around to see the biggest smile on my sister's face, which tells me she thinks I'm full of shit and that whatever happened between Adrian and me was a bigger deal than I let on.

Shit.

# Chapter Eighteen

An hour later, we're saying our final goodbyes to the newlyweds before they head out, when we discovered that Stefan did, in fact, hook up with a girl last night and waltzed into the villa with a fresh face and a skip in his step. He wanted to get a jump on packing his gear and excused himself just after.

I changed into something that made me look less like I'd just fled a cult. Now we are gathered in the foyer of the Villa. Josh is loading the luggage into their car when Gianna turns to me and Adrian. "You have my permission to kidnap my sister every day until she decides to leave."

"Sure thing, captain!" Adrian gives my sister a salute, like they're in on a secret at my expense. "You guys let me know if you need anything on your travels." He hands Josh an envelope with their itineraries for the next few weeks. They nod and thank Adrian for taking care of everything. I hug my sister and Josh, and wave them off as they head down the dirt road with "Newlyweds" written on the back of their car, holding back tears and a sob in my throat.

Adrian hands me a coffee, but holds the bag of pastries just out of reach. "You ready?" He smiles, holding out a hand. "Your chariot awaits."

I roll my eyes and walk past him to his car, but immediately stop when I see the cherry red vintage car in front of me.

My jaw drops. Speechless.

"She's pretty to look at, isn't she?" Adrian steps up beside me. "She cost a pretty penny, too. Don't be fooled, I worked hard for her." He looked at me like that statement was important for me to know. Great.

I finally find my words, my heart beating fast. "I can't believe you have a classic Alfa Romeo. Is that why they also call you *Romeo*?" I tease, unable to help myself.

"Perhaps, but my family's been calling me that for years before I purchased this beauty." He smiles, light and warm. I'm beginning to understand why they call him Romeo.

He opens the passenger door just before I could move to grab it myself. This man. I climb in and get settled, taking a sip of my coffee—Hazelnut. I hold myself back from moaning into my cup. How did he know that was my favorite flavor?

One word. Gianna.

And why does it taste better than anything I've ever made in my life? The nutty flavor and the sweetness explode in my mouth.

I realize I was so wrapped up in my coffee that I've forgotten my surroundings. Easy to do when it tastes so damn good. I look over and find Adrian looking at me with amused eyes. "Italy really knows how to make the best coffee," he says with a curve to his lips. "No judgments here, moan away." And now my cheeks turn pink while I shove my face with a buttery pastry.

Definitely not moaning. I have willpower after all.

We're driving through the countryside, the windows down and the smell of lavender and dust drifting in. I watch the scene unfold before me. The Tuscan landscape feels like slipping into a dream you never want to wake up from. The narrow, winding roads twist and bend through golden hills that roll like soft waves beneath a sun-drenched sky.

I could settle here. It's so peaceful and full of life. It's the type of place I could paint every day and never tire of its beauty. I see myself dancing in fields of sunflowers as they tilt their golden faces toward the light. I would mirror them, wearing a sun dress to match their texture. I imagine standing tall with the rows of cypress trees lining the roads like sentient beings, guiding you toward quiet hilltop villages where terracotta rooftops peek out from ancient stone walls.

Yeah, I could get used to this real-life painting. I glance over at Adrian and wonder where he's taking me. Part of me likes not knowing, but the planner in me is curious.

"Where are you taking me? A museum, perhaps?" I ask as we curve down a back road flanked by olive trees. So many olive trees.

"No, that would've been too predictable," he says, grinning. "Besides, museums are full of what's already been done. I want to show you what *could be*."

His words settled somewhere low in my chest, even if it sounded like he was dissing my favorite pastime. "I'll have you know, museums are fascinating." I gawk, watching his dark locks dance across his chiseled face. "Where beauty and creativity burst within each art piece. Each is written with history and foundation for art, highlighting the human experience."

His eyes meet mine with a smile full of intrigue. "Yes, but looking in the past robs you of your future. Trust me. Let me show you other places that are brimming with life and artistry you have yet to experience."

I keep my gaze fixed forward, replaying his words. It feels like a warning I know too well—asking more means knowing more. And knowing more about Adrian? That's where it starts—how people lose themselves. That's how I could end up somewhere I can't crawl out of, if I'm not careful.

As the silence grows, so does my curiosity. I should probably just let it go, but it's gnawing at me, and in the end, my inquisitive nature wins. "Do you like being called Romeo? I mean, is that what you prefer? And your answer may very well be the deciding factor on whether we can even be friends." I hold his gaze as he lets out a full belly laugh, and oh my god, it's delicious.

Like hot buttered rum, soothing and rich as it coats everything in me.

Shifting his head back and forth between me and the road, his infectious smile made me smile. "*Si,* I knew you had spark in you. A fire that burns hotter than you let on. I like this about you, Eve. A truth for a truth, then. I will tell you my name for yours. Eve sounds like a nickname as well, is it not?" I glance at him, curiosity tugging at the edge. I'm caught off guard by the sincerity in his voice and how it feels like we've been friends for a long time.

Easy. Comfortable. Safe. And that's what unsettles me. Because with him, my secrets feel dangerously close to spilling out. And I'm terrified of revealing too much.

"Evolet," I reveal, twisting my hands in my lap while looking out at the rolling hills and passing olive trees. Anticipating his answer. Slowly, I bring myself to look at him again, and all humor is gone from his face. Left in its place is the most serene smile.

"Evolet," he reverently rolls with perfect accented English. Like just saying my name brings him life. "*E molto bello.* That is very beautiful. *Grazie.* Thank you for sharing with me."

"Now, to give you my name." A look that sends my stomach into a frenzy, his voice carries a hint of formality. "Adrian Amoroso." He pauses before saying, glancing at my face. "Most people call me Adrian, but occasionally, earlier acquaintances from my early days as a teenager, will call me out as Romeo." There's a hint of nostalgia in his pretty blues that both lightens and dims — that shift piques my curiosity, but I don't ask.

Not yet.

"I like that name way more. Can I call you Adrian?" His hands grip the wheel a second before he looks at me again. With heat. It warmed my face despite the cool morning air.

"*Si*—the way you say it sounds sexy. I love when it leaves your lips."

Oh. Oh no.

The words spill out easily, like it's nothing. But it knocks the air right out of me. My thoughts scatter, my words vanish. I have to turn my head, just to collect myself—to pretend I'm not unraveling with every casual compliment he throws my way.

This man is dangerous.

Not in the way that sets off alarms, but in the quiet, unassuming way that sneaks up on you. The kind of danger that doesn't feel like falling—until you've already hit the ground.

And I know myself well enough to see the edge when I'm standing on it. If I stay too close to his warmth, I'll melt.

I'll give in. And there'll be no coming back from that.

Our first stop on this spontaneous kidnapping was a tucked-away painter's studio in a sleepy village, run by an elderly couple who barely spoke English but lit up when Adrian greeted them in Italian. The walls were covered in chaotic beauty—unfinished canvases paused, but not forgotten, still waiting for the chance to be complete.

To make it whole.

A blend of palettes stained with decades of color swirled with texture, while the light filtering in through cracked shutters danced across the brushstrokes.

It was breathtaking.

I took a moment to stop in the center of the room, silent, while Adrian wandered ahead. I run my fingers along the edge of a wooden table splattered with dried paint. The smell of turpentine is present, mixed with a blend of oil and earth. It fills my lungs and sparks a memory of me painting flowers I discovered while walking home after school one day.

That was a good day.

It was *before.*

I continued to wander along walls filled with softly lit, golden-hour depictions of the Tuscan countryside, with vineyards, olive groves, and winding roads. They are famously painted by many artists over the years, captivating visitors near and far.

Many watercolor paintings of misty morning fog rising over fields, with silhouettes of distant farmhouses, fill another wall. That seems to be a popular choice. My personal favorites are the intimate renderings of sun-dappled cobblestone streets, weathered wooden doors, and flower boxes overflowing with sunshine-yellow geraniums.

The studio was brimming with life and love for art, a studio I see myself owning and teaching in. A pulse fluttered in my stomach, soothing an ache that's been festering for way too long. A forgotten dream, bubbling to life within me once more.

"You okay?" Adrian asks, quietly returning to my side.

I nod. "This... this feels like what I used to dream about. A place to be free in the pursuit of creation, surrounded by like-minded artists." I gaze around the studio, still in awe.

"Then maybe it's time to start dreaming again," he offers his arm, waiting for permission. I hesitate for a moment, looking for a hidden agenda in his eyes. There isn't one, at least not one I see. I thread my arm through his, and then he's pulling me into another room filled with bigger canvases painted with different mediums. "Bigger perhaps?"

"Hmmm. Perhaps." I give a noncommittal response because a war is raging inside my body. Being here brings up so many memories and emotions I wasn't prepared for. It feels about fifty/fifty good and bad. Adrian doesn't let go of my arm. Instead, he tugs me alongside him as if I've always belonged there. I'm trying not to lean too far into him, but failing miserably. It's like he knows, and I'm thankful for the quiet support.

After perusing the studio and the little shops surrounding it, Adrian takes me to a hillside town I hadn't even heard of, where we wander through cobblestone alleys and stumble across an impromptu artist fair. With color bursting from everywhere, I can't hide my wide smile as I take it all in. Children draw with chalk on the ground in different swipes and swirls, old women selling pressed flowers delicately managed with aged hands, a man sculpting clay in the shade while opera plays softly from a tinny speaker.

So simple, but grand in the best way.

Adrian ducks into a tiny shop with a quick *Be right back.* And a playful look.

He emerges with a sketchbook and drawing pencils, then hands it to me without a word. I look at it like it was a dare and look up to see the challenge in his eyes.

"You don't have to finish anything," he says, "You just have to start." My eyes seek his, trying to find some hint of judgment, but there is none. He is honest, sure of himself, and of me for some strange reason.

I have no idea why.

Reluctantly, I follow Adrian to a sun-warmed bench on the edge of the town square, sit down, and stare out with the sketchbook resting on my lap. I watch. I wait. I observe. After what feels like too long, I open the book and let the pencil move, sketching the sculptor's hands

I saw at the artist fair, the flower vendor's wide hat and wrinkled skin, Adrian's profile as he leans against a tree watching me—not possessive, not intense.

Just *there*.

Just *seeing*.

I try to quiet my mind and let my hands move without thinking—just sketching whatever finds me. It's messy, uneven. None of it is beautiful, not really. I'll probably tear it all up later. But for now... I'm here. The light is soft, the breeze carries a sweet scent, and I let myself belong to the moment.

Adrian doesn't speak. He doesn't fill the silence or interrupt my drawing.

He just sits nearby, scribbling in a notebook—not close enough to touch—but close enough to feel his steady and solid presence. Like he's part of the landscape—*real* in a way that's almost unnerving. And even though I don't look up, I know he's still there. And somehow... that makes me braver.

In my bravery, I can be who I want to be in this moment right now. I can be the artist I've dreamed of becoming. Staying in my comfort zone has led me down a long and lonely road of pain and suffering. Maybe it was time to veer off on an unknown road that leads to a destination I can be proud of. The problem is not knowing the destination, but all the unknown curves and bumps along the way. What if I get even more lost than I already am?

What if that destination changes and I can't find my way again? Going down a terrifying road I haven't yet explored doesn't feel brave. It feels irresponsible.

It feels like a place I may not come back from.

However, moving forward is forward, right?

Right.

# Chapter Nineteen

By sunset, we end the day by the sea. A quiet cove, he claims, is "his secret," even though I strongly suspect half the village knows about it. The cove cradles the sea. It's not grand or dramatic, but it steals my breath just the same. Adrian leads me to a flat rock by the edge of the water, setting a soft blanket down before we watch the sky melt into pink and orange, the horizon stretching out.

The ocean is serene and comforting. I love the sound of the waves lapping at the shore, playing tag that brings a smile to my face. The water is a surprise—clear and impossible blue, not the theatrical sapphire of postcards. I love how it touches everything like a lover's hand tracing skin. It deepens to jade as it draws away from the sandy shore. I don't just feel like a visitor, I feel a part of a cinematic landscape. The ocean brings a serenity to the storm living and breathing inside. Like I could whisper my secrets to the waves, and they would listen and then carry them away completely.

What a beautiful feeling. I could come here every day and not grow tired of its comfort.

"You do this for all the tourists?" I tease, toes hanging in the water.

"Only the ones who look like they've forgotten how to live," he replies easily, tossing a pebble into the tide.

"I haven't forgotten." My eyes drift away from his. "I just...needed a reminder." I needed this change of scenery and, to be honest with myself. Today has been amazing and sparked more than I can handle, dangerously close to a wildfire if I don't reel it in. So many ideas, and I don't feel like I have the time to execute them into a single painting for the art submission. I can't think past that. Every time my thoughts search for answers, my stomach tightens and twists.

He looks at me, no smirk, no joke—just the kind of stillness that makes you feel like it's okay to be comfortable inside your own skin. "Well," he says softly, "I hope you'll stay long enough to remember the rest."

And for the first time, I didn't immediately push the idea away. I could get used to this. This place. These people.

This feeling like I belong here.

Italy was no longer just a place I ran to.

It was starting to feel like a place I could *begin from.*

And Adrian?

He wasn't trying to save me.

He was just lighting the path I hadn't dared to take alone.

The problem is, the darkness hasn't gone away with miles of ocean. It's just sleeping. Waiting.

And I am scared of that silence.

What will happen when it awakens?

They say not to live in the past, and while I am trying to crawl my way forward, it feels like a weight pulls me down for no reason at all. When I move forward and make progress, an obstacle is shoved in my path, blocking the way. It's discouraging, yes, but it's also the life I've become used to. I stopped doing what I loved because of the cruelty I felt at the time. But doing nothing hurts more. Becoming numb to everything was slowly killing me, until I was drowning in the pain of the past and not seeing my successes for the gift they were.

"You know, the ocean holds more secrets than we could ever know in a lifetime, and yet, we keep searching to uncover its treasure. Some say the ocean holds no memory, but I beg to differ," Adiran says, looking out into the sea with reverence and respect. "These celestial waters cradle tradition and swallow pain like it was meant to. Like, its purpose was to always be unpredictable so humanity couldn't control it. It's perhaps the only thing that can withstand time and cleanse the world of its darkness. It holds the power to swallow up anyone or anything at any given moment and erase them. In the same vein, acts of love are embedded and entangled in motion within the endless surf."

I don't even know how to follow up on something so profound and beautiful; it rivals even the most stunning or articulate paintings I've seen. "I love your perspective, it gives me hope that it could possibly wash away my pain, my sorrow. I want to believe that I could someday create meaningful art that portrays that kind of passion. I would love to leave that kind of legacy for others to enjoy, to evoke that kind of emotion when they enter my gallery." I let out a soft laugh, a little shaky and unsure. "At least, that's my pipe dream, if you will. There is still so much to accomplish between now and then. If I am even capable of such a thing."

Adrian looks at me, like I am the best thing he's ever seen, and it unnerves me. I feel like I don't deserve his praise. "Oh, I believe you will. You will, Eve," he repeats. "I see the passion simmering underneath, it's in your veins and in your soul, waiting to be set free. It's going to be stunning what you create. Every stage will get you closer to your happy ever ending. Just wait and see." His eyes are glowing, and I can't help but believe him.

Even if it's small and timid.

The stars begin to dot the twilight sky by the time we wander back up the hill from the cove, sand still clinging to our feet, the air cooler now and humming with crickets. Our time by the ocean was simple and exactly what I had needed. Time to rest.

To *breathe*.

Adrian reaches for my hand and slowly slips his fingers against my palm, warm and secure. My breath stutters, just once, before I can steady it. I feel his warmth all the way up my arm and into my chest. His thumb barely grazes my skin, the gentlest pass of warmth that somehow unravels the tight knot sitting in my chest.

I don't look at him. I don't have to. His presence settles me like an anchor, quiet and unmoving. The kind of calm that asks nothing and gives everything simply by being there.

My fingers tighten around his, just a little, and he answers with a soft squeeze, as if to say *I'm here*.

*I'm not going anywhere.*

We reach his classic Alfa Romeo parked beneath an ancient olive tree, and instead of getting in, he spreads the sketchbook I'd used earlier across the hood of the car. The pages flutter in the breeze, containing rough pencil strokes, unfinished lines, quick moments I didn't even remember capturing. Uncertainty shadowed among the scenes if you were looking closely enough.

And Adrian always looks too close.

"You still think you're lost," he acknowledges, not looking at me, just flipping the pages gently. "But I see someone who's slowly mapping her way back to herself." He brings his eyes up to mine. "You think uncertainty is a bad thing, but really, getting lost is the best way to find yourself again. Ditch all the pretense of what you think you should do, and reach out towards your surroundings, feel your way back."

His voice was so soft, it almost disappeared into the night. I wrapped my arms around myself, the wind biting a little now. And before I can stop myself, the words fall out.

"I end relationships before they even get a chance to start," I whisper into the dark. "I push others away when it becomes intense, and I make everything harder than it has to be."

Adrian turns toward me, still as stone.

"I tried to shrink. To soften the edges. I stopped painting. I stopped asking for more in my life because every day was a struggle. And event ually... I stopped recognizing who I was when I looked in the mirror."

I stare at the gravel beneath my feet, blinking fast. "My Ex left because *I* pushed him out. I'm pretty sure he was going to propose, and I had to put a stop to that. I won't get married. Not ever."

There it was.

The wound.

Not festering, not bleeding anymore. But tender. Real.

Adrian doesn't rush to fill the space.

He just takes a step closer and reaches into his bag for his keys. "Wait here."

I watch, confused, as he ducks into the car. He rummages for a moment, then comes back with something wrapped in a soft piece of linen. He hands it to me with care.

I unwrap it slowly, hands slightly shaking.

A small wooden box fits perfectly in my palm. Worn, hand-carved, and painted with tiny details—a fig tree, the sea, a sun rising behind Tuscan hills. Inside was a set of watercolor paints.

They looked old. Loved. Beautiful.

"These were my mother's," he says quietly. "She was an artist. Never famous. But everything she touched had color until she gave it up."

I look up, stunned. "Adrian... I can't—"

"They've sat in a drawer for years," he interrupts gently. "Waiting for the right hands to bring them back to life." He presses a paintbrush in my hands, curling my fingers around it with his warm hands.

My throat tightens.

"I see color in you, Eve. Even when you don't."

The tears come fast, no longer held at bay. I press a hand to my mouth, unable to speak. I look away to hide the vulnerability that presses at the edge.

Adrian steps closer, his hand resting lightly on mine over the box. "You don't owe me anything. I just want you to know... You are not alone. You have a beautiful light within, ready to shine." He lifts my chin with his fingers, light and comforting, his eyes piercing my soul. "Only if you allow it to."

We stand there, surrounded by quiet, ancient trees and the hum of a sleepy ocean town. And in that moment, I didn't feel like I had to apologize for who I was or who I wasn't. I didn't have to fill the void or hide from the awkwardness or shame. The awkwardness I usually feel is gone. I don't feel eclipsed by Adrian's sun.

I feel warmed by it.

I lean in, just enough to let my forehead rest against his chest. His arms wrap around me with the kind of care that wasn't trying to hold me back, only hold me still for a moment.

And I let him.

Because in that second, I realized I didn't need to be saved.

I just needed someone to believe I was worth finding again.

The real me. The lost me. The vulnerable me, afraid to be seen.

And maybe, just maybe, I was starting to believe it too.

# Chapter Twenty

The warm sun spilled across the wooden floor of the old upstairs studio next to the kitchen that Stefan had cleared out for me before he left for the Dolomite climb. It smells like citrus and turpentine, with open windows, breathing in the sweet lavender fields and the earthy scent of far-off hills.

It was perfect.

I make a quick call to Nikki to check in and FaceTime Arlo. Nikki flips the camera, and suddenly Arlo's giant, judgmental face fills my screen. His whiskers practically poke through.

"Arlo!" I gasp, a lump forming in my throat. "Hey buddy, how are you?" He blinks once. Slowly. Offended. I smile, with tears welling in my eyes.

Nikki snorts. "He's been staring at the door every morning like you're going to walk in and carry him around like a princess."

"More like a reverent King," I say, leaning closer until all I can see is my own reflection in his pupils. "Hi, my boy. My furry soulmate. My—Arlo, are you even looking at me?"

Arlo pointedly turns his head to lick his shoulder. Full betrayal.

"Wow, he's moved on."

"He hasn't," Nikki says, lifting him like Simba. "He's just mad I wouldn't give him a third breakfast."

Arlo lets out the most dramatic yowl—a noise that sounds like he's narrating a tragedy.

"See?' Nikki says. "He's thriving. And possibly manipulating me."

"Good, keep spoiling him," I tell her. "If he forgets me, I'll never emotionally recover."

"He won't forget you," Nikki snorts again. Then she lifts Arlo's paw and waves it at the camera. "Say bye to your mom!"

Arlo meows, loud and indignant, like he's being forced to do press for a movie he didn't sign up for.

I grin so hard my cheeks hurt. "I love him."

"He knows," Nikki says. "He's just pretending he doesn't for the drama."

After saying a teary goodbye and holding Nikki's encouraging words close to my heart, I stare at the blank canvas propped against the wall.

It was massive. And quiet. Daring me.

Adrian had dropped off another shell-shaped pastry, this one dusted with powdered sugar earlier this morning, but left shortly after. "This is something you do alone," he'd said with a smile, kissing the top of my head. "I'll be close, though. Just in case you need to scream." He's shown up every day, sometimes with pastries, other days simply to walk with me around the property or take a swim in the small pool.

Now, I stand barefoot in front of it, my fingers smudged with charcoal, paint tubes scattered like candy around my feet. I have no idea how to begin.

And I was terrified.

Because starting again isn't gentle. It's violent. It shakes the old dust loose and asks: *What do you still have left?* I start with a mark. Just one—sweeping and fast, dark across the white.

Then another.

And another.

I didn't sketch. I didn't plan. I just *moved.*

Memories pour out in color. Brushstrokes that bled from my heart-break in Boston. The metallic ache of silence from parents gone too soon. The warmth of Gi's laugh as it echoes through the villa's kitchen. Adrian's hand on mine, that night under the fig tree.

And deeper still. My childhood.

The way I used to draw to keep my siblings quiet when Mom worked double shifts.

The way I *felt* when I created art with no rules.

How I *belonged* to myself when I created.

Hours passed. The light shifted. My back ached, and I didn't care. Paint clung to my arms like armor. My eyes burned from the deep focus, but I kept going. By nightfall, the outline of a new began to emerge.

It wasn't pretty. It wasn't tidy.

But it was *honest.*

A self-portrait. But not of my face.

It was a landscape of emotion. A war between grief and hope, chaos and calm. It was scars in color, stitched with golden light and shadows that still trembled like my hands did now, waiting to see if there's more.

It's been years since I felt this way, maybe never. I wasn't painting to prove anything. I was painting to *feel everything.* I was painting to clear the cobwebs of doubt that had been etched into the dark corners of my mind, begging my hands to hold steady. After hours of relearning, orienting myself with technique and composition, I stepped back from the canvas.

With arms streaked with ochre and blue, my hair tucked in a knot, and breathing like I'd run a marathon—I smiled. I felt lighter, and warmth spread across my chest. A gentle truth unfurls inside me.

Because now I knew something for sure—something that had only whispered before.

I was still an artist.

Not in spite of the pain.

But *because* of it.

And I am ready to fight for this next chapter—with every brushstroke, every mistake, and every piece of myself I'd once tried to hide.

I'm no longer hiding.

I am seeing in FULL color.

Three days have passed, and the studio is in chaos—paint-splattered rags, dust motes dance in the morning light, and canvases lean against every wall. But it's the half-finished self-portrait watching me from the corner with eyes of forgiveness that haunt me. I stand up from the stool and cover it with a piece of fabric. I couldn't finish it, I wasn't ready yet, but I didn't want to throw it away either. It felt too close to tapping into the darkness I've kept away since being here.

I dip my brush into a swirl of cool colors, watching the bright colors come to life. Cerulean. Sapphire. Navy. Teal. And a little touch of Gold. I mix them, not carefully, but with abandon, letting instinct guide me instead of fear. Each stroke feels alive on the surface.

Having the villa to myself has given me the space needed to focus and create. The landscape hums beyond my window, but inside, time slows. For once, I don't think about perfection. I don't think about what anyone will see when they look at what I've created. I just *feel*. The cool drag of paint against canvas. The thrum of music low in the background.

The pulse in my wrists reminds me I'm still here, still creating. Still flowing.

When I finally step back, the canvas is wild. No symmetry, no plan, just color colliding like a sunrise after a storm. It's like no time has passed since I stopped painting. I feel just as alive as I did when Papa placed my first set of watercolors in my hands. A precious gift. I feel that now.

Painting *is* a gift. I'm realizing just how much I've missed it.

A soft knock at the door pulls me out of memory. "Someone's been busy." Adrian's smooth voice brings a smile to my face and goosebumps across my skin. His presence is growing on me with each passing day. His encouragement nestles warmly in my chest, while his touch sends fire to my stomach, burning and teasing.

When I turn toward him, I find that his hands are empty. I scrunch my face in a frown, and then internally berate myself for expecting him to show up with pastries and coffee. It's his fault, naturally. I wipe my forehead with the back of my hand, feeling the heat of the day. "I was just thinking I needed to take a break," I say, washing out my paintbrushes.

Adrian approaches my latest creation. "I like how wild this one is. There's fire and passion in the reds, while a calming, more peaceful emotion is captured here." He points to the lower part of the canvas. He's right. The brushstrokes are softer and more blended, while the fiery colors are painted with more rigid, chaotic strokes. I can feel the heat of his stare on the side of my face while I hold my focus on the canvas before me.

"I didn't have a plan," I say, voice soft. "I just needed to start somewhere this morning, and it turned into this." I point in front of me.

"I like seeing what you create." Adrian dips his head so I can see his eyes. Sincerity written on his face, which is what I admire about him. I don't have to guess what he's feeling. I feel it. Even when I don't want to, it makes me breathe a little easier knowing.

"Thank you," I softly say while cleaning the rest of my mess.

"If you are not doing anything, I would like to invite you to a picnic. It would be on the property, so no need to do anything extra." I glance up at him, and his eyes meet mine with an inviting smile. "I have everything we need, too. Just say yes." There's a glint in his eyes that has become bolder over the last few days. I'm nervous about where this is headed.

"Okay," I nod, with a small smile curving my lips.

"*Perfetto*. Meet me out by the pool in 15 minutes."

"I'll just freshen up a bit, then."

He leans down and kisses my cheek. And when I look up through thick lashes, he's beaming. "See you soon." Once again, my belly does that flutter thing that leaves me flustered.

After changing into a sundress and applying a layer of mascara, I head out to the pool, where Adrian takes my hand in his and leads me through the row of olive trees up to a small hill. Just under a big olive tree, in the shade, I see a linen blanket laid out with a few pillows and a basket at the edge. A charcuterie board filled with a selection of meat, cheese, grapes, figs, and bread sits in the middle. It looks amazing. I love a good charcuterie spread. I also spot a wine bottle with two glasses on a wooden round for stability.

"Adrian, this is beautiful." I look at him and give a warm smile to show my appreciation. He's really taken care of me this week. The warmth of the sunshine is almost too much, but the shade looks soothing.

"You put so many hours in the studio, I felt like you could use a nice change in scenery." He helps me sit comfortably on a cushion and takes a seat on the other side of the food.

"It's a nice change."

Being this close to him, I can see his skin heated from the sun's rays. He's lying on his side, propped up on his elbow and forearm. I swear he smells like citrus and something else I can't quite point out, woodsy maybe. I almost roll my eyes, feeling like a cliché in a romance novel. I tell myself it's all part of the lore of hot men having this innate scent that draws you in. If it were true, Adrian would annoyingly have it, I'm sure. I let my eyes travel the length of the torso, his white linen shirt open, unforgettably attractive.

This last week has been spent in the studio, pouring my heart into painting anything from grief to little details over the years, to the breath-

taking beauty of what I've seen here, and to everyday life rendered poet-
ically. I've created a wide variety, sketching in my book and painting on
canvas, and I still feel like I am just getting started. I'm hesitant to finish
the self-portrait, as feelings of inadequacy rear their head whenever I get
close to a breakthrough. Painting my face pulls at the deep parts I've kept
hidden for so long.

Adrian's right. I needed this. To break free and just relax.

He takes that moment to look back at me, catching me admiring his
physique.

He smirks. So annoying. "Whatcha looking at?"

"Nothing." I quickly look away, plopping a purple grape in my mouth
to keep it shut. I do not need to lead this man on. "Just thinking of
painting and feeling unsure how I'm going to move forward." I take a
glance at his perfect face before turning away. I can't look directly at him
right now. It's like staring directly into the bright sun. I stare across the
rolling hills, watching the white puffy clouds move through the blue sky.

I've seen this landscape in so many Renaissance paintings, but nothing
compares to seeing it in person. I will forever smell this place every time
I see a painting or picture. It's peaceful here. I could see myself living in
one of these old houses, with a vineyard, a simple life. That in itself feels
decadent, even now in the middle of all this uncertainty.

"Sometimes I think I got it all wrong. Giving up painting, then thinking I can just pick up years later without consequences. Like, who do I
think I am?" My gut tightens low in my stomach. I stuff a slice of meat in
my mouth with a chunk of cheese and chew slowly through it to distract
me.

Adrian sits up and pours us another glass of a white chilled wine
called Pinot Bianco. It's light, crisp, and fruity, perfectly paired with

our meat-and-cheese spread. He hands my glass to me and looks at me cautiously.

"What makes you think it's the wrong choice? Did someone say that to you?" He asks, taking a sip without taking his eyes off me.

I hesitate. "Well...no. But what if I'm making the wrong choice? What if I don't finish in time because I simply cannot find the technique that feels right?"

Adrian's gaze is sharp, searching. Like he's trying to pull the truth from what I'm not saying. "Sounds like a lot of what-ifs to put in motion before you've even given it a chance." I could see the questions piling behind his eyes, hungry for answers I wasn't ready to give.

My cheeks feel warm, my clothes damp from the unusually warm afternoon. "I've just learned over time, I don't have control over much of anything." I look down at the blanket, feeling raw, the tension growing in my chest. I take another sip of wine, hoping it helps ease my mind.

Adrian hums before I feel a warm finger direct my chin to the side to meet his eyes. I take a measured breath through my nose, stunned into silence. "*Finché c'è vita, c'è speranza,*" he says in a soft voice. Adrian speaking Italian is something I never thought I would crave to hear. And while I have Italian heritage, I never learned. He makes me want to know it. It's beautiful, and especially decadent when it comes from his lips.

"What does that mean?" I whisper as he lets my chin go—already missing the contact. I sit up a little taller.

"As long as there's life, there's hope," Adrian says, all heart and certainty like he's quoting some ancient truth. I blink, caught off guard by how easy he makes it all seem—as easy as breathing. Which is hard to do sometimes.

"How do you do that?" I ask, tilting my head.

"Do what?" A smile ghosted across his lips.

"Walk around radiating sunshine like it's your job. Seriously, how are you always so damn hopeful? Is it something in your coffee when you wake up in the morning, or are you just genetically annoying?" I had to break the tension somehow.

He chuckles, slow and low. "Maybe I used to be the opposite. Maybe I've already seen how dark it can get."

That catches me off guard. I search his face, but he's still smiling—just softer now, like the light's still there but it's learned to survive the shadows. Like me. "Turns out," he says, voice quieter now, "hope shines brighter when you've been through a little hell."

His words linger in the space between us, heavier than his smile lets on. *Maybe I've already seen how dark it can get.* That line sticks, makes my curiosity flare, and my mind reels with possibilities. There's a story there—buried behind the light in his eyes.

I want to ask. God, I want to know.

But I don't.

Because the way he says it—so calm, so careful—it tells me he's not ready to hand that part over. And I can't afford to go digging.

Not when I've already started feeling more than I should.

# Chapter Twenty-One

"Well, I guess that makes you the resident optimist around here," I mock and lean back into the pillow, trying to cover the tremble in my voice, "Every tragic girl needs one of those, right?" I laugh lightly, uncertainty betraying me. My smile holds, but it wobbles at the edges.

Adrian cocks his head as if he's trying to figure me out, too. "Maybe so." His words are steady but full of curiosity. He pours more wine into our glasses and spreads a sage and fig jam on bread. The spread is so good. Simple and elegant. He was very thoughtful with this picnic.

I take a deep breath and let it out slowly. I cannot get attached, even when he makes it so easy to be in his space. There's too much at stake with my heart. My life. I can't afford any distractions, and he is one of the biggest challenges standing in my way. Because I can get lost in his charm. His steadiness. I can see myself falling into a free fall and never reaching the bottom. How can one person make me feel so much in so little time?

I need to focus. Painting needs to be at the forefront of everything. Romance is not in the cards for me, and yet part of me wants to wrap up in the moment he offers. He's determined to take care of me and relentless in his approach. But he's also a gentleman who is patient. And persistent. Which makes saying no impossible.

"I am here to rediscover myself in my artistry, not to be romanced." I finally say, hoping he gets the message. The last time I was romanced was with Conner, and we know how that ended.

Instead of a scowl or a look of frustration, Adrian's face lights up like a Christmas tree.

His laugh is loud, with a deep rumble that lights me up inside. Shit. I could wrap myself in his laugh like a cozy blanket. It makes me want to make him laugh over and over.

"As soon as you enter Italy, *mi bella*, you accept the invitation of being romanced. If not by the love of your life, then the cities and landscape will do it for you. Romance isn't limited to love stories or relationships. It's an all-encompassing love for beauty, how human potential shapes us all, and the way art and culture connect us. It's what inspires or enchants us to this day. Romance is everywhere and is in everything. Even as an artist, you will learn that through each creation. And it will magnify your life."

I look at him—really look—and for a second, the world stills. His eyes, impossibly blue, seem to hold more than just color; they hold questions, truths, maybe even pieces of me I didn't know I'd lost. And that smile—easy, a little crooked, completely disarming—undoes a longing I've kept tightly wound for far too long.

I've never met anyone like Adrian. It's not just the allure of where he's from or the way he carries stories in his voice. It's deeper. He feels... *undeniably alive*. Like the kind of person who sees through the surface without trying to, who notices things most people miss.

And somehow—he sees me. The *real* me.

It's terrifying, but it was also an almost-hopeful feeling, fragile and brighter. Since arriving in Tuscany, everything has felt more vivid, more awake—but *this*... this is different.

I have no clever words. No shields. Just a quiet, full feeling in my chest, I don't quite understand. And once again, I think—maybe I don't need to.

Seeing the beautiful landscapes of Italy reminds me of the stories my dad relayed to me about this place. I could listen for hours to anything he told me while strolling the museums in Boston with him or simply sitting on his lap as he described his love for us. His family. The grief still feels fresh to this day, even after all these years. I'm not sure I will ever not hold this heartache close to me. A part of me wants it, to remind myself that he's still here.

Adrian gives me hope, reminding me of my dad's positive energy. A balance to my dark.

"I guess I feel that way every time I walk into a museum. The grandeur of it. The over-the-top gold statements." Museums are alive with history, holding a slice of serenity that engulfs me. It's why I love walking into one whenever I get the chance. They tether me like my dad used to, which helps me stay grounded instead of feeling out of control. They provide a connection I had lost so many years ago when my dad died, and that same fateful day, I had lost my mother to depression. Making that the beginning of a downhill spiral I had been falling into and desperately wanted out of.

"Well then, I guess I have some competition then. Better step up my game." Adrian says with confidence. I roll my eyes. No, he does NOT need to step up his game because it's already too much.

We both gaze out into the sun setting on this full day. The colors light up the sky with deep oranges, bright yellows, the lightest pinks, and the softest purples.

It really is magical and romantic here.

The temperature drops, setting off little goosebumps up and down my arms and legs, and I shiver slightly. I bring my legs closer to my body, tucking the fabric from my dress to keep out the chill. Adrian seems to notice, and without saying anything, he wraps the softest blanket around my shoulders and legs. And then sits closer to me after moving the food out of the way, wrapping his big arms around me. I decide to just not overthink it and lean into him, watching the day fade into the night.

It feels good, right now at least. Which always feels great at first. It's the "after" that seems to go to shit, creating massive problems for all involved. I try to shove those ugly thoughts to the back of my mind and enjoy the moment.

Adrian will eventually have to understand that this can't go beyond friendship. I don't ever want to put him at risk of clouding his light with my shadows. He deserves so much more than someone who is screwed up in the head. Carrying a shitload of baggage and sharp pieces that seem to collect with each passing day.

I can't help but wonder what it would be like to live here after my education is complete. I see myself not just living here, but thriving. If only I could calm the storm inside. The ache I feel when I let those dangerous dreams flourish is equal parts exhilarating and terrifying.

If I think too much about dreams forgotten, I'll want them all to come true, and that's just not reality. The truth is hard, but I need to remind myself to focus on one thing at a time. I just have to get my art submission in.

Watching my family chase their dreams with more ease and passion I hadn't felt in years was difficult because they make it look so easy. Seeing their own happiness unfold before my eyes is all I could ask for. Raising them was one of the greatest challenges I had faced while still being a child myself. But it was worth it, and I would do it all over again to watch them grow up into the amazing humans they are today.

And this trip is a gift, even I recognize, that comes once in a lifetime.

Expressing myself verbally has always been a challenge, even when I was little. A little too reserved and a lot in my head. Only when I was drawing or painting did I feel free. Dad used to say I would grow out of it eventually, once I found the thing that would change everything.

He was right.

I look back on that now, a little sad. If he were here now, what advice would he have for me? Or if that day when the light dimmed— never happened— how would I have chosen differently given the chance to?

Adrian leans back on his elbows, eyes on the sky, but his words are clearly meant for me. "You know," he says, his voice calm and steady, "you've got this way of carrying silence like it's a language. Most people try to fill it. You let it breathe."

I blink, caught off guard. "Is that a compliment or a very poetic way of calling me quiet?"

He chuckles, glancing at me now. "It's a compliment. Trust me—I don't give those lightly." His tone is sincere, almost reverent and it settles the unease in my chest. Once again, I don't feel like I need to explain myself.

Not to fill the silence. Not to run from it.

I smile faintly, eyes drifting back to the sky. "Guess that makes two of us then."

He doesn't press further. And somehow, that says the most.

I glance over at him, keeping my voice soft, almost unsure to ask, "You ever feel like... you're not quite yourself, until you're far from everything that was supposed to define you?"

Adrian looks at me like he can see through whatever walls are still standing. He doesn't answer right away. He takes a slow breath, as if he wants to choose the words carefully, not out of fear, but with a kind of ache in the way he looked at me.

"I think... sometimes it takes being far away to remember who you truly are. Or to meet the part of you you've been quieting for too long." He says it so gently that it feels the words sink beneath my skin. I turn to him fully, heart thudding a little harder.

His eyes hold mine, steady and unguarded. Then he adds, "You don't have to try so hard around me, Eve. I see you. And I like what I see, even when you're not performing or protecting anything. Just you."

The wind catches my breath before I can find it again. I stare at him, stunned—not by the boldness of the words, but by how safe they make me feel. How real.

For a long moment, I say nothing. I just let the warmth of his words settle.

Then, I smile. "You really are dangerous, Adrian."

He laughs softly, eyes never leaving mine. "Only to the lies we tell ourselves, *bella*."

I let out a soft laugh at his reply, but there's a tremble in it I can't hide. I turn my face slightly, unsure of what to do with the sudden vulnerability pressing against my chest.

Adrian doesn't move quickly. He doesn't crowd me. But he shifts a little closer—just enough to feel the warmth of his presence, like the sun that's dipped just below the edge of the hills. My breath catches again. His body close to mine, his warmth, makes me feel safe, like a night light in the dark.

He reaches out slowly, giving me time to pull away—but I don't. His hand finds mine where it rests against my thigh, his warm fingers brushing gently before settling over my cold ones.

It's not a claiming touch. It's an offering.

The resistance in me melts away.

I turn toward him fully, knees brushing his on the blanket. My free hand rises before I realize it, as if pulled by something quiet and magnetic, and I trace the edge of his jaw with my fingertips. Light as breath. His eyes close briefly at the contact. Waiting. An invitation.

When he opens them again, there's nothing playful there. Just that steady, earnest heat that's been there, building all along. He brings his hand up over mine and holds it. The contact sends warmth throughout my body.

He leans in—not fast, not tentative either. I hold my breath, his lips hovering, waiting for a split second before they claim mine. It isn't fire or urgency. It's *recognition*. An unfinished novel finding its ending. Or maybe it's beginning.

The kiss deepens, slow and deliberate. His lips are full but firm. No one's rushing, no one's pretending. My fingers slide into his hair, pulling at the silky strands. He pulls me closer, his hand resting at the small of my back, grounding me. Holding me like a precious gift. I could easily stay here.

We move our lips in a dance that feels like heaven, surrendering to the moment in an openness I can feel through my entire body. It's like taking a full breath after holding it captive for so long. My body softens beneath his touch.

Willing.

Adrian slowly pulls back, I can tell he doesn't want to, just barely, foreheads still touching—his breaths fanning across my face in small bursts.

"I didn't expect this." My voice was barely above a whisper.

Adrian's thumb grazes my cheek, his own breath a little unsteady. "Neither did I. But I'm not running from it." I close my eyes, holding onto the moment just a little longer.

He tugs me closer, and we stay like that, not wanting to break the bubble we just created. I push everything out of my head and relax into his warmth.

His steadiness. His everything.

What if I don't want to push him away like all the others?

What if I get to keep him and this life here in Italy?

What if?

# Chapter Twenty-Two

Morning slipped in quietly, like a secret. The sky above the olive grove was pale and golden, the trees casting long, dappled shadows over the dry grass. A few birds chirped somewhere in the distance, and a soft breeze rustled the leaves overhead.

So peaceful. Comfortable.

I blink against the light filtering through the branches. For a second, I'm not sure where I am. Until I realize my head is resting on a very manly chest, with an arm curled around me like it belonged there.

I freeze.

We fell asleep.

We fell asleep outside, and I'm still in yesterday's dress. Curled up on a worn blanket with a man I'd kissed for the first time only hours ago. And yet... I have never felt so safe. I'm not immediately pushing away the idea of being in his arms. Another first for me.

Adrian shifts beneath me making a soft noise—half sigh, half groan—as he stretches.

I tilt my head to look up at him. "Did we seriously sleep out here?"

His eyes crack open, heavy with sleep but glinting with amusement. "Seems that way. I vaguely remember declaring this the most comfortable patch of earth in all of Tuscany last night."

I laugh, low and warm, surprised at how good it feels to laugh first thing in the morning, without being assaulted by anxious thoughts.

"And I let you convince me of that? Pretty sure that was the wine talking."

"I don't recall a protest of any kind," a crooked smile forms on his mouth. "Though you did mumble something about olive trees being better company than people."

I roll my eyes while smiling, remembering our conversation. Easy and effortless. The grass clung to my dress, and there were probably creases on my cheek, but I really didn't care.

Not here, with him.

I should be running for the hills, but for some reason, I want to stay planted here next to Adrian. He has a way of disarming even my most insecure thoughts.

Just then, a voice called out from a few rows down the grove, breaking the hush of the morning. "Buongiorno?" It was Marco, the villa's landscape caretaker, his wheelbarrow squeaking behind him. I like Marco, he is one of my favorite people since he gave me a ride to the vineyard. He has a very homey presence. Like you can tell him anything and it wouldn't faze the old guy, because he's lived through hard lessons. His deep wrinkles and uneven teeth make me smile.

Adrian sits up quickly, trying to blink the sleep from his eyes. He's very rugged in the mornings, and somehow that makes him even more attractive. I stifle a laugh, grabbing the blanket and pulling it over my shoulders.

Marco spots us and approaches, eyebrows raised. "Ahh... romantic night under the stars, eh?" he says in accented English, clearly enjoying himself. "Careful. The olives gossip." Giving us a toothy grin while pointing up to the trees.

I bury my face in my hands, laughing helplessly now. Adrian just grins and gives a mock salute. "We'll keep that in mind, Marco."

As Marco moves on, whistling, I look over at Adrian, shaking my head. "I can't believe we got caught by a man pushing a wheelbarrow of compost."

"It's a rite of passage," he says solemnly. "Means it's officially a Tuscan romance now."

I can't help but chuckle and relax into the warm blanket. Adrian is looking at me again—not in a way that demands anything, just *being* here. Present. The same way he had been the night before. He reaches out, catching a stray hair and putting it behind my ear. He pulls back slightly, unsure, not his usual confident self.

I reach for his hand, surprising even myself. "I actually slept. Outside. I can't recall the last time I did that."

He laces his fingers through mine, gently. "Me too."

We stare at our joined hands, not knowing what comes next. And I don't want to know. For once, I just want to *be*. Right here. Right now. I just hope my sharp edges don't cut him too deeply. Because as much as he wants to believe he sees me, he doesn't see how deep these cuts go.

No one does. I've kept them hidden too well, even from myself. My memories, my emotions, my depression. All simmering below the surface. And the pain that goes with it.

We sit in silence as the sun rises over the hills, our fingers slowly threading together like it's the most fragile thing in the world. I can feel the weight of his thumb brushing against mine, steady and warm.

And still. I can't breathe all the way in.

I don't know what this is between us, what it's becoming, but I don't want to dissect it or demand clarification. I just want to *feel*. To exist in this exact moment, wrapped in the hush of shared breath and soft glances. With Adrian. However long I'm allowed.

But beneath the stillness, a flicker of unease twists in my chest. Tight. Sharp.

Even now, as his hand holds mine, there's a part of me already bracing for the fall.

He doesn't see it. Not this, not what's inside.

He sees the fire, the independence, the soft curve of a heart trying to heal and not the jagged pieces of memory and trauma still buried inside, fractured. Unreliable. The ones I shoved down, I even forgot where I hid them, until he came along and started making me feel again. Deeper than Conner ever could.

And feelings? They scrape against the old scars like glass across bone.

I close my eyes, just for a second.

Because I want to stay in this moment more than I want to protect myself from it.I want him, and all the unspoken things he brings with him. The calm, the questions, the *maybe.*

Even if my edges bleed through. Even if I'm more wound than skin. And God, I hope he's strong enough to hold me anyway. My smile holds, but it wobbles at the edges. Before either of us can say anything more, the sharp ring of Adrian's phone slices through the quiet, pulling us out of the moment.

He sighs, pulling it from his pocket and glancing at the screen. "Work," he mutters, already half-standing. "They probably want something last-minute and entirely impossible."

"Ah, the joys of being talented and dependable," I say, grateful for the break in tension but oddly disappointed too.

He grins, tucking the phone under his ear. "Don't miss me too much," he says with a wink as he walks away, voice already shifting into professional charm.

I watch him go, the warmth he left behind fading slowly, like the last rays of sun slipping behind a building. Part of me wants to call him back. The other part—the smarter one—reminds me: *Don't get attached.*

Still, I can't help but think—whatever story he's not telling...

I already feel it pulling at the edges of mine.

After a shower and leftovers from yesterday's picnic, I braid my hair and put on a soft pair of linen coveralls in sage green with a white top. They have spatters of paint on them, reminding me that my hands have been busy and my creativity flowing. I take a sip of my second coffee and get to work. I glance at the self-portrait on the wall, but then shake my head and start a fresh one. I try several different strokes and colors, but nothing feels right.

The canvas looms before me, too expectant. I sit frozen, brush in hand. A streak of light filters through the blinds, slicing the studio into bars of gold and shadow. Dust drifts lazily in the air—everything moving but me. I take a deep breath, try to breathe through it, and let instinct take over. But my chest feels too tight. Every idea that once sparked inside now feels lost. Like a flickering candle snuffed out.

My skin prickles beneath my clothes, a crawling itch that no amount of scratching can reach. The deadline sits in the back of my mind like a ticking metronome—too loud, too close. My leg bounces as I dip the paintbrush in a mess of color, forcing my wrist to move. But the stroke looks wrong. Too harsh. Too meaningless.

"Come on," I whisper to the canvas, as if it's to blame.

The stool screeches as I push it back and stand up. I look around the studio, the walls seem to close in—the old sketches pinned up like witnesses to my failure. I want to scream, to tear the canvas apart and start over, but I can't find the energy.

Instead, I stand still in the middle of the room, breathing hard. The brush trembles between my fingers as paint drips to the floor. Tiny, accusing splatters of color I can't seem to control. The silence is unbearable.

And still, the canvas awaits.

I get so lost in my own world that I don't hear Adrian walk into the studio until warm arms wrap around my middle, a bag of pastries in one hand, and a cup in the other, the smell of coffee awakening my senses. "I brought provisions," his silky smooth voice soothes the chaos in my head.

"I could kiss you, right now." I grab the coffee and turn around to face him with a smile on my face.

"Well, I won't say no to that," he says, wiggling his eyebrows—his eyes sparkling with hope.

I go up on my tiptoes—keeping eye contact as if I'm going to kiss him—but instead go for his cheek at the last second.

"You play dirty," Adrian says, his lower lip caught lightly between his teeth.

"Oh, what did you bring me?" I ask, taking a sip and letting the heat of the liquid burn away thoughts of doubt. He showed up at the perfect time, stopping what could have been a very steep downward spiral.

"*Bombolone*. It's a soft donut rolled in sugar and filled with pastry cream." My mouth waters. "While the American donuts are usually cut from dough, the bomboloni dough is formed into balls."

"Oh my god, that sounds so delicious." I reach for the pastry when Adrian hands me one, not caring if I get messy. I close my eyes as the butter and sugar hit my mouth, chewing slowly, reverently. Powdered sugar clung to my fingertips and lips, unapologetic and divine. It wasn't just a pastry—it was a taste of comfort. Of summer mornings in hidden piazzas, of Nonnas laughing over flour-dusted counters. As the last bite melted away, I knew one thing for certain: Adrian had slowly slipped into my mornings with these pastries, and I wasn't mad about it.

Adrian didn't say a word—just watched, leaning casually against the wall with his arms crossed, a knowing smirk tugging at the corner of his mouth. The bombolone sat half-eaten in my hands like a soft, golden promise, its sugar-dusted surface already leaving faint fingerprints on my skin.

"You're staring," I say, around a mouthful of donut.

"I'm admiring," he corrects, voice warm with amusement. "This is a sacred moment. I'd be a fool to look away." His eyes light up while his lips curve in the way that makes my stomach flutter, again. I roll my eyes but take another bite anyway. My eyes flutter shut, shoulders relaxing like I'd just stepped into a hot bath. A soft, involuntary sound—half-sigh, half-moan—escaped my lips.

Adrian's mischievous smirk widened. I'm in trouble.

"Oh," I moan, lips dusted with sugar, "this is... dangerously good."

"Should I leave you two alone?" he asks, lifting his espresso to his lips with mock seriousness. "You're making me feel like the third wheel."

I laugh mid-chew, hand flying to cover my mouth. "Shut up."

He grins, pointing to my face. "You've got sugar on your nose."

"No, I don't." I reached to wipe it, but he was already leaning forward.

"You do. Right..." He reaches up and gently brushes his thumb across the bridge of my nose before I can blink. "There." He brings his finger to his mouth and sucks it off. "It's charming. Like edible war paint."

I gulp down the fire that's making its way up my throat. The touch was fleeting but enough to still my movements, a breath caught halfway between flustered, and a warmth spreading low in my belly.

He takes a step back, eyes never leaving mine. "Told you. Sacred moment."

My eyes flutter, bombolone still in hand—my heart now racing for reasons that had nothing to do with the pastry.

Adrian breaks the spell by looking around the studio. He steps slowly around, careful not to disturb anything. I hope he's not judging the half-finished canvas in different sizes propped against the walls. Or the brushes resting in water jars and notebooks stacked unevenly beside old sketchbooks. Every attempt lacked the depth I was looking for.

The space felt sacred, almost. But all I could see were imperfections in the technique I was using. I feel stuck, and I don't know how to move past it. Getting lost again, in my thoughts, I don't catch Adrian in time when he moves toward a small table near the back, where a leather journal sits cracked open, its spine tired from years of secrets. My secrets. Those jagged pieces I've written down in raw and messy handwriting, for no one's eyes to see but my own.

Adrian glances at the open page. But it was enough.

One page, torn halfway through. A sketch with messy, urgent lines—of two hands reaching but not touching. And beneath it, a passage written in sharp, slanted script.

*He left without warning. Just silence and hearts that shattered instantly. A beautiful art piece was deeply cracked that fateful day. I stopped painting after that. For years, the dark crept in and spilled its contents, snuffing out the light. What's the point in beauty if it keeps slipping through your fingers? My heart will never recover and will never be able to fill the void he left behind.*

Adrian stills. I know he read the passage; it's written all over his beautiful face.

All flirtation gone.

He closes the journal gently and backs away, "I'm so sorry, Eve. I didn't mean to read it. Is this why you protect your solitude so fiercely?"

I look away, swallowing hard through the tears that threaten to fall. "I'm not asking you to talk about it," Adrian steps closer, "but I need you to know, if you're holding back because you're afraid of breaking... I get it. I've been broken before, too."

My eyes lift to his. He doesn't push. He just reaches for my hand, slow and steady, like he had that night in the courtyard. This time, I let him take it. His softness comforts my hard edges.

"You are not alone," he says. "I see you, and the scars don't scare me. Your scars are welcome here, Evolet."

My shoulders tight, and my stomach clenches, a breath shudders out of me.

Not from fear.

From the unbearable tenderness of being *seen* and embraced in a challenging moment. To have someone discover the darkest parts of you, and still show up day after day. The way this man opens me up and tenderly cradles what's broken leaves me speechless and confused. The feeling of being practically strangers and yet familiar frightens me. It's like he knows my excuses before I even have a chance to give one. Like, he's felt them before, too. And that shatters me even more if it's true. If he's been broken like this. Then maybe he could help me heal the most deeply scarred parts of my mind.

My soul.

"Let's go for a swim." He takes both hands in his and lifts me off the stool. "It's going to be another warm afternoon and I know a lake nearby that is mostly secluded. Get a chance for you to relax." His willingness disarms my stubbornness and I easily give in.

There's something disarming about Adrian's face—like the universe couldn't decide between rugged and gentle, so it gave him both. His dark hair curls just slightly at the ends, always a little unruly like he's been running his hands through it, which he usually has. And then there are his eyes—clear, impossibly blue, the kind that catch the light and hold it. I've watched them storm, soften, and burn. They say more than his words ever could.

His jaw is strong, always dusted with short stubble that makes him look like he belongs in an old black-and-white film, somewhere between the hero and the heartbreak. When he smiles, really smiles, it's like watching clouds part after a long, heavy rain.

It's rare and worth everything.

But it's the quiet moments that undo me. When he thinks no one's watching and his expression turns inward, often softened by a memory, or maybe pain—I see the pieces he carries. Like he's been touched by loss and knows the deep cavern of grief. And yet he never hides. Adrian wears his emotions openly, with the same strength he carries in his broad frame, tall and steady like the hills that raised him.

He's not afraid to feel. To love.

And every time I look at him, I realize—I'm not just looking at a beautiful man. I'm looking at someone who's survived and still chooses softness. Still chooses *me*.

"Okay, yeah. Let me clean up here, and I'll meet you downstairs." I slip a quiet smile to assure him I won't be long. It's a gorgeous day, but my anxiety is fierce, reminding me of what's brewing inside me, and I fear I won't be able to get by with brushing it away. I'm going to have to face it. And soon.

He gently kisses my hands, then leaves the studio.

This man is slowly warming parts in me that have been cold for so long. His attention feels like the glue that could actually hold my cracks in place. However sweet, it's still a dangerous way to think. I try to push the negativity away as I finish cleaning and grab my stuff for swimming.

Maybe the water can wash away the doubt. I can only hope.

# Chapter Twenty-Three

The late afternoon sun dripped gold over the hills as the lake shimmered like liquid glass. The olive trees rustled in the breeze, and the only sound was the splash of water as Adrian broke the surface with a dramatic gasp.

"I swear you did that just to show off," I called from the rocky edge, one foot already in, and the other hesitating.

Adrian brought me to one of the most dreamy lakes I have ever seen. It's serene, crystal-clear, and deep-blue freshwater embellishes the landscape that takes my breath away. It looked so inviting, that is, until he jumped off a perfectly good rock and then dared me. This man once again challenges my existence in a way that is both exhilarating and intimidating.

I question my sanity. And his.

He slicked his hair back, the water teasing around his broad shoulders. "I didn't realize casual swimming was a competitive sport now. But if it is... I'm winning."

"You're impossible," I say, easing myself in with a sharp inhale. The water was colder than I expected—cool and smooth against my skin, like silk with teeth.

"Come on," Adrian teases, treading water just far enough that I'll definitely have to work for it. "Thought you were braver than that." He challenged me with a wicked grin and a sparkle in his eyes.

"Oh, I'm brave," I shoot back, rubbing my arms in false bravado. "Just smart enough not to trust a man who smirks like that in a remote body of water."

"That's a very specific phobia."

"Hard-earned."

He laughs and drifts closer, "Guess I'll just have to earn your trust, then." The water swirls around him, tanned skin glistening from the sun's reflection.

"Mm. Good luck," I say with as much conviction as I have, but it comes out softer than I meant it to. I keep my eyes off his muscular frame. It's the most skin I've seen, and my cheeks are pink and not just from the sun.

Before I give it any more thought, I jump in the freezing lake with a girlish scream and end up splashing the smile right off his face. I call it a win in my book, if I were writing one. Writing seems way more daunting than painting, so I'll just keep to my paints and brushes. I gasp for air as I breach the surface, shivering for many reasons I do not care to name.

We tread water for a moment, quiet but not uncomfortable. His eyes search mine, the playfulness still there, but there's a deeper current that simmers underneath. A simmering heat that has my body warming up just a little. Okay, maybe a lot.

"You always keep your guard up like this?" he asks, voice lower now, more intimate. More dangerous to my willpower.

"Only around men who smile like they already know my secrets." Who am I kidding? Normal Adrian is dangerous, wet Adrian is downright sinful.

He inches closer, to where I can feel his heat but not his skin, his eyes looking like clear glass from the water's reflection. "I don't know your secrets, Eve." His hand brushes the side of my arm underwater, a gentle current of touch. "But I'd like to."

My breath hitches. The lake, the sun, the silence—it all feels too perfect. Too still. Like the feeling of holding my breath for too long. Ready and waiting. My body vibrates, anticipating his next move.

"You think you're ready for them?" I ask, the flirtation is still there, but now threaded with a truth we weren't quite ready for. That I was ready for.

"I don't want perfect," he murmurs into the space between us. "I just want *real*. And right now, this... you... feels like the most real thing I've had in a long time." I can't look away from his fierce gaze. Demanding I come clean and meet him.

My hand finds his in the water, fingers brushing fingers, slow and searching.

"Adrian..." I can't tell if I say his name like a plea or a warning. Both make my heart beat faster and tangle my mind in knots.

Before I can say anything else, he leans in. I watch as a water droplet drips down his face just before his lips meet mine, warm—tasting like salt and something sweeter. Curiosity. A steadiness past all the pain.

I wrap my legs around his waist as he pulls me closer. This moment feels weighted with a desire for more. A dream I have always wanted but was too scared to ask for. Here in the safety of his arms, I feel brave. I feel a tremendous yearning for a deeper connection.

With Adrian, I want to surrender the walls I have spent years building to keep others out. But I am still wary. Still fearful of the unknown. Fearful of losing him like I've lost my parents.

We stay there, tangled and content with our combined heat, the water no longer feeling so cold. The rolling hills behind us fade behind our closed eyes, and the sound of our hearts racing louder than the wind through the trees.

His hands roam my body, massaging from my legs up my back, settling on my neck and in my hair, tugging with passion. He's everywhere. I sigh into his mouth, pulling away to look into his blue eyes. I love the way his eyes soften when he looks at me—like I'm not just someone he sees, but someone he *remembers*. His jaw is strong, marked by the faintest stubble, and when he smiles—really smiles—it tugs at the corner of his mouth like it's a secret only I get to witness.

"What are you doing to me?" I study his face, not really looking for an answer. Adrian wasn't the kind of man who demanded attention. He simply existed in a way that made the world feel softer.

Made me feel softer.

"Exactly what you do to me. *Sei sempre nei miei pensieri.* You are always on my mind." His words soothe an ache in me while setting fire to the walls I no longer care to keep up. Wanting things I cannot have is how others get hurt. And I don't want to hurt Adrian. But I can't pull away either. This feels different.

We hover in the water, lips still tingling from the kiss, full and flushed. He presses his forehead lightly against mine. The lake cradled us in silence, the kind that doesn't demand words. It feels safe here in our bubble.

Adrian lets out a slow breath, his fingers tracing soft circles along my back in the water. "I should probably tell you something," his voice barely above a whisper. "Before this gets... deeper."

I pull back just enough to see his face. His usual grin is gone, replaced by a rawness that surprises me and an edge stripped of charm. My stomach bottoms out, but I keep my face as neutral as I can. I try to remove myself from his hold, but his arms tighten around my back, holding me in place.

"You don't have to," I offer, though part of me already wants to know—maybe needs to hear his words. Better to stop this before it goes too far.

"No, I do." He looks past me, toward the fading horizon. "Everyone always assumes I'm this hopeful guy because I've had an easy, happy life. That I float through the world untouched." He pauses, eyes darkening in contrast to the sunny sky. "But that's not why I hold onto the light."

I stay quiet, letting him go at his own pace. Hoping his words keep flowing.

"There was a time I didn't think I'd make it to thirty," he confesses, voice tight. "I was stuck. Angry. I lost my brother when we were kids. He was only eleven. And after that, it just... it changed everything. Mama never recovered. My father disappeared into himself. And me? I tried pretending none of it mattered until I couldn't anymore."

The water ripples between us, cool against the heat rising in my chest.

"I had a choice," he continues, staring straight at me now. "Live in the dark... or run toward the light like my life depended on it. Because, at one point, it really did." His head dips down as if he's trying to hide his pain. But I see it clearly, a familiar pull from the depths.

I reach for his cheek, bringing his eyes level with mine, brushing a drop of water away. Or maybe it wasn't just water. "Adrian..." I whisper. Staring directly into his crystal blues.

His smile returns. Smaller this time, but real. "So yeah," he says, "I flirt, I joke, I wake up every day trying to find the good. But not because it's easy. Because I know how easy it is to forget it's even there."

I lean in, my lips brushing his again, slow and certain. "Thank you for telling me."

He closes his eyes like the words were a balm for the cracks. Cracks I know all too well.

"Thank you for listening. I never want to mask anything with you." His words soothe the ache growing in my chest for him. His past is dark, too, and yet his sunshine is just as bright today as on any other day. While my dark cloud hovers endlessly, casting shadows.

We stay like that, bodies close, heartbeats syncing in the hush of the lake, the sky burning orange above us. No more hiding. Just truth, tangled in warmth, and the silent promise of more.

The sun dipped below the hills as we returned to the villa, our skin still damp, hair curling in the leftover lake breeze. Dusk beautifully draped in gold, the air rich with rosemary and woodsmoke from nearby chimneys, as I imagine friends and family gathering for the evening or enjoying a quiet night in. Everything felt hushed, like the land itself was resting.

Peaceful.

Inside, Adrian moves through the old stone kitchen like he's been there for years. Barefoot, sleeves rolled up revealing corded muscle and tanned skin, a towel slung over one shoulder. Tendrils of his damp hair curl in his eyes as he looks down at the stove. The French doors were open to the terrace, where I currently sit, with a perfect view of the kitchen, letting the scent of onions and garlic simmering waft through the air.

With a sketchbook in my lap, left untouched, I toy with the charcoal stick, smudging black dust onto my palm. The quiet was comforting. But my mind still reeled from Adrian's words from earlier at the lake.

*He saw more than I thought.* And somehow, he hasn't run for the hills.

His pain matches my own in a way I was not expecting. I can't imagine losing one of my siblings. I wouldn't survive it. Losing my parents at such an early age ripped me open and flayed the most precious part of me.

Slowly and painfully, it's become recoverable. Broken, but slowly being put back together. Like a mosaic. A work in progress, yes, but still there.

I get up and walk to the doorway, needing to stretch my body when thoughts feel too heavy. "You cook now, too?" I sneer, leaning against the doorway, watching him slice fresh tomatoes with maddening ease.

Adrian glances over his shoulder, smirking. "Only the important things. This one's my Nonna's recipe. She used to say if a man couldn't make a decent pasta, he wasn't worth marrying."

I laugh, the sound surprising even me. "High stakes."

He shrugs. "Lucky for you, I'm a man of many talents." He gives me a knowing smile and wiggles his eyebrows. His confidence is so ridiculous, I can't help but smile back with a shake of my head.

The kitchen glowed in the low light overhead, and the stove's simmer sent tendrils of steam into the air. Adrian walks over to the bottle of red wine and pours me a glass without asking, then hands it over with a casual brush of fingers. A light touch, but it sends a little shock of warmth right through to my core.

"So what is it? Your Nonna's famous...?"

"*Pasta al forno*," he says with mock seriousness. "It's rustic. Soulful. Slightly chaotic—like most of my family."

I wander closer, unable to resist the smell. Cheese. Garlic. Basil. It fills the space, making it feel homey. Cherished. He reaches across me to grab a dish, his arm grazing my waist. Not accidental. Not rushed. Just warm and steady, like the way he looks at me.

"You know," my voice is soft, as I watch him layer pasta and sauce, "If you keep this up, I'm going to expect a homemade meal all the time."

He glances up at me and lifts his shoulder. "Maybe I've been waiting for someone like *you* to cook for."

The words should've made me roll my eyes. Instead, they settle into my chest, warm and terrifying. I make a noncommittal noise, turn, and step onto the terrace. Something inside grows, a feeling I can't quite decipher yet. But I know it's close.

A soft shuffle of feet moments later, slow and careful, shifts my attention to the French doors. The warm lights twinkle above, and Adrian steps into view, looking at me with heat and awe, like he's waiting for permission to erase the distance and take what he wants. Me.

"Hey," he greets me. I sweep my gaze over his face, seeing nothing but admiration, which makes me want to share more of my thoughts with him.

"I used to think love was this... burning thing," I explain, voice low. "A wildfire. Like my parents' love. If it didn't consume you, it wasn't real. I didn't realize it could smolder quietly and still mean something."

Adrian didn't speak. He waited, breath held in the space between.

"Will you sit with me for a moment?" I silently plead, knowing what I am about to reveal to him. I need his presence closer—at a touchable distance. He takes the seat next to me, thighs pressed against mine.

The silence between us wasn't empty—it was full. Full of what he'd shared earlier, of the way the truth had softened in him, and in me. Giving me the courage to share a piece of me I haven't let out in so very long.

I rest my head against his shoulder—willing the confidence in my voice that I don't have—our bodies pressing together in the stillness.

"I don't talk about them," I reveal, the words barely more than a breath. "My parents."

Adrian doesn't say anything, just turns his head slightly, listening.

"My dad died when I was six. A car crash on the night of Stefan's birth. An unfortunate circumstance involving a mother and her son on a very stormy night." I swallow, trying to ignore the tightness rising in my throat. "And it was. One second he was here, the next..."

His fingers brush mine, a gentle reminder: *I'm here.*

"Six years later, my mother followed him in death, leaving us orphans." My voice wavered, but still I continued, "I think part of me died with them," I confess. "The part that believed in stability and safety. I stopped painting and letting people in after that. I didn't see the point. Everyone leaves. Or worse—gets taken. My focus was on Gi and Stefan. Nothing else mattered but keeping them safe."

I look at him then. "So I built walls. High ones. Told myself I was fine behind them. Strong. Untouchable. I'm honestly surprised with myself for telling you. I haven't told anyone this."

Adrian nods slowly, his eyes never leaving mine. "But you're not behind them right now?" That simple truth broke loose in me.

"No," I whisper. "I don't know why, but... You make it feel like maybe I don't have to be."

He cups my cheek, a tender gesture that grounds me. "Because you don't." The words sink deep, past all the walls I thought I still had up. I lean in and press my forehead to his, eyes closing.

"I'm scared," I admit. "Of what this could be. Of what I could lose."

"So am I," he answers back, voice low and honest. "But maybe that means what we have is real. Or what it can be if you let it."

"I'm terrified," I reply. "Because I feel myself opening a wound that has long since been opened. Wanting what I have never asked for before. And I promised myself I wouldn't put someone through that kind of uncertainty. Or lose myself completely."

Adrian's hand moves to the back of my neck, firm but gentle. Pulling my head up to meet his pleading eyes. "You're not losing yourself, Eve," he says softly. "You're becoming more *you* without all the other noise.

And I'm not here to take anything from you. I just want to walk beside you... even if you never fully let me in. Even if this never becomes more than what it already is. I feel like I've already won, just having this time together. You have also surprised me."

His words continue to unravel everything inside my chest. My eyes blink against the sting of salty tears. Slowly and deliberately, I lean my head against his shoulder. My body is still tense, but less so when I am around him. I stare at my fingers that are still dusted with charcoal. My heart is pounding—but not in panic this time.

"You already are more," I whisper into the space between us.

Adrian doesn't press further; he simply sits with me and holds me in his arms. I love that we don't have to talk often or fill the space. He's becoming someone I could easily exist with. Share my secrets without feeling judged for how I feel. These big feelings take up so much space in my head. I wish I could just let them all go. They feel trapped within me, putting pressure in places and causing pain in my body.

Someday soon, the dam will break, and I don't want anyone nearby when it does. I'm afraid of the damage the wake would cause.

We finish the evening with a romantic dinner under the soft cicadas in the trees, twinkling lights over the table set for two, as a warm breeze dances in the drapes by the door. It's my kind of perfect. With a man so caring and attentive, I see myself losing the battle of keeping my heart in check.

I am already falling. I fear I have passed a point of no return. I hope for Adrian's sake that the damage is recoverable.

# Chapter Twenty-Four

It's been four weeks in Italy, and somehow, I still haven't set foot in a single museum that felt almost sacrilegious in a country steeped in centuries of art and genius. When I asked Adrian if he'd come with me to Florence for a day of gallery-hopping, he gave a theatrical sigh and muttered about "tourist traps and never-ending lines." But beneath the grumbling, there was a glint of amusement in his eyes. He was already reaching for his keys before I finished asking.

Florence, with its crumbling facades and marble saints, was waiting. And I was ready to be lost in its masterpieces.

The yellow sundress I picked out feels soft and flowy on my skin, matching the lemon and fig trees perfectly. It reminds me of the canary-yellow dress Papa picked out for our first visit to the Renaissance wing of the museum, because he said I looked like sunlight. He would point out every brushstroke as if it held the world's secrets, and he couldn't wait to share them.

Cool marble, old books, the faint smell of coffee on his breath. I can almost hear his voice low beside me, telling me to look closer, that art always has more to give if you let it.

A tear slips down before I even notice it, landing right on the embroidered flower on my left breast—right over the heart. I let out a small laugh. Wet and shaky. Because of course I'm crying over a sundress. But it's more than that.

It's him. It's me.

It's all the versions of myself I thought I'd lost. And grief never goes away.

I turn toward the mirror. The dress flares softly around my knees, fluttering like it remembers who I used to be. I look up and see the girl who stared up at the paintings with wide eyes and believed she could make something beautiful, too. A warmth spreads across my chest and settles within.

I swipe my cheek, and a small smile sits proudly on my face.

"Papa," I whisper, "I hope you are proud of us, of me."

And maybe it's the lighting, or maybe it's the dress. Or maybe it's the strange ache of leaving home for the first time—but I feel it.

That warmth in my chest. A nudge. To see Art and History collide with color and texture. My heart feels ready to burst at the thought of finally seeing Florence in a way that would have made my Papa smile widely.

I hope I don't annoy Adrian too much with my enthusiasm. I'm beginning to learn he does not enjoy large crowds or places that were a tourist's dream but a local's nightmare.

Neither did I, but this was a milestone I wouldn't give up.

Adrian picked me up in his classic car once again. This time without the top off. I appreciated that. My hair was already a frizzy mess with all this humidity. I eventually gave up trying to tame it and let the curls be in their natural state.

Wild and unpredictable.

Florence greeted us like a painting coming to life—ochre rooftops glowing beneath the late-morning sun, narrow streets unfolding in a mosaic of cobblestone, rich in history. The air smelled faintly of espresso and pastries—one of my personal favorites. And the stone was warmed by centuries of footsteps. I practically vibrated with anticipation as we crossed the Arno and headed toward the Uffizi, which held one of the largest collections of Renaissance Art.

Adrian, true to form, wore a smug half-smile and sunglasses like he was allergic to the city.

"Try not to look so thrilled," I teased as we joined the line outside the museum.

"I am thrilled," he says flatly. "Can't you see me vibrating with joy?"

"You're vibrating with judgment."

He cracks a grin. "Just mentally preparing to stare at paintings of sad saints and suspiciously muscular angels for the next few hours." I shake my head and playfully slap his arm. I guess he doesn't have to like everything. He'd be too perfect.

But once inside, the artwork worked its spell—even on him.

The Uffizi was cool and quiet, the outside world muffled behind thick stone walls and gilded frames. We wandered through halls where time bent around us, Botticelli's *Birth of Venus* practically glowing from its pedestal.

I stood there in awe, trying to take in every curve of the goddess, every pale wave of foam, while Adrian leaned in close and whispered, "If you ever emerge from a seashell like that, I'll write sonnets."

I nudged him, laughing. "You'd write limericks at best."

"Fair point. Still," he added, softer now, "she's something."

"Yeah, she is." I've seen many prints of her, but nothing beats seeing the canvas in real life. Not only do you see the texture, but you can see the colors without enhanced vibrancy. I notice the curves of her body and the long face framed by her hair. She bears an expression of sweetness but also a subtle melancholy. I see a familiarity in her. Like holding up a mirror.

A reflection.

In the same room, we lingered in front of *Primavera*, and I couldn't help but notice the way Adrian watched *me* more than the painting. His gaze wasn't performative—it was curious, attentive, like he was watching me find a piece of myself I hadn't seen in a while. The little girl in me delighted in walking the ancient halls. It brought me back to when I held my Papa's hand, listening to all the stories he told me about the Renaissance paintings.

*"You know, Eve, the oldest paintings made have a story to tell us even today. They hold their own secrets and messages hidden in brushstrokes and composition. There is so much yet to explore."* Papa always lit up when he talked about art, searching for a deeper meaning to everything.

This feels like right where I belong because he planted those seeds of curiosity in me and watered them every chance he had. I didn't fully know it then; I was too young. But I see it now and wish I had more time with him when I was older. To soak up his wisdom when I could understand it more.

"You know," Adrian's deep voice fills the room without it being loud, especially when it's right behind me, peppering my skin with goose-bumps. "This painting is one of the most mysterious paintings in all of Art history. Want to know why?" Of course I do, and he knows that. But it's the way he shifts closer to stand right behind me, pressed up against me, that has my heart pumping a little faster.

I keep my eyes forward, waiting for his answer.

"There is a silence in *Primavera* that speaks louder than words—a hush between the leaves, where myth breathes and desire lingers. Botticelli does not paint a scene. He paints a spell."

His fingers graze the inside of my left arm, barely touching, just enough to set my skin alight. Every nerve leans into the contact—slow, deliberate—like he's tracing a secret only he knows. I hold my breath, acutely aware of every inch he touches, and every inch he doesn't.

"Each figure moves as if caught mid-thought, half in this world, half in another, whispering secrets only the heart might hear if it leans close enough." I can feel him pressing in more, wrapping his hand to my stomach, drawing my body into his.

His voice feels like a whisper dancing along every nerve ending, "Venus stands not as a goddess, but as a question. Serene? Perhaps. Distant? Even more so. See how her eyes are turned inward, as if she knows that love is never simple and tinged with the ache of becoming." I can't breathe.

My body is frozen in place. Adrian's words are so poetic, so enticing, they draw me in like a damn Venus flytrap. My breath stumbles, heart pacing to the rhythm of his touch.

I am. Hooked.

Pressing closer to my back, he brings his right arm up to point out some of the details of the painting. I can feel his breath on my cheek. "To her right, Zephyrus lunges, fierce and blue like the west wind, chasing the nymph Chloris who will bloom into Flora."

Long fingers make small, slow circles around my navel, heat blooming everywhere. But it doesn't stop his articulation of the painting. "A transformation that feels less like myth and more like the truth of every woman who's ever been touched too roughly, then taught herself to flourish anyway." My voice is silent, but my heart is bursting, and my legs are shaking.

He brings both arms around me, holding me tight as if he knew I needed to be grounded. To feel safe. I itched to know more. No one has ever described paintings this way. This is exhilaratingly new. Breathtaking passion is wrapped up in Adrian's deep voice, and I am soaking up every word. But he is far from being done.

This man.

His mouth touches my right ear, softly whispering, "And then, there are the Graces—spinning in their impossible grace, all soft limbs and veiled intentions, their dance forever suspended in a moment just before the fall or in surrender. Cupid floats above them, blindfolded, bow drawn, in warning or a promise, it's never clear. That's the magic of it."

His mouth trails little kisses down my neck as his words and heat fill my senses. My eyes fall closed, internally mapping his hot mouth on my over-heated skin, feeling like I will combust at any moment.

"*Primavera* does not give answers. It tempts you with scentless orange blossoms, and glances not quite met, with the tantalizing mystery of spring itself: beautiful, fleeting, and always just out of reach." Adrian places a lingering kiss on my neck. Letting the weight of his words settle deep within me.

Am I the temptress? Am I the one fleeting and out of reach?

Do I want to be?

The air around us felt charged. I couldn't speak. A familiarity stirred inside me, sudden and fragile. A hush that echoed. A longing too large for words. Not for the art alone, but for whatever *truth* Botticelli had buried within it. The way Flora scattered her flowers was like pieces of herself.

The Graces danced, not for others, but *with* each other, free in their own unspoken language. Venus watched it all, calm and untouchable, as if she had known heartache and transcendence and found them to be one and the same.

I swallow hard, my throat tight. My heart beat frantically.

I could feel it—wild in my chest pressing against the inside of my ribs, aching to be let out. A voice that hadn't been used in years. A part of myself that had gone quiet in the noise of becoming what others expected. Of what I pushed down. Forgotten. A memory hovered on the surface but was still out of reach.

Adrian held me, sensing the shift in my body—my mind, quiet now, hands secure in front of me. He didn't interrupt the storm that was warring inside.

But he was *there*.

Grounded. Still. A presence he kept showing me it could be healing for me. I glance at him, eyes wide with fear and wonder, battling for space in my heart.

"Why does it feel like... something just cracked open in me?" I whisper with a trace of sorrow.

Adrian looks at the painting, then at me. His gaze was steady and warm. "Maybe because you're finally letting yourself feel what you've needed to feel."

I let out a breath that trembles as it leaves pursed lips. A release of tension held for many years. "Don't let me shut it again. Please." I say out loud, but also trying to convince whatever was whirring inside my chest.

Adrian's hand brushed the top of my hand in tiny circles, a gentle tether.

"I won't," he says softly. "But I think you're strong enough not to."

"Just hold me. Please." I ask, my voice tight and unsure of what to do with this revelation.

"I wasn't planning on letting you go anytime soon, *Tesoro*."

We stayed like that for a while longer until I didn't feel so frayed at the edges. Adrian never once complained about leaving or told me to get my shit together. He held me close until I was ready.

Later, we ventured to the Accademia, where it houses the largest collection of Michelangelo's sculptures in the world, and a thick crowd gathered around *David*. Adrian stood back at first, arms crossed, eyes narrowed. Then he leans in, "He looks like he's judging me."

"Probably because you mocked the Uffizi gift shop." I side-eye him with a little grin.

"He didn't *have* a gift shop."

I laughed, but then looked up at Michelangelo's masterpiece and felt a lump rise in my throat. The sheer scale of it, the delicate power in every carved tendon—it wasn't just art. It was grief and beauty and defiance chiseled into stone.

"He made this out of something broken," I say quietly, almost to myself.

Adrian looks over with curiosity in his eyes. "What do you mean?"

"The marble. It was a discarded slab. Too flawed. And Michelangelo turned it into *this*." I gesture to the sculpture, letting out an exasperated sigh, feeling stirs deep inside me. "It makes me wonder what beauty we're still carrying, even after we've been broken."

He doesn't make a joke this time. Instead, he gently takes my hand, threading it into his, and pulls me into his chest. His cedarwood-citrus scent floods my senses, instantly releasing the tension I've been carrying. I am quickly becoming addicted to Adrian's hugs. And other things.

We spent the rest of the day wandering—from the echoing Duomo to tiny side galleries with flaking frescoes and barely legible plaques.

At a sun-drenched café in Piazza della Signoria, we sipped wine and watched artists sketch tourists on benches. A violinist played a slow and aching tune near the Loggia, and the whole city seemed suspended in a kind of romantic hush.

Adrian leans across the table, eyes soft behind his sunglasses.

"You really love this stuff, don't you?" he asks with a serene smile on his face.

I nod. "It makes me feel like the world has more to say than we ever give it credit for."

He looks at me a moment longer, then smiles—not the usual cocky smirk, but gentle and inviting. "You make me want to look closer." I can't help but match his tender smile, my heart beating a little faster while I take another sip of wine.

Later, as the sun began to dip behind the terracotta skyline, we stood on the famous stone Ponte Vecchio, the river flickering below us like melted gold. Adrian brushes a strand of hair from my face, his fingers linger against my cheek while leaning on the stone's edge.

"I never thought I'd feel this again," he says while he studies my face.

"Me either." I cover my hand over his and turn my face into his palm, placing a gentle kiss in the center. I knew he didn't mean the city. And neither did I.

"*Vieni qui*. Come here." He leans in for a kiss, soft and slow—while Florence shimmered behind us, its ancient heart beating still, watching two people fall, quietly, into more. "I like the taste of your lips on mine, *Tesoro*."

"I can't argue with you there, *Romeo*."

# Chapter Twenty-Five

We're driving back to the Villa after a long day of playing tourists and enjoying all the shops and ancient alleyways, all part of Florence's charm. But it's the way Adrian keeps looking at me that has my insides coiled with heat and my heart racing like a horse running free. There's a wildness in him he never tries to tame, and god, it draws me in. His jaw is dusted with stubble that would scrape deliciously against my skin if I let him get close enough.

And I *want to.*

Those ocean blue eyes? They don't just look at me—they consume. Stormy, electric, and full of things he hasn't said yet, like he's holding back just enough to drive me mad. Or perhaps he's waiting for me to say yes. To close the small gap I've kept for safety. His safety. But what wrecks me most is the way he looks at me—not with hunger alone, but with heart. As if all that muscle, all that strength, was built not for power, but for protection.

For holding fragments. For holding *me.*

He'd been built like he was made to be leaned into. There's nothing delicate about him— all rough edges and heat, and yet, his touch is always slow and careful. Reverent, like I'm a dream he never thought he'd get to touch. I feel the same way about him. Everything he is and stands for is all I have ever wanted in someone. To feel cherished in a way without pity staring back at me. To be consumed and let go of the weight of all I have been carrying. To find someone willing to share the load and still love me through it all.

It feels like a dream, not real. Reality has a way of ripping me apart until I don't recognize myself. I didn't for the longest time. Until him.

"You keep looking at me like that, and I won't be responsible for what happens next, Eve." His voice is like a sinful caress across my skin. A caress I am craving like it's my last breath.

I bite my lip, "You know exactly what you are doing to me, don't you?"

His eyes meet mine, gold flaring to life in his crystal blues. "I'm not a mind reader, but if it's the same thing that you are doing to me, then yes. We seem to have the same effect on each other." I stare a beat longer before turning to look at the passing landscape. Trying to think of all the ways this is bad for both of us, and coming up short. All rationality has left.

Desire takes its place.

The villa is quiet as we pull up, except for the occasional chirp of the endless cicadas and the intermittent rustling of trees. The scent of rosemary and lemon still lingers from the cleaners as we step into the empty foyer, but it's the warmth in his eyes that fills the room more than anything.

Adrian takes my hand in his and turns me towards him. "I had a delightful day, Evolet." He brushes his other hand over my cheek in reverence. My eyes are glued to his, waiting. The air is charged as I hold my breath to hear what he says next, what he's thinking.

"I cannot escape you," his voice low, strained, and full of heat. "You live in the quiet spaces of my mind, a whisper threading through every thought. Each time I close my eyes, there you are—a dream I never want to wake from. Please tell me you feel it too?"

As he draws nearer, his lips caress mine, featherlight, his stubble scraping ever so slowly, sending sparks throughout my body. Just as I thought it would. I don't think—I don't push or break away. Instead, I lean into his hold and let go.

"Come upstairs with me?" I ask, with an invitation for more. He stares into my eyes for a second before nodding, and then I lead him up the staircase. My heart feels like it's going to burst out of me. He follows me into my room, but then excuses himself for a moment and slips into the bathroom.

I take a moment to calm my racing heart and sit at the edge of the bed after setting my purse on the table by the window. I close my eyes and blow three breaths, in and out.

*One. Two. Three.*

I open my eyes and see him standing in the doorway, shirt half-unbuttoned, his skin still kissed by the sun, that signature hint of a smile playing on his lips—patient, sure, and devastating.

I meet his gaze and hold it. "Like what you see, *Tesoro?*"

For once, I don't question what comes next. I don't overthink or second-guess or listen to the part of me that always pulls back. Right now, it's just us. My thundering heart. The quiet hum between bodies that no longer wants to pretend.

I stand up and step closer. He doesn't move—not yet—but his eyes darken just slightly, like he's waiting to see if I'll really let go.

"Yes... I do." My fingers brush the edge of his collar. He exhales—slow, deliberate, his hands find my waist, drawing me in like he's done it a hundred times in dreams he'd never admit to.

"I can feel your heartbeat." He places his hand above my heart." Is that for me?" I hum in response as his lips meet mine, warm and unhurried, tasting like wine and the quiet kind of want that grows under the skin quietly until it can no longer be contained.

The kiss deepens, and that longing inside me loosens. The knot in my chest. The ache in my ribs. The fear that's kept me from feeling too much, too fast. It all unspools in the way he touches me—like I'm not something to be fixed, instead, I'm already whole.

Treasured. *Tesoro.*

He lifts me gently, guiding me backward toward the bed, the old wooden frame creaking beneath us. The air shifts, thick with heat and curiosity, neither of us stopping or slowing down. His hands are firm, but his mouth—his mouth is soft and tender, mapping my collarbone and worshipping like he's waited too long to touch. I tilt my head back, letting his mouth worship the dips and curves.

His fingers slowly go to the buttons of my dress, pausing to look at me for permission. I nod once, and he continues to unravel the fabric from my body, slowly. "You're shaking," his voice thick with desire and a slight shake in his hand. I've never seen Adrian nervous.

"So are you," I whisper. His nervous chuckle releases some of the tension in my body, helping me relax in the moment. He continues to undress me while his eyes search deeper, like he's trying to see beyond the skin, to my soul.

Fully exposed to him, his gaze is all-consuming. Fire, simmering before, now a raging inferno. "Do you trust me?" He asks, as he moves down my body, kissing between my breasts before trailing down my stomach, stopping to kiss each hip bone. A breathy moan leaves my mouth in response. "Yes." Tingling skin makes me feel like I am floating from his touch.

"*Sei così bella.* You are so beautiful. I feel your heart's yearning. Nothing is more exquisite than your trust. Your passion. And I want to breathe it all in. I need your want, your desire. I don't just want your body, Eve—I need your heart's invitation. Please surrender it to me, so I may claim your heart, your openness."

Adrian's words wrap around me, unfurling a part of me that lay dormant. Hidden. Now that it's awake, it's burning hotter than ever before. A fire I can never contain or snuff out again. My body softens around the truth and opens deeper than before, spreading wider. I let go. Breathing out a gust of air—I release the cage to my heart, feeling freer than I have ever felt before.

He sheds the rest of his clothes. Taking his pants off slowly until he lies bare in front of me, just like one of the statues, and yet, no statue comes close to how striking Adrian is. An Adonis, yes, but more than that. More of... everything.

He steps closer, and the space between us tightens. Heat rolls off him in slow, deliberate waves, and suddenly I can't think, can't breathe. I can only feel the way my pulse stumbles in my throat. It burns in me—a relentless yearning in a place no water could reach. It wasn't just thirst; it was hunger wrapped in longing. My mouth goes dry and floods all at once.

An ache curling low in my belly and a wildfire behind my ribs, smoldering in silence, growing louder with every breath he took near me. And no matter how close he got, it wasn't close enough. Because I didn't want *just* closeness.

I wanted *collision*. I wanted to be known in the way rain knows drought.

And not even the ocean could drown this need.

I want him—God, I want him with a need that borders on painful. His gaze drops to my lips, slow and purposeful. The way he looks at me feels like he's already touching me, tracing every place he knows I'll break for him.

"I need you," I whisper as he climbs on the bed. My body leans toward him. My skin tingles, tightening with every inch he closes, every breath that blends with mine. I thread my fingers through his hair, tugging him closer, and let the noise in my head go quiet. And when his fingers brush my hip, I gasp into his mouth.

I'm undone by his touch, and he knows it. He knows exactly what he's doing to me, and I'm helpless to want anything else.

He gazes into my eyes and breathes with me. Each breath felt like an anchor, holding my heart and body in a deeper embrace. My name sounded like a sacred prayer on his tongue. *"Evolet, ll mio respiro; my breath."* His body moves against mine in reverence.

Passionate.

The space between his breaths feels infinite.

As my body shifts in pleasure, his body shifts in awareness, never letting me escape his full presence. He doesn't hold back. He knows where to touch me, how to touch me, setting my body alight. I move to kiss him again, more forcefully.

He smiles against my assault, pulling away slightly, teasing me. I push him just enough and roll on top of him, yearning for more. And suddenly he pounces—me on my back as he pins me beneath him. "Is this what you wanted?"

"Yes." I gasp as his legs open mine. But he waits. Breathing with me. As one.

I feel his hardness and the force of his belly pressing against mine. He looks into my eyes a second before he moves to kiss my full breasts, gently nipping between kisses, meeting my eyes again. Adrian's adoration of my body is obvious, but so is his passion, which has me opening my legs wider to draw him in. "Your body is divine, Eve," He says, kissing my neck and then moving to my collarbone. Kiss, kiss.. "Each curve reminds me of the hills of Tuscany." His lips move to the dip in my belly, warm and wet. "Every valley that dips and meets the rivers."

Every touch lights my body on fire, a rush of sensation makes me feel like I'm floating. "Please, *per favore...*" I moan and plead for him.

"I'll do anything for you, *Tesoro*. Especially when you ask so nicely in my native tongue." I barely have a moment before his deep voice commands my attention. "Eyes on me, Evolet, I want to see your face when we become one." He brings his hand up to my chin to guide my eyes to his before he enters my body with one agonizingly slow thrust. I let go of a breath I didn't know I was holding.

It was *inevitable*.

Like a storm that had waited too long to break.

His hands tangled in my hair, and mine clung to him like gravity had shifted and he was the only thing tethering me to the earth. Our kiss was fire and salt and breathless devotion, a desperate kind of knowing that we'd crossed a line that could never be uncrossed.

And we didn't care.

I surrendered to him completely. Incoherent words disappeared into stifled moans and breaths that he claimed with a searing kiss. One after the next in a tidal wave. Every inch we touched felt like a revelation—like we were writing a new language with our bodies, spelling out everything we'd tried so hard not to say. My heart cracks open, not in fear, but in love and adoration. A cry bubbles up in my throat, unable to hold back anything right now.

He kisses me harder with each thrust, like he was starved for only what I could give. And I gave it. Freely. Recklessly. As if I, too, had been walking around half-alive, waiting for this ruinous kind of beauty to find me.

We didn't make love so much as we *fell* into it—wild, tender, and imperfect. A beautiful, intimate mess of limbs and whispers and trembling mouths. And in that tangle of need and skin and heartache, we found a deeper connection than desire.

We found *relief.*

Not the kind that fades with morning, but the kind that settles into your bones like truth. Like belonging. Like finally being seen, all the way through—and continued our descent anyway.

Time slows as we both fall over the edge. Our breaths mingling, he stops moving to wipe a tear from my cheek. I open my eyes—without realizing I closed them—and his gaze penetrates into me as deeply as his thrusts. I close my eyes again, feeling too much, but his deep voice has me opening them.

"Don't hide from me, Evolet, *my breath.* I want all of you. Even your cries. I want the depth of the ocean with you." In Adrian's arms, the past doesn't matter. The future doesn't chase me.

There's only now.

And I let myself feel it all.

The room fell into the shadows of night, the linen curtains moved slowly, as a breeze slipped through the open window. The moon spills silver light across the terracotta floor, soft and uneven, like spilled milk on warm stone.

Adrian lies beside me, one arm draped over his forehead, the other curled loosely around my hip, making soft circles like he's afraid I might disappear if he lets go completely. His skin is still warm against mine, damp in the crook of his elbow. The soft cadence of his breath anchored me to the moment.

We haven't said a word in minutes. Maybe more. And yet, the silence between us wasn't empty. It was full—*charged* with a promise neither of us dares to name just yet.

I lie on my side, watching the curve of his mouth as it twitches in thought. There's a softness to him now, stripped of sarcasm and cool bravado. Just a man, with salt on his lips and vulnerability framing his jaw.

"You're quiet," I whisper, my voice nearly lost in the stillness.

He turns his head slightly to face me. His blue eyes, dulled in the dim light, still manage to find mine with unsettling precision.

"I'm just... trying to remember every second," he breathes with a lazy smile, and it knocks the breath from my lungs.

It shouldn't. We barely know each other. The last few weeks have been filled with more depth and adventure than I have ever experienced. And yet, I understand. Me too.

Because what just passed between us wasn't supposed to feel like *this*. It wasn't supposed to feel safe and terrifying all at once. Like letting someone into a room you've kept locked for years.

I run my fingers along the edge of the sheet, heart drumming a steady ache in my ribs. "This wasn't what I expected," I admit, barely above a whisper.

Adrian shifts, his hand finding mine under the blanket. He doesn't lace our fingers together—not yet. Just rests his palm against mine. Skin to skin. Honest and open.

"No," he says, quietly. "But maybe that's the point."

I turn my face into his shoulder, "Hmmm. Mmm." I hummed, inhaling the salt of skin and distant pine from outside, and let myself rest there. Let myself *belong* in his arms—for a moment, and maybe longer.

Outside, the night stretches on—full of stars that dot the night sky as an owl hoots in the distance. And inside, two people who were practically strangers lie tangled together, hearts whispering truths not quite ready to say aloud. At least not me.

Not yet.

But soon.

Maybe.

# Chapter Twenty-Six

The first light of morning slips through the shutters, casting golden stripes across the bed like brushstrokes on a canvas. The air is still, faintly scented with the floral, sweet lavender, and the strong aroma of coffee brewing somewhere in the villa.

I stir, the sheets tangled around my waist, the weight of the night still draped over my skin like a memory I don't want to wash away. My eyes flutter open to find Adrian already awake, sitting on the edge of the bed. He's watching me with a softness that makes my cheeks heat. His gaze is tender and thoughtful, like he sees more than just what's on the surface.

He reaches out and softly traces small circles on my bare back, his fingers whispering secrets across my skin, awakening every quiet place I thought had forgotten how to feel. He leans in, kissing me with the same kind of passion he did last night, making me want to tangle with him. Over and over again. Whatever Adrian sees in my eyes has his lips shifting into a devious smile.

"Good morning, temptress. Insatiable little thing you are, aren't you?" he says, voice low and rough-edged, sleep still clinging to it.

God, even his voice is devastating in the morning.

I smile, but it's a tentative one. I'm not sure what we're waking up *into*. Whatever line we crossed last night, we're standing on the other side now. And yet, the weight of it doesn't feel heavy. It feels... grounding.

"Do you always look at people like that when they wake up?" I ask, stretching beneath the sheets.

"Only when they steal the entire blanket and leave me for dead," he teases, but there's a warmth there that brushes against me more tenderly than his hand on my back, relaxing my mind.

I glance down and realize, yes, I am cocooned in most of the sheet.

I laugh—soft, breathy—and he leans forward to press a kiss just below my shoulder, and just like that, I melt into the mattress. I move to lie on my back, pulling the sheets up higher around my chin, needing a little separation to wrap my head around what happened between us last night.

Neither of us says anything for a long moment. Just the shared silence of two people who know this wasn't supposed to happen, at least not this soon, but aren't sorry it did.

"You okay?" he asks, eventually. And it's not casual—it's careful. Like he knows the difference between good and fine. Like he's asking if I regret it without forcing the words.

I meet his gaze, and there it is again—*that face*. The one that holds stories he hasn't told me yet. The one that tells me I'm not the only one who carries ghosts.

"I am," I say, voice honest. "But I'm still... figuring it out."

He nods slowly. "Me too."

His hand reaches for mine again, fingers brushing lightly—not grabbing, not assuming—just offering. I let mine slip into his, warm and unhurried.

There's no rush. No pressure. Just morning light on tangled sheets where casual had stopped feeling like casual. I trace lazy circles on Adrian's chest as he tucks a piece of crazy morning hair behind my ear for the third time.

"*Baciami*? Kiss me?" Adrian's voice is low as he both asks me and commands me at the same time, removing the uncertainty, and replacing it with knowing he regrets nothing—putting me at ease to let go and soak up the moment.

In his arms, I can be anything I want to be.

Adrian had a date planned—a romantic one. But not in the way people mean when they say that. He told me it wasn't about grand gestures or perfect timing. It was about showing me *his* Tuscany—the quiet corners, the secret flavors, the places you only find when you stop rushing.

It was perfect.

In Boston, the city's business magnified my schedule, so it was refreshing to just sit back and relax, enjoy the countryside of Italy. This is the kind of date that I looked forward to.

He met me just after sunrise at the villa, my hair still slightly messy from painting, my sunglasses pushed up into it, and a curious smile toying with my lips. He told me to dress however I felt comfortable. I felt giddy and a sense of freedom that lifted a little off my shoulders.

Adrian leaned up against his classic red Alfa Romeo, holding a warm espresso in a tiny paper cup and a flaky sfoglia filled with cream. His signature move is coffee and pastries. It was quickly becoming the way to my heart.

"No better way to start a day," he told me as we leaned against his car, the soft pink light brushing the rooftops of the town behind us. "You trust me, sì?"

I nod, laughing. "God help me—I do."

We didn't go far. Just a few winding kilometers into the hills, windows down, morning breeze curling through my fingers as I rested my hand out the window. The scent of cypress trees, lavender, and freshly tilled earth filled the car. A combination that was starting to feel more like home with each passing day.

We stopped at the vineyard where we had our "blind date" before the tour buses arrived. We wandered through the vines with glasses of chilled white wine in hand, dew still clinging to the leaves. I could feel his eyes on me as I closed mine, tipping my face to the sun. At that moment, I fell in love with Italy a little more. Maybe more than a little.

It felt like a life I could build and familiar in a way that made me feel closer to Papa. But it was also a choice waiting to be made.

A path I could call mine if I allowed it.

Later, we walked through the open-air market in a sleepy village square. The old stone buildings breathed their history into my ears. I ran my fingers over handwoven linens and tasted pecorino dipped in honey, laughing when it dripped down my chin. Adrian wiped it with his thumb, lingering on my lips while gazing in my eyes.

I had to remind myself to breathe.

For lunch, we sat at a small trattoria tucked beneath an olive tree. No menu—just what the little old lady was making that day. Handmade pici with wild boar ragu, bread still warm from the oven, and wine that tasted like summer had kissed every grape.

But it wasn't the food that made me quiet. It was the view—hills rolling like velvet, dotted with stone farmhouses and sunflowers turning their heads toward the light. My chest loosened as I breathed out.

"I could stay here forever."

Adrian said nothing. I didn't need him to. He just smiled and reached across the table, taking my hand in his and tracing lazy circles into my palm with his thumb.

A tether.

When the sun began to sink, we drove to a cliffside overlook where no one else goes. Adrian spread out a blanket, and we watched the sky melt into a hundred shades of gold and rose. I rested my head on his shoulder and took a deep breath in, then out. A breath I hadn't truly breathed in years.

"Why are you being so good to me?" I ask softly.

Adrian kisses my hair.

"Because Tuscany is beautiful," he breathes, "but it's more beautiful when you see it through the eyes of someone falling in love with it... and maybe, with someone in it."

I turned to look at him, his eyes shining in the fading light.

He kisses me, slow and reverent, and it feels like worship.

For a moment, the whole countryside stood still.

The stars arrived slowly, one by one, like they, too, were waiting to see what might happen next. The air had cooled, but not enough to chase us away. Crickets hummed softly in the tall grass, and in the distance, the low rustle of olive branches swayed in the breeze.

I pressed against Adrian on the blanket, shoes kicked off, feet tucked beneath me, eyes fixed on the sky like it was telling a story only we could hear. The moon hadn't risen yet, so everything was bathed in that in-between light—where time feels suspended, and silence becomes its own kind of conversation.

Adrian turned to look at me. "Tell me something you've never told anyone."

I smiled without looking at him. "That's dangerous."

"So is staying in Tuscany with a stranger."

I laugh, softly. "Pretty sure you are staying with me, *sir*."

"Touché. I'm beginning to crave that laugh of yours. " He says as I turn to face him, his hand finding mine in the space between us.

"I've never felt more myself than I do right now," I say, barely louder than the wind. "Makes me wonder who I was before this trip."

Adrian brings my hand to his lips, kissing the inside of my wrist with tenderness, like a promise. "I wouldn't want you to be anyone other than who you are, Evolet." He says my name like it's the only oxygen he's breathing. It sets my lungs on fire.

We lay there a while longer, a stillness settling between us that doesn't need filling. The kind of comfort that usually comes with a couple who've been married for years and yet are newlyweds at the same time.

At some point, Adrian tugs me gently into his arms. Like I'd always belonged—my head against his chest, his chin resting on my hair. His fingers traced idle shapes along my arm, like he wasn't really even aware he was doing it. I felt every single one.

The night deepened.

I looked up at Adrian. His eyes lingered on mine, a quiet invitation. That look again—the one that made my pulse kick up before my brain caught up.

"*Sono pazzo di te.* I'm crazy about you." There was a reverence in his voice—desire softening into awe—and I forget how to breathe. It was becoming the sound I waited for, the one that sank under my skin and refused to leave.

"I'm mildly crazy about you, too," I say with a little tease in my voice. This moment feels heavy and light at the same time.

"Does that scare you?" He asks, drawing in a long, grounding breath.

"Yes," I whisper back, my voice trembling, but with hope in my eyes.

Then, he kisses me with no hesitation. No light teasing. Just the deep, unhurried press of lips that speaks a language neither of us needed to translate. It was the kind of kiss that came not from wanting, but from knowing. And I wanted to know more. More of him, and more of Italy. His hands touched my jaw, while mine found the back of his neck, pulling him closer. His fingers sink into my hair, my breath catching as he leans in like he'd been waiting to do so since the moment we met. As if it's the first time.

We didn't rush. There was no need. It felt like all the moments before were special, but this was weighted with a sacredness that matched all the love stories ever written.

It was ours.

Time folded in on itself—moonlight painting silver across our skin, the hills holding our secret, the whole night wrapped around us like a second blanket. He laughed softly into my mouth when he whispered in hushed Italian, and I didn't even care that I didn't understand it.

I didn't have to.

Because in that moment—beneath the stars, we were wrapped in each other's warmth with endless possibilities on the horizon. Nothing needed explaining.

We simply *were*.

# Chapter Twenty-Seven

The following day, after a long stretch of painting, Adrian took me out for a late lunch. After we wandered slowly through the narrow street just beyond the café, the late afternoon sun cast long golden streaks between the shutters and terracotta walls. The last bite of panna cotta still lingering on my tongue, the silky smooth custard imprinting on my soul. Adrian walked beside me, hands tucked into his pockets, his gaze not-so-subtly drifting toward me every few steps.

"You've got that look again," I say without turning to him.

"What look?" he asks, feigning innocence.

"The look that says you're about to get me into trouble."

He chuckles low in his throat. "I'm just walking with you."

"Mm-hm." I glance over at him, smirking. "And undressing me with your eyes."

"That's unfair." He places a hand over his heart and smirks. "I'm a gentleman."

"You're a menace."

"Only mildly."

We round the corner into a quieter alleyway, where ivy curls around cracked stone and flower boxes spill color over the windowsills. Adrian slows to a stop and looks over at me with a new kind of stillness—less teasing now, but no less electric.

"I've been thinking," he says.

"That sounds dangerous."

He steps closer, enough that I could smell the faint citrus of his cologne, the warmth of espresso still clinging to his breath. "I want to kiss you again."

My breath catches, stilling my thoughts. "Again? Like right now?" I look around us, watching people pass us by, like it's no big deal.

His eyes drop to my mouth. "Yes. Like the other night... but slower."

My heartbeat vibrates in my throat, wild and free. "And if I say no?"

He tilts his head slightly, a lazy grin pulling at his lips. "Then I'll behave. But if you say yes..." His voice drops again to a velvet murmur. "I promise I'll make it worth your while."

I stare at him, every nerve in my body suddenly alive, crackling beneath my skin. My voice comes out softer than intended. "You're trouble, Adrian Amoroso."

He steps even closer, one hand gently brushing a loose strand of hair behind my ear. "Then stop looking at me like you want to get in trouble with me. *Evolet Moretti.*"

A second later, I lean up—just slightly—and whisper against his lips, "Okay. Kiss me." And he does. His mouth finds mine, and the world narrows to the heat of his lips and the way he takes his time memorizing me. My breath catches. I taste him, feel the deliberate pressure as he deepens the kiss.

His lips taste like the red wine he had at lunch, warm and bitter, mixed with the caramel left behind from my dessert. It was the kind of kiss that didn't just melt my insides—it rearranged them. One hand was cradling the side of my face, thumb gently tracing the edge of my jaw, the other resting lightly against my waist, like he still couldn't believe I was real.

Our breaths mingled, warm and unhurried, as if we had all the time in the world.

Just feeling.

And for a while, it felt like we did. No clocks. No distractions. Just this.

The world had gone soft around the edges—until his phone buzzed sharply in his back pocket. He didn't move at first. I felt the vibration through him, then the brief tension in his shoulders. The kiss faltered, lips hovering just above mine now, eyes still closed.

The phone buzzed again.

Adrian exhales, a low hum of annoyance—or maybe reluctance—and pulls back just enough to rest his forehead against mine. "Of all the times..." he mutters, and I could feel the smile trying to pull at his mouth even as the moment slips away like the tide going back to sea.

I blink a few times, still trying to return to my body. "You can get it," I whisper, voice breathless, though I wasn't sure I meant it.

He leans away with a groan and fishes the phone out of his pocket, glancing at the screen. The moment his eyes landed on it, something shifted. Subtle, but there. The glint in his eyes dimmed just slightly. His thumb hovers over the screen—undecided, maybe—but then he silences the call and slides the phone back into his pocket.

"All yours again," he says lightly, turning his attention back to me with that easy, roguish grin that had undone me more times than I cared to admit. "Sorry about that. Apparently, the universe gets jealous."

A hesitant laugh escapes me, but a sliver of curiosity wedges itself between my ribs.

He didn't say who it was.

And I didn't ask.

Because until now, I hadn't had to share his time with anyone—not really. It had been just us, tucked away in this strange, beautiful bubble with sexual tension and wine-soaked nights.

Still, I catch the faintest crease in his brow as he leans in again, but it disappears quickly. It smoothes over with a kiss to my cheek and another murmured apology. And maybe I should've pressed. Maybe I should've asked who was calling, and why it stole something from his expression for just a flicker of a second.

But instead, I let myself fall back into him—into the heat of his mouth on mine, the way his hands anchored me so effortlessly.

Because I trust him.

And I wasn't sure I was ready for what I might hear if I did question it further.

I wasn't looking for anything more. It just sort of happened.

As we finished the perfect date, my mind lingered on that phone call. What if I was keeping him from something important? He'd had a whole life before I arrived in Italy, which made me curious to know more about his life here.

His past. His present. A possible future.

But the words stuck in my throat. What if asking meant learning he would no longer show up at the Villa? What if it confirmed what I already suspected? I shake my head, letting out a breath. I should just focus on my art submission anyway. That thought has me nervous for a different reason altogether.

Because the deadline was just around the corner.

The villa was quiet in that soft, golden way only morning could manage. The breeze drifted lazily through the open shutters, carrying the scent of warm stone, lavender, and something earthy in the distance. I'd wrapped myself in Adrian's linen button-up—still faintly smelling of him—and padded barefoot onto the terrace, expecting to see him return any moment with our usual: a hazelnut latte, a cappuccino, and a white paper bag filled with flaky, cream-filled pastries from the café down the hill.

He was never late. Not with coffee. Not with me.

I leaned against the railing, scanning the path that wound through the olive trees below, squinting toward the village. No sign of him. I check the time again. *Twenty minutes late.* Not dramatic. Not unreasonable. But... off.

I tried not to read into it. Tried not to remember the call from the night before, or the flicker of shadow that had passed across his face before he'd masked it with a kiss and a joke. Still, a subtle unease crept in.

I go back inside, pacing once around the kitchen, aimlessly moving spoons and teacups like it would give my hands something to focus on. I glance at the espresso machine on the counter. He hadn't used it this morning.

Which meant he'd gone into town.

I open the door to the bedroom and scan the space—his shoes gone, his leather wallet still missing from the nightstand. He hadn't just gone for a walk. He left with intention.

I found my phone and checked for a message. Nothing.

Back on the terrace, I sat at the small mosaic table and pulled my knees up to my chest, resting my chin on them as the sun began to climb higher. Still no footsteps. Still no Adrian.

And then a thought bloomed—quiet, uninvited.

What if that call hadn't just been a disruption?

What if it were the excavation of a truth that would leave a lasting hole in its place?

I hated the way my stomach clenched around it.

He wasn't mine to control. I knew that. This wasn't that kind of story. But I had grown used to being the center of his world, even if only for a short, borrowed season.

The sound of a car door closing jolted me from my thoughts. I stood, too quickly, my heart thudding in my chest. Adrian appeared a few seconds later, rounding the bend with the paper bag and coffee tray in hand. His sunglasses are pushed up in his wind-tossed hair, and he looks infuriatingly handsome as ever.

But as he stepped closer, I noticed it again—it's in the way he walked. Distracted. Like he'd come from somewhere else entirely before remembering where he was supposed to be.

"Sorry, *amore*," he says easily, offering the coffee like a peace offering. "Detour. Ran into a neighbor's dog, who decided to follow me halfway through town."

I raised an eyebrow, taking the coffee. "The legendary Tuscan pastry delay?"

He grins, but it doesn't quite reach his eyes.

"I brought extra." He sets the bag down in front of me. "To make up for the tragic wait."

I take a sip. It was perfect, of course. Everything he did was usually intentional. But I stayed quiet. Watchful.

Because the Adrian I knew didn't get *distracted*. Or maybe I was just spoiled before.

I smile anyway, brushing my lips against his cheek as I pass by.

But the seed was planted now. And no matter how sweet the pastries were, the question had begun to rise.

Who was on the other end of that call?

And why, for the first time, did it feel like he wasn't fully mine?

The light in the studio was all wrong.

Too sharp, too harsh. It splintered through the tall windows, as if trying to expose me rather than warm me. I shifted the canvas again, just slightly, but it didn't help. The colors looked dull. Flat. The composition was nearly there, but the feeling—the soul of it—wasn't.

I dipped the brush into a mixture of phthalo blue and raw umber, swirled it like I knew what I was doing, and pressed it to the canvas with more force than necessary. The stroke bled wrong, uneven. I cursed under my breath, stepping back, hands on my hips, trying to see it with fresh eyes.

Nothing.

It didn't speak.

It just stared back at me, half-finished and hollow.

I ran a hand through my hair, fingers catching on paint-smudged strands. I was *so close*. I could *feel* it—this thing I was trying to say with color and texture and shadow. But it kept slipping just out of reach, like a name you almost remember, like the ending of a dream that evaporates the moment you wake.

Adrian's voice echoed in my head, *"Don't overthink it. You already know what it's supposed to be."* God, I hated how easily he got in, how even his absence could take up space.

I hadn't seen much of him the past couple of days—more phone calls, more half-smiles, more moments when he was there but not really with me. And I told myself it was fine. We weren't defined. We weren't making promises. The nightmares hadn't helped either.

Last night, I woke in a cold sweat, the sheets tangled around my legs, my breath tight in my throat. I couldn't remember the details—just the feeling of drowning in something I couldn't see. I reached for Adrian, but the other side of the bed was cold.

Just like the brush in my hand now. Cold. Useless.

A sudden wave of frustration surged through me. I flung the brush across the room. It hit the floor with a clatter and left a smear of burnt sienna across the pale tiles.

I pressed my palms to my face and exhaled through clenched teeth.

Get it together. But I couldn't. Not today.

There was too much noise in my head. Too many unfinished thoughts about him, about this piece, about myself. The doubts crept in quietly and fast, like mold beneath the surface.

*What if I can't finish it?*

*What if it's not enough?*

*What if I'm not enough?*

My gaze snapped back to the canvas. I stared hard, as if sheer willpower could force it into worthiness. But it just looked back at me like it knew better. As if it had seen all my cracks and decided not to trust me either.

I sank onto the stool, arms resting on my knees, chin dropping forward. The silence in the studio was deafening.

And I thought, not for the first time. I don't know how to do this. Not the painting. Not the art. Not falling for someone who might be pulling away without telling me why.

And still... I didn't stop trying.

Because even in the doubt, even in the mess of it all, I still wanted to finish the painting. I had to believe I could find my way through.

Even if it meant getting lost first.

# Chapter Twenty-Eight

Five days before the submission deadline, I'd finally reached the last layer of my painting. The final shadows. The golden lines. It's nearly done.

I should feel proud.

I should be celebrating.

But Adrian never came back after he left this morning, when he said he had "a few things to take care of in Siena." There was a tightness in his voice I hadn't heard before and he looked away too quickly.

Now the air felt heavier than the wine I opened after the last brush-stroke of the day, and a strange stillness clings to my shoulders. I Face-Timed Gi to let her know how close I was to finishing my painting. After the squealing and many congratulatory remarks, she now looks at me through the screen with worry. "You okay?"

I nod. "Just tired. And... something feels off."

"Feels off? How so?" She asks. I haven't told Gi of what happened between Adrian and me, so I am hesitant to reveal how close we've become. How deep the connection between us is. And I am afraid to speak about it to anyone; I don't trust us yet to put a label on it.

"I'm not sure I should say anything. It could be nothing. But..." My voice wavers at the thought of voicing what I care about.

"It's okay, you can tell me, sis. I may not know heartache like you do, but I'm here for you. Is it Connor again?" Gi inquires, having no idea how hard I have fallen for Adrian.

"It's Adrian." I look at her on my phone, feeling weird to have this conversation without her here in person. "We've been seeing each other over the past couple of weeks. And then... he, uh... he slept over."

I stare at Gi through the screen, trying to gauge her reaction. It's when she doesn't smile with excitement that has my heart dropping into my stomach.

"Last night? Or a while ago?" Gi questions, with a frown on her face. I don't like the combination.

"A few days ago, but we have been hanging out since you guys left for your honeymoon," I reply, anxious about her response.

She hesitates. Then says, "There's something I think you should see." She pulls out Josh's phone. Her expression was careful—like she didn't want to be the one to unravel a truth, but knew she couldn't protect me from it either.

The screen showed a photo. Adrian. Standing just outside a gallery in Siena. Next to a woman. Laughing. Close. Familiar. Their bodies angled in a way that screamed history.

And the caption, *Congratulations to Viola and Romeo on launching their new service with Luxury Travel Agency—Paris, Florence, and beyond!*

My stomach drops. I didn't speak. I couldn't. The image spoke louder than any words ever could. He hadn't told me about this.

About *her*.

Why? Who was she? Was he leaving? Was she the reason he never stayed anywhere long?

I knew he worked with a Travel company but I didn't know he was working on creating his own business with a partner. That's something he would've mentioned right? I would hope he felt comfortable enough to let me in. But maybe not.

Suddenly, my whole body vibrates with questions I didn't want to ask. Why didn't I ever ask him more about his job? Why didn't he say anything? Does he even live nearby?

Had I been a *pause* in his journey, while I was making him part of my destination?

"I didn't think anything of it, because you hadn't mentioned him lately. I didn't get the impression that he was with someone when I met him; otherwise, I never would have suggested it. I'm so sorry, Eve. I feel awful."

"Neither did I, and he was right in front of me." After a bit of catching up, I ended the call, not wanting to chat any longer.

I was swept away in the moments, not caring about what that could mean for me in the near future. Because I still thought, on some level, that this was temporary. And I didn't want to invest too much. But my heart did already. And I don't know how to stop it.

I didn't text him. I didn't pick up when he called.

Instead, I shut everything out and headed up to the studio to paint away the confusion long after midnight until I couldn't feel the pain.

I didn't cry. Not yet. I have to get this submission done.

But I felt the wall around my heart slowly rebuild itself—quietly, efficiently, out of instinct.

The version of Adrian I knew—the man who brought me pastries, who kissed my forehead under a fig tree, who gave me his mother's paints—was now tangled with a version he hadn't shown me.

Not dishonest, exactly. Just... *hidden*. And I didn't know which one to trust.

The next morning, he showed up at the locked gate with that lopsided smile, a bag of oranges, and hopeful eyes. I didn't go down. I watched from the upstairs window, unseen. And I let the silence answer for me because I feel the cracks split wide open.

Not shattered, but deepened.

I needed to protect the part I was finally beginning to trust again.

And the person I was was finally becoming.

The next day, the hour blurred into the next, and I painted furiously. I wrapped a new canvas, feeling the creative tide rise to the surface, and I surrendered to it. I painted everything I had in me, screaming to come out. Screaming for recognition, the voice was not quiet. She was loud.

Fierce.

I reached for every color on the tip of my paintbrush, thrashing at the canvas, I swiped, I blotted, I teased color over color. Parts of it start in one and then mix in the middle.

Then she formed, out of the greens, the golds, and the blacks. Lips rising from water, but still a touch of color, the cold didn't reach that far yet. Surrounded by nature, still feeling the weight of it all.

Life. Love. Defeat. Self-doubt.

The crumbling ache of the pain felt with each torturous lesson thrown my way. She emerged from the depths of the darkness that had plagued most of her life.

My life.

The bone-aching heartache seeped into other areas of my body, causing discomfort and damaging thoughts. I gazed at the painting and saw it reflected back. A self-portrait I did not dare to attempt until now. I can feel it, the creative wellspring, reachable and attainable.

I have realized it's always been there, but I was too afraid to tap into it. Too scared to tap into it too early in fear of it disappearing or not being enough to finish what I set out to do. But here I am, painting through the pain. Brushstroke after brushstroke flaring to life with every new breath.

I am creating. I am enough. I AM AN ARTIST.

Tears flowed down my face, dropping onto the palette of messy color. I kept going. I mixed the tears in with the paint—sweeping my brush—adding detail after detail. Swirls and lines that shape and blend into the emotion I am feeling.

Hurt. Freedom. Conviction. Passion. Darkness. Love. All of it.

Even through the cracks, I am melding the pieces of myself together. Until. There she was, a mosaic of emotions, a masterpiece worthy of submission. A blend of my past and present made new.

Made whole.

I stepped back from my creation, and took a breath. I breathed in all the tension of the years past, hiding in the pain and depression. Afraid to move forward in anything and then releasing it through a long, languid breath. "*Let it go, Eve.*"

More tears welled in my eyes, but I didn't hold them back. For once, I let them build freely, without trying to stop them or make myself feel numb. I felt every ounce of this monumental moment. Because I fucking deserve this success.

This moment of absolute truth manifests itself through this painting. I will never make myself feel small again. If anything, this process has shown me that I am capable of more than I realize.

That, even when things are difficult, or it feels too much, I need to take the time to paint, to create. I need to pick up the damn paintbrush and just start. It doesn't matter where I am, or what I've done in the past—showing up for myself is the best thing I can do for my heart and for my healing. I matter. My art matters.

*My art matters.*

I am so proud of what I've created. I close my eyes, my face wet with tears, and yet, I never want to forget how I am feeling right now.

I wish Adrian were here right now so I could show him. He was a pillar I wasn't expecting, and in his absence, I've realized how important he'd become in my life. It scares me to know how much of an impact he's made in this short amount of time, and I fear I'll royally mess up what we have. I just hope we can recover.

Whatever he is going through, I know we need to talk. I know for certain he would not be dishonest with me without a reason. A reason I robbed him of, with my heartache.

A storm rolled in without warning. Heavy clouds crawled over the hills like bruises, thunder rumbling in the distance. The air in the studio thickened, but I kept my focus on the canvas in front of me. My mind was wild tonight. My body a blur of motion—brush in hand, fingers stained with deep, aching colors—red, ash gray, indigo so dark it looked like night had bled onto the canvas.

I hadn't spoken to anyone all day. I don't remember the last time I had a bite to eat. A longing ached in my heart, and something stirred inside, as if it were cracking open.

Not like glass. Like Earth.

I am nearly finished. I rub the spot in between my breasts, stepping back from what I created. My skin prickled with awareness.

The piece was a towering abstract figure—a human form, but not whole. Fragmented. Veins of gold thread stitched along the edges of the breaks. There was grief in it. Fury. But also surrender. A woman disintegrating and rebuilding herself all in one motion with soft, blurred edges.

A flash of lightning lights up the room, breaking me out of my haze. Heart pounding after the crack of thunder that follows. And then, it hits me.

A single memory. A buried one. Shoved down for years.

I was nine. In a cramped classroom with several girls at the same table as me. We were all painting something that made us happy. I painted swirls, dots, and splashes of all the colors on my palette. A girl, the mean one, laughed at me and declared my art was "horrible" and "messy." I didn't pick up a paintbrush for a month after that.

Then another. A professor I admired stood over my final project. He'd called me "emotionally indulgent." Said my work was "messy" and "too feminine to be serious." He said I didn't have *discipline* and that art wasn't therapy.

And I'd believed him.

I stopped painting that week for good.

The memories struck like lightning—sudden, bright, and paralyzing.

My breath caught. The canvas blurred in front of me.

"Not now," my voice tight and my heart beating wildly.

*Not now.*

But it was too late.

My lungs refused to open. My hands trembled violently. The air pressed against my chest like it wanted me to drown in it. I stumbled back, knocking over a jar of brushes. They clattered across the floor.

"No—no," I whisper, crouching, holding my chest. "Not again."

Tears streamed down my cheeks while my pulse thundered in my ears.

I curled in on myself beside the canvas, fingers digging into the floorboards. The panic roared inside my head—this terrible chorus of *you're not enough, you're too much, you don't belong here, you'll never belong anywhere.*

And then—a voice.

Not outside. Inside. Soft. Familiar... Mine.

*They were wrong.*

*Your pain is not a weakness. Your story is not an indulgence.*

*You make beauty out of truth. That's what art is.*

My breath hitched. Shallow. But it came.

Slowly, I pressed my forehead to the floor and let the storm pass through like a wave, my body shaking, but relieved that the panic didn't take me out. Not this time.

I rolled to my back, still and wrung out, staring at the ceiling through tear-blurred lashes. The painting loomed above me like a monument. It was unfinished, but alive. Brutally, achingly alive.

And for the first time, I saw it not as proof of my brokenness, but as a mirror of strength.

The panic hadn't destroyed me. It had *delivered* a truth: I never stopped being an artist. I had only stopped *trusting* that I was allowed to be one.

Outside, the storm faded. A sliver of moonlight slipped in through the open shutters and landed across the gold veins on the canvas. They shimmered.

I inhaled a breath. Deep. Real.

I wipe my face with the sleeve of my shirt and pull myself up, picking up the brush again. With hands still shaking—but not retreating—I lean into the light.

And kept going.

# Chapter Twenty-Nine

I decided to take a bike ride along the dirt road to put some distance between myself and my painting. Even though the journey was rough, I am proud of myself for surrendering to the process and finishing it. At least, it feels finished for now.

Which is why I needed space to avoid critiquing my work and just soak in its completion. Sometimes I wonder whether, when I get to the end of it and am ready for submission, I will actually follow through. And while those thoughts are dangerous, stepping out into the slightly cooler afternoon sounded better than throwing all of my progress out.

I'm riding along the rugged road for about an hour, as the cool breeze dances in my hair, when the faint aroma of woodsmoke mixed with a delicious punch of garlic. I see a small house tucked back among an olive grove, its charming size blending into the landscape's beauty.

As I approach the gravel road leading up to the traditional farmhouse, I see an elderly woman walking with a basket and a bright orange shawl draped across her shoulders. She has a bit of a lopsided gait, but you can tell she is a strong woman. As I get closer, I hear a melodic song with an upbeat tune playing on her lips. It brings a smile to my face.

When I'm within talking distance and the tires crunch under me, she turns around to see where the sound is coming from, a gasp escaping her. *"Ciao! Mi hai fatto paura, cara. Da dove vieni?"*

I stop immediately and get off the bike.

Not quite understanding her Italian, I politely say, "Sorry, my Italian is still rusty. Do you speak any English? *Parli inglese?*" She shakes her head no, but motions for me to follow her. Curiosity getting the best of me, I look back at the direction I came, and see no one around for miles. I decided to just follow, walking my bike next to her.

She mumbles in Italian, but I have no idea what. So I continue to follow her. She has a very relaxed presence, making it feel like I don't have to fill the space at all. It reminds me of another certain local that has been taking up space in my mind.

I miss him.

It's been two days, and I haven't reached out yet. I needed time to wrap my head around how fast we'd moved in our very short relationship. Do I even want to be in a relationship? There was a reason I left Connor. But when I am with Adrian, it feels different. Serene. I can be myself around him. But does he feel like he can be himself around me?

As we get closer to the house, I see the lush gardens to the right, filled with vegetables and herbs. In a pen just beyond, I see chickens, goats, and pigs. Out in the pasture are a mix of cows. Black dotting the horizon. The olive grove sits just beyond the backside of the country home.

This place has been thoroughly taken care of. All the little touches are thoughtfully placed. Flowers of all shapes and sizes line the front, giving a very lively cottagecore vibe. The house itself is pale yellow, with a terracotta roof, which I notice is popular here. As I look around, I notice, out of the corner of my eye, that the old woman has a serene smile on her face, one that feels familiar. Like she knows me somehow.

I have never seen her before in my life, and yet she feels safe.

"Is this your house?" I ask, pointing to the villa and the surrounding area, knowing she doesn't understand my words, but hoping she recognizes my inviting gesture.

"Sì, *benvenuto a casa mia. Mio nipote mi aiuta qui.*" She nods to the house and points to the animals. "*Sono molto fortunato. Benedetto. Venire.*" She gestures towards the door, walking up the small steps. Before she even opens the door, I am assaulted by a waft of onion, garlic, and basil.

Familiar.

I follow her inside the door, after I lean my bike against the railing, when a blend of emotions runs through me as I take in the quaint living space. The house is full of rustic charm, exposed beams, and a staircase leading up to a second floor. The woman sets down her basket on a wooden island in the middle of the open kitchen and hangs her shawl on the hook by the door. She then reaches for the basket, pulling out the perfect loaf of bread. She grabs a knife and cuts thick slices, placing them on a wooden tray.

She then pulls out what looks like whipped butter and generously spreads the butter on the loaf. Grabbing a linen napkin, she then holds them both out to me in offering. Of course, I take it, not denying a healthy dose of bread and butter. The food seriously tastes way better here in Italy. It actually makes me feel depressed just thinking of going back to the States and eating garbage.

I bite into the bread loaf, instantly picking up the generous amount of honey in the butter, and I melt. Healthy moans accompanied by nods of my head.

This pleases her. I am so wrapped up in this immersive experience, I don't hear the door open until a deep voice carries across the space.

"Well, I haven't heard that kind of moan yet. I think you're holding out on me, Evolet." I know that voice.

I whip my head around toward the door in shock.

"I..I didn't. Um, how are you here?" I am stunned. Seeing him here, so unexpectedly. Speechless and confused, Adrian walks over to the old woman, who has her arms open wide for a hug. I watch in fascination as this big man engulfs this petite woman in a familiar way that says "family," and that's exactly what I hear coming from his mouth, "*Nonna*," Grandma.

This is Adrian's grandma. I'm at Nonna's house.

I keep shifting my weight, feeling like I'm witnessing a moment of personal significance.

They continue to speak in Italian to each other, with the occasional glance from Adrian and that little smirk that drives me crazy. I stand there, watching in equal parts awe and confusion. I wring my hands together in front of me, as the bread is forgotten on the table.

Why didn't he tell me his Nonna lived so close to the Villa? But then I remember my sister mentioning he had a connection close by to the vineyard they were getting the wine from for the wedding. This must be the connection she meant. I feel so selfish for not asking more about Adrian's life here. I blame myself for diving in too soon. I've never felt this way before, and it took me by surprise.

Probably Adrian too.

After what feels like an uncomfortable amount of time, I clear my throat and wait for an explanation. Adrian replies to my question, "Eve, this is my Nonna, Elena. Nonna, questo *è il mio respiro*, Evolet." Nonna looks at me with a new twinkle in her eye and a wide smile that takes my breath away. It's familiar, maternal, welcoming, and warm. She steps toward me, pulling me into a strong embrace.

Taking a step back, she grabs both of my hands in hers and kisses them both. Water stings my eyes from the gesture, but I smile back and nod in return. I don't know what else to say. She's caught me off guard. Tilted my axis just like her grandson.

*This family.*

I try not to read into it. Although I am feeling big feelings right now, I'm unsure where to put all these thoughts and emotions.

"Adrian...." I say his name, is it a question? A statement? Shit, I have no words. I look up at him only to see emotion in his eyes. He wasn't expecting this either. He looked at me like I was the only thing in the room.

"Where have you been?" I ask, unsure, I want to know the answer.

"I've been working and then staying here to help Nonna. We lost my grandfather last year, so she's been needing extra help with the land. We are preparing to sell the house so she's closer to the rest of the family in Puglia."

"Oh, how devastating. I am so sorry." I look back at his Nonna, "*Mi dispiace.*" She looks at me again, tears in her eyes, but a warm smile, and nods.

"*Gracias. Mi bella.*" She turns back to cut more bread and serves Adrian a couple of slices.

"I had no idea you were going through all of this." I wave around the kitchen and look out the window by the dining table. "I am so selfish." I quietly say to myself.

Adrian walks up without saying anything—and wraps me up with his big arms that comfort me in only the way he can. I know I am safe here. I know we have things to discuss, but it feels good to be grounded in his masculine citrus scent.

"Can we talk for a minute?" He asks, pulling away and leading me to a big table in the dining area.

"Of course," I say, my heart racing, but I follow him.

"Did I do something wrong? To offend you?" He looks at me with hurt eyes, not the usual warmth I've seen every day.

"Do you have a girlfriend?" I just come right out and ask. I'm not usually this forward, but the suspense is eating away at me.

He blinks. Wide-eyed and speechless. "Are you serious? Do you think I would be in a relationship with you if I were?" His eyes search mine, trying to make sense of my question.

"I, uh...saw a picture of you with a woman you're in business with and was unsure. And then I realized I haven't actually asked much about your life here or about your family." I look down at my hands, picking at the side of my nail. "I'm sorry," I whisper.

Adrian lifts my chin with his finger until I meet his eyes. "Evolet, there is no one but you." His face is genuine, and I can't help the sob that escapes me. Viola is my business partner and a long-time friend —nothing more. She handles most of the meet-and-greets with our travel company as well as the Luxury details. I handle the schedules mostly and connections in each city."

"Oh," I manage to say, while wiping tears from my face.

"I didn't want to bore you with the details because you needed to focus on what was in front of you with the art submission. And I was still trying to woo you." He smiles that wicked smile that disarms me. And I laugh.

"I'm so sorry for jumping to conclusions. I should've asked."

"It's okay, you are here now, and what a lovely surprise that was!" He pulls me in for a kiss, and without saying more, we embrace and let go of the awkwardness of before and enjoy being together again.

We all end up outside in the back living space —an inviting terrace with stone pavers and a pergola that has seen better days, its wood worn.

It doesn't matter, though; the space feels like a well-loved home with years of fond memories.

Memories only time could paint such a lovely landscape full of stories. The sides are adorned with fragrant herbs and flowers of all colors, I'm certain Adrian's Nonna lovingly cares for. This place holds a certain kind of magic that only one can make in the presence of family.

I'm sad to think of it being sold off.

I see how Adrian's Nonna admires her grandson. The way she holds her hand on his arm as they talk and laugh, sharing stories, sharing their time. Emotion swirls inside me —a wild storm of love and appreciation, rather than fear and emptiness, for once. I let my gaze wander over the trellises with climbing wisteria, providing shade and also a romantic setting paired beautifully with the setting sun. The golden light warms everything in its path.

It's perfect. It's magical. It's everything.

After a delicious meal with an extraordinary wine, I am leaving filled with *more*. More of this Italian culture and landscape. More influenced and inspired to create. More of everything I could ever have imagined since arriving so lost and broken. And Adrian. He is the one who surprises me the most.

With him, I feel a future I hadn't allowed myself to imagine.

It both scares and excites me.

The dark doesn't feel so black with his light shining like a beacon on stormy waters.

He's my lighthouse.

# Chapter Thirty

The ocean was quiet, wrapped in a hush like being in the eye of a storm, and moonlight spilled over the tide, casting silver shadows across the sand before me. The beach stretched endlessly, sand pulling at my feet like it wanted to keep me. I was looking for something—had to find it—but every time I tried to remember what, the thought slipped away like water through my fingers. My heart hammered against my ribs, too loud, too fast, though nothing had changed.

Or had it? The horizon bent at the edges.

Then came the whisper in the wind. Not words—just *need*. Raw and sharp.

I was small again, running along the beach with no end. I wore a white shift dress and was barefoot. My voice didn't carry as I kept calling out to the emptiness until a scattering of thick paper swirled at my feet. Paintings I did when I was little. Each one had my name scrawled on it in a child's messy handwriting.

Then two doors appeared in the middle of the beach, one white, one black. My parents materialized out of nowhere, smiled at me, and walked through the white door. I rushed at the door in what felt like slow motion, but it was locked.

I clawed at it, sobbing, *"Please—come back. Take me instead."* I pounded on the white door until my hands were sore and aching from the assault. I turned to see if the black one was unlocked, only to realize

I *was* the door. My white dress shifted into a black one in my adult body. Tendrils of black smoke wrap around my trembling legs and sore arms. It crawled up around my throat and squeezed. I clawed at my throat trying to ease the pressure, but it didn't let up.

I frantically searched the beach for someone to help.

But there was no one. The pressure squeezed tighter, dotting my vision with black spots and bringing me to my knees.

A scream caught in my throat—waking me up in my bedroom at the villa.

I sit up, gasping. Chest heaving. Skin damp with sweat. The walls of the room look warped in the dark, still halfway inside the dream. I press my hands over my face, trying to calm the tremor rocking through me and the shake in my breath. My heart ached in a way I couldn't name.

I reached for the empty space that Adrian filled the other night. His presence had anchored me these past weeks; now the storm I helped feed over time is back to claim me for good. He was staying at his Nonna's tonight for an early doctor's appointment in the morning. I wish he were here.

I jump out of bed, grab a washcloth from the bathroom, and wet it with cold water from the tap. As cold as I can get it, then place the cloth on my face and neck, while trying to steady my erratic breathing. I stare at my reflection in the mirror in the dark—a faint silhouette. I can hear the rain softly pattering on the roof. The sound soothes some of the unease in my gut, calming my racing heart.

Nightmares have been a very common occurrence over the years, but this one was different. This nightmare felt sharper, and the darkness that'd been far enough away feels closer to the surface. I feel like this panic attack came out of nowhere. I close my eyes and place my hands over my chest. Praying for the darkness to fade away when it feels acute and ready to strike again.

Deep breath in. One. Two. Three.

Breathe out. One. Two. Three.

In and out, I repeat several times until the danger I felt fades away into the night. I move to the balcony of my room and look out at the stormy sky. The sweet smell of rain teases my nose, while the cold humidity claws at my skin.

What am I going to do? I am so tired of feeling this way. Feeling so unsettled. I thought Italy was the answer. And maybe it still is. Even though I've painted and fought through my emotions, the darkness still threatens what I've worked so hard for. Slowly. Torturous and painfully repetitive. What am I missing?

I wrap myself in my oversized sweater, hugging my body like armor.

I will get through this like I always have. The path is unclear, but I know I need to finish my art piece. Even if it feels like it will never reach its final state, the finish line is constantly moving. Can I complete this monumental painting and find a completion I can be proud of? Or will I always feel this sense of dread and vulnerability, letting it capsize my creation? I let the thought swirl, knowing that's the panic talking, but somehow I know this isn't the end of it.

It's not done haunting me.

The art submission is due tomorrow, and time—like everything else—feels like it's slipping through my fingers. I sit before the canvas, surrounded by other canvases of varying sizes, each at a different stage of finality, staring at a painting that should feel like triumph. But it doesn't.

It's *good*. Maybe even remarkable. But not *enough*.

There's something missing—I can't name it, can't see it, but I *feel* its absence like a dull ache in my chest. I study every brushstroke, every layer of color, waiting for a spark, a whisper, some kind of revelation to rise from the canvas.

But nothing comes.

My hair is piled on top of my head in disarray, while a cold cup of coffee sits on the floor beside the stool. My thumbnail is raw, bitten until it bleeds, and still, I chew without thinking—another unconscious ritual in a long line of self-doubt.

I can't start over. There's no time. But I can't bear to send this version either, not when it feels incomplete. *What is missing?*

The question from last night returns, curling itself around my ribs like smoke.

*"What am I going to do?"*

And this time, I don't have an answer. I stand up and pace the floor in front of the painting that should be finished, but I can't seem to finalize it. It feels too demanding, accusing. Its brilliance feels like a lie. All I see are flaws—edges too sharp, colors too restrained, emotion that never made it from my chest to the canvas.

It's supposed to mean something different.

It's supposed to *be* something *more*.

But instead, it feels like an imitation of someone I thought I could be.

*Crack.*

My knees buckle before I even realize I'm falling, crumpling onto the floor in a tangle of limbs and shattered resolve. The sob that escapes my throat is raw, ugly, involuntary—years of exhaustion rising to the surface all at once.

*Crack.*

"I can't do this," I choke out to the room, to the painting, to no one. I cover my face with my stained hands, hiding tears that burn as they fall. "I've failed. Again. I'm not an artist. I've been pretending this whole time."

*Crack.*

The door creaks open behind me, but I don't look up. I can't. Let them see me like this—defeated, humiliated, undone. I don't want to shield myself any longer.

"Eve."

His voice is soft, almost reverent.

My body stiffens, wiping my eyes with the back of my sleeve, hating how vulnerable I feel. "Please don't," I whisper. "I feel too raw, it's too much."

But Adrian steps inside anyway, closing the door behind him. He doesn't speak, doesn't judge. Just walks over quietly and kneels beside me on the paint-splattered floor. "I wasn't sure if I should come over," he says after a beat. "But... I saw the light on. And I brought you something."

I finally lift my gaze, eyes puffy and rimmed with red. In his hands, wrapped in worn brown paper and tied with a bit of charcoal-stained string, is a sketchbook—his sketchbook. I thought I saw him drawing in it one day.

"I wanted you to see it," he says gently, placing it in my lap. "I've kept it a secret because I wasn't sure I should share it... that is, until I knew you felt the same way about me that I do you."

"Oh, Adrian." With trembling fingers, I open the book. Page after page of raw sketches and honest lines, all showing different emotions in each. I flip through it slowly, as if touching a sacred document. I let my fingers softly graze the charcoaled lines.

"This... this is me," I say, voice breaking.

"It *is* you," Adrian murmurs, placing his hand over mine. "It's how I see you. Strong and yet soft. Vibrant with emotion, with swirls of light and shadow blended beautifully together. You take my breath away, while giving me breath at the same time." I look at his swirling blue eyes, his words matching the emotion there. "You've never lost her. You've just been trying so hard to prove to everyone you are more... you forget that you're already enough. Just the way you are."

I feel a shift, and my heart folds in on itself, surrendering. "Adrian, these drawings are beautiful. I don't know what to say."

I lean into him, burying my face in his chest, his arms closing around me with warmth and quiet strength. "You don't have to say anything, Evolet. Just let me hold you until you are ready to get back up and continue your journey. This painting is a masterpiece, Eve. I know you haven't seen it yet, but you will. You will, *Tesoro*."

It's not perfect, but it's there. It's on the canvas and for now, I let myself believe—not in the perfection of my art, but in the worth of my voice. In the hands holding me together. In the small, steady light flickering just beneath the darkness.

The line I've been toeing finally breaks. I'm not giving up. Not tonight. Not with Adrian beside me.

# Chapter Thirty-One

Today is the day. I turn in this art piece that has been a monumental journey, but I am finally here. I have to drive it later to Florence after a few more touches. I feel like I could have done better, but there's no starting over. What's done is done.

Time to move on.

The villa has been my home for the past weeks, and I love that Adrian snuck his way into my world here. Adrian, the man who has been drawing me in his sketchbook for weeks in all shades of charcoal and magnificence, into each shadow, highlighting a creative side I admire. He's always told me he sees me differently, but last night, he showed me. He shared his art with me, a beautiful gesture I will forever cherish.

Soft light slipped through the slats of the curtains, stretching long across the rumpled bed. I blink into the quiet, my body still humming with the warmth of last night, I turn my head on the pillow to Adrian beside me.

One arm curled over his chest, the other stretched toward my body as if he was searching for me in the night. His hair is tousled, with dark waves falling over his brow, and his mouth—the mouth that teased my body with pleasure—was slack with sleep, boyish and unguarded.

I watch him sleep as my heart beats wildly in my chest.

*God, I am falling for him.* He is so handsome.

So. Mine. And I want to be his.

I reach out gently, letting my fingers graze the stubble along his jaw and the curve of his lips, memorizing him in this rare stillness. The weight of my affection settles, not heavy like before, but light and warm, like a secret I no longer have to run from.

Suddenly, without opening his eyes, Adrian smirks. "If you keep staring at me like that, *Tesoro*, I'm going to start thinking I'm the pretty one in this relationship."

I let out a soft laugh, my cheeks flushing as I pulled my hand away. "You talk in your sleep now?"

"Only when beautiful women can't keep their hands off me," he murmurs, cracking one eye open.

"You're impossible," I smile as I tuck the sheet a little tighter around myself.

He rolls toward me slowly, snaking an arm around my waist, and tugging me close until my body is flush against his. His voice drops, rough and low from sleep. "No, I'm serious. The way you were looking at me... I felt it. Like you were painting me with your eyes."

"Maybe I was," I whisper, breath catching as he presses his lips to the hollow beneath my ear.

"I hope it was a nude," he teases, mouth brushing my skin. "You know, for accuracy."

I laugh, swatting at his shoulder, my heart pounding. The air shifts—heat blooming in my belly, my breath shortening as his hand slides along my spine, slow and deliberate.

"I like this version of you," I say softly, brushing my nose against his. "Lifelike, more playful. In my arms. Warm." His hum of approval vibrates through the rest of my body, sending a scattering of goosebumps across my skin.

He kisses me then, slowly and deeply, like he has all the time in the world to learn the lines of my body again and again. I let myself lean in, let myself *feel*—not with fear, but with longing.

No masks. No second-guessing.

Just Adrian.

And the quiet, undeniable truth snuck into the space between us.

I was falling—boldly, irrevocably—in love.

After a delayed start to the morning and a healthy dose of "spirited" distractions, I turned my phone to silent and got to work finalizing this art piece for submission. Every submission will be different, but the requirements were clear; it had to be a self-reflection of our art. It had to personally represent style, technique, and composition.

I feel like I've finally achieved that. Setting up varying-sized brushes and colors, I settle in for the next couple of hours in the studio I have come to appreciate and embrace.

What a journey this has been. I am thankful for the lessons while also staying cautious that even when this is submitted, the work is not done. I have a long road ahead of me and lots of decisions to make, but they don't feel so heavy today.

I am grateful for this opportunity.

Adrian made himself scarce but occasionally brought in coffee and pastries to curb my appetite and motivate me forward. Also, to sneak in a few heated kisses. I had to push him away, though, otherwise I'd be ready to throw the towel in.

I'm so easily swayed.

Brushstroke after brushstroke, the truth settles in, heavy but grounding. The canvas, once still and accusing, now opened up like a living, breathing thing. The little details that once eluded me—the shadows too soft, the light too timid, the colors that never quite spoke—now came alive, igniting beneath my fingers with a fire that had been missing.

A flame I thought I'd lost to the darkness.

Each movement of the brush felt purposeful, not forced but instinctive, as though the painting had been waiting for me all along. One line led to the next, each shape unfolding with rhythm and grace, building a quiet symphony of emotion that poured from a depth beyond technique.

My hands moved on their own, fueled by a rawness toward a quiet conviction that I *was* enough. I didn't think. I just *felt*. My shoulders loosened and I could breathe all the way down.

Swirl after swirl, stroke after swipe, I breathed another layer into the canvas with every color I had once been too afraid to use. Golds as bold as defiance. Blues as deep as grief. Reds as urgent as love. It wasn't perfection I was chasing—it was truth.

*My* truth. Messy, aching, and radiant.

I lost track of time. I let go of the fear of failure. All I knew was this moment—this rhythm of creation that pulsed with passion and light.

This was no longer just a painting.

It was *me*.

I wasn't afraid of being seen in this way. Of being critiqued or judged for creating my heart's desire. I wasn't thinking with a critical mind, but a creative one. One I had lost along the way.

I'm proud of this journey. This painting. This mosaic of messy, fractured pieces of raw emotion mixed with light and shadow. It wasn't perfect, but it was perfect for me.

And that was *enough*.

The sun had made its way across the sky, casting golden rays through the window into the studio. The painting still sat on the easel, finished—its presence shining a beacon of light after years of darkened shadows. I stand in front of it with my messy hands gripping the brush after its final pass over the canvas— eyes glassy, mind quiet, and a heart so full I could burst.

I didn't hear the phone buzz at first.

It buzzed again, then again—insistent, urgent. I fumbled for it with tired hands, barely glancing at the screen before answering.

"Hello?"

Silence. Then, a sharp inhale.

"Eve," my sister's voice broke on the other end, trembling. "It's—it's Stefan. There was an accident. He was climbing the final ascent in the Dolomites. His rope snapped, and he fell. The rescue team got him out, but—"

She choked on a sob. "They don't know if he's going to make it."

Time stopped.

My knees buckled, one hand bracing against the wall—stamping a messy print from hours of painting as the phone slipped slightly in my grip. The words echoed in my skull, disjointed, surreal—*accident, rope, fell, don't know.*

My mouth fell open, but no sound came.

"No, no—" I whisper finally, shaking my head. "Not Stefan. No, please—"

"We're flying out now," Gi says, crying openly now. "Josh has already called the hospital in Venice to let them know we will be there. You need to come, Eve. You *need* to. I love you, sis."

The call ended.

*Crack.*

I stood there for a moment, staring at the floor, my breath coming in shallow, broken gasps. My heart thudded violently, as if my body couldn't contain the storm building inside me.

My baby brother. My little spitfire. The one who fiercely climbed trees was not afraid of falling. The one who always told me that the world needed my art, even when I didn't believe it myself. *Stefan.*

*Crack.*

A strangled sound escaped my throat as I sank to the floor. I pulled my knees to my chest, pressing my forehead against them, rocking my body gently with each wave of grief.

*Crack.*

Tears came—not graceful, but guttural. Ugly. Full of all the things I hadn't had the strength to say to him lately. I sobbed until my voice broke, until there was nothing left to give.

*Crack.*

When I finally looked up, the afternoon light had shifted. The clock on the wall read *4:45 p.m.* The submission deadline was in fifteen minutes. I told Adrian I wanted to drive to Florence alone to submit the piece on my own. Something I needed to do, and I failed. I wouldn't be able to make it. He even left his car for me to use, and that time has passed.

And now, all I can do is just stare at it, empty. *Numb.*

Everything was unraveling—my future in art, my strength, my brother's life. All slipping through my hands at once. I let out a hollow laugh, bitter and small.

"Of course," I whisper to the silence. "Of course, this is how it ends."

I didn't think. I didn't second-guess. I just got in the car and drove.

No destination. No plan. Just instinct.

*Crack.*

The final crack hit hard and fast, and I was not prepared for what happened next.

# Chapter Thirty-Two

## "Lost In the Deep End"

*I'm in over my head.*

*I'm slipping.*

*I want to give in. It's too much.*

*I'm lost in the deep end. I'm afraid there's no way out.*

Dark, thick clouds obscure the sun, dropping the temperature as I walk along the deserted beach. The crashing sounds of the stormy sea feel like an invitation welcoming an old soul, with the bitter air caressing me in its embrace. *Home.* I track the big swells as they crash into the giant rocky cliff just ahead, a cathartic scene before me.

They hold firm against the elements with such strength, beating after beating, and yet the destructive evidence of rock at the base—broken off over time — tells me that, even after many years of harshness, it gave way.

Forever changed. I amble toward the big rocks, digging my bare feet in the bitter sand.

I had to get away. I had to drown out the noise in my head and the storm brewing in my chest. I wasn't surprised to find myself at our spot by the ocean Adrian took me to on our date. Where the ocean felt serene and clear before, it is now a tumultuous grey, like my heart right now.

It's better this way. I can't seem to outrun storms. Storm matches storm.

Heavy raindrops fall onto my already sensitive skin, each drop seeping through to my bones, sending shivers that coil and wrap around like icy fingers. The wind howls, and the sky splits open with a violent crack of thunder, drowning the world in its ruthless demand.

Here, beneath the storm's merciless gaze, I am raw.

Exposed. Yet free.

No prying eyes, no suffocating expectations. Just the chaos inside, echoing the fury above. I am everything and nothing, a contradiction unraveling in the downpour.

I am so tired. Tired of the mask, of pretending I'm whole when I feel hollow, drained. All I want to do is fade into the storm.

*Be nothing.*

As much as I would have loved to be a successful artist or have my dream job, it feels so out of reach because of the chasm of pain that festers, digging its claws deep within, while granting unlimited access to my mind and body for so long. My darkened soul stirs restlessly just like the darkening clouds stretching and unfurling over the sky above. I feel like disappearing altogether, into this dark thing ready to consume me completely.

Oh god, *Stefan*! How can I possibly live without him? I should have called Adrian. I should have driven to the airport, yet this is where my feet brought me.

The pain feels unbearable to carry, festering into the deep cracks, widening, and expanding until I'm raw inside and out. Every time I look for a way out, I'm shoved into another tunnel so dark, so unforgiving, there's no way forward. No light, only shadow.

I wrap my sweater closer around me, fighting off my racing thoughts, and trying to protect the ivory maxi dress I love to paint in, almost sheer now from the downpour. I remember looking at it at one of the shops in Florence when Adrian took me to the museums.

*Adrian.* He was an unexpected twist in my story and possibly the perfect man for me, but I don't want to snuff out his light with my shadows. I release a long breath, emptying my lungs. Adrian shines; you can see him radiate all over, no matter the location. So thoughtful and full of life—He's perfect and I am broken.

*Opposites.*

Watching his passion reflect brightly in his eyes is quite stunning; they dance with possibilities and a future. A future he made me believe could happen, with his determination. But the damage of my past will always bring me here. I'll always feel the need to drop everything and protect my siblings, even if it robs me of my dreams. Because I will not abandon them like my parents did. I will always put them first. I can never give him what he needs, what he deserves. Because he deserves the world and every beautiful thing in it.

Not some broken, shattered, jagged pieces that will never be whole. *Not me.* I'm just not strong enough, even when he says that I am.

I want to believe it. Trust it. But he deserves better.

*You'll never be enough.*

*Crack.*

Unforgiving tears mix with the fresh stormy rain, striking my face as a reminder of reality. My eyes fall shut, feeling the storm within swirl and widen, a dark thread that coils around my soaked body. It tightens, constricting like the grasp of unseen hands, dragging me deeper into a place where light has long since drowned. The wind shrieks in my ears, a mournful wail that drowns out thought, out hope–out everything. The rain beats against my skin, relentless, cold, and uncaring.

*"Who do you think you are, Eve?"*

*Crack.*

The small whisper slithers through the air, thin as mist, yet it coils around my name with an eerie familiarity. My eyes snap open, breath hitching as a chill laces through my spine, colder than the storm itself. I turned, slowly, rain streaming down my face.

Who was that? I searched for the source, but I saw no one. Did I imagine that? My eyes scan the beach, but still, there's no one.

No one anywhere.

How strange. The thought slithers through my mind, leaving a cold, uneasy feeling. My forehead crumples, my skin prickling as if unseen eyes trace my every movement. Shaking my head, I force myself forward toward the bluffs ahead, my steps unsteady.

Maybe I am crazy.

Looking back to where the car was parked, every instinct screamed to turn back. Still, I can't help but let my thoughts wander and swirl just like the storm while my feet carry me forward aimlessly, my hands squeezing tight around the softness of the shawl. I move slowly along the cold, wet sand, the fabric of my dress clinging to my legs in protest.

There's peace in letting go of expectations of the world. Of drifting into the emptiness and walking alone to free the swirl of emotions. *What do I feel?*

The wind continues to howl, a furious, wailing thing, shoving against me with invisible hands as if trying to push me back—a warning. The ocean is a seething, monstrous void now, its whitecaps foaming like bared teeth over black water. The waves surge and crash, vengeful, as though the sea itself is alive, watching, and waiting. I stare into its churning depths, mesmerized, as if it's calling my name, daring me to step closer.

Suddenly, a high-pitched scream snaps me back into the present. That sounded like a girl. I jerk my head to my right, searching for the owner of the panicked scream. My eyes are wild as they scan the beach, trying to find its source.

*"Help!"* The scream is raw and strangled—barely more than a gasp against the storm's merciless roar. My head jerks toward the water, my pulse hammering. Through the sheets of rain and the furious waves, I catch a flash of white, vanishing under the waves and then reappearing.

*Who is that?*

My breath catches as I spot a head, bobbing, disappearing beneath the waves before resurfacing—helpless against the monstrous pull of the tide. Panic grips me like a vice, ice-cold and suffocating. A sharp pain slices through my chest. My body moves before my mind catches up, feet stumbling. The wind shrieks, whipping against me, as if warning me to stay back. But I can't. I won't. She goes down again.

"Oh my God! Hold on!" I yell back to her, a strangled cry ripping from my throat. Where did she come from?! "I'm coming! Hold on!" I shout over the storm, but my voice gets lost in the howling wind. My heart is threatening to beat out of my chest, but I don't let that slow me down. I have seconds to think, remembering I'm not the best swimmer, but I don't see anyone else nearby, and I am not about to leave a child helpless to drown. I keep running.

The sand eats away at my feet from the impact, and my legs threaten to give way as I rush to save this stranger. Oh gosh, how did she even get out there? I didn't see any parents around at all. Please, let her be okay. *Please*. I say a silent prayer. I hiss as my feet hit the cold water, icy and breathtaking, stealing the remaining heat from my body. The wind bites at my face.

I try to focus as I scramble to reach her. The water surges around my skin—curling and wrapping itself in its harsh embrace. Not an embrace you could survive in.

"Where are you?" I whisper to myself. I frantically search the waves, my arms feeling heavy against the current, back and forth until I see her head bob above the water.

She's not screaming anymore.

The silence is worse than the storm, worse than the waves, worse than anything. My chest hurts, and dread curls tight in my stomach. An unbearable weight drags me down even before the water does. Am I too late? Was I so lost in my own mind that I didn't hear her sooner? The thought claws at me, a sharp and merciless thing.

Whispers flit in my mind.

*Why did you even try? You knew how this would end.*

*Crack.*

Words of regret and shame fill the quiet spaces, yelling loudly.

*You're too late. What makes you think you could ever be strong against me?*

*Crack.*

I push out those thoughts even though they barrel through me over and over again, just like the tumultuous waves threatening to pull me under. "I'm coming! Hold on!" I bellow again so she can hear me, to know someone is coming for her.

The moment my body is fully submerged, the ocean seizes me—wrapping around my limbs like cold, unrelenting hands. The current is strong — too strong, dragging me down. I fight, kicking, thrashing, my arms burning from the effort, but the water is heavy. I finally breach the surface, gasping for air, willing my lungs to expand with every panicked gasp.

"Help!" she cries above the water. I snap my head toward her thin, shaky voice.

"Just keep going." The words leave my lips in a breathless, wavering plea, meant more for myself than for her. My limbs are weak, my strength fading, and I feel the vast, endless black of the sea is all too willing to take me.

I see her hand reach up a few strokes away as I propel my body forward and grab her hand the moment I come into contact—her head out of the water, her eyes meeting mine. Aquamarine eyes... eyes that match mine exactly, her chestnut hair mirroring the chaotic tresses as a result of the storm. This girl looks familiar.

Everything fades away for a split second while we stare at each other. A moment in time. "Don't let me go, please." Her whimpering voice cracks my heart. The desperate plea was etched all over her porcelain face. My throat constricts when I try to tell her I am here to help.

Before I could respond, a giant wave crashed over our heads, splitting us apart, violently shoving us underwater once again. No! I anxiously look through the rolling waves, but it's no use; the tide is too strong and I will my body to reach the surface. When I do, I look around, but I don't see her.

The storm is upon us, cursing the ocean and anyone caught in its wrath. The waves surge and crash like a beast unchained, pushing us further apart. It strikes again and again. My arms burn, my lungs scream, but I push forward, fighting against the utter chaos. The current is relentless, clawing, twisting like hungry fingers.

Salt water slams into my face–again, again, and again–filling my mouth, stinging my eyes, choking the breath from my lungs. I sputter, gasping for air, only for another wave to strike, stealing what little progress I've made.

My limbs are shaking, my body straining. I can't stop. If I do, the ocean will claim us both.

*You are going to drown here.*
*Crack.*

# Chapter Thirty-Three

## "I Hold You"

I fight with everything I have to reach the girl. I can't see her in the ebbs and flows, the ups and downs of the water. My breaths are short and too fast as the salt water invades my face, my breaths shallow, my body trembling.

"I'm so sorry," I barely whisper to myself. The pain never ends.

*She's gone. Give up.*

*Crack.*

Where did she go?

Another tidal wave pushes me under, my arms growing heavier against the force of each wave, my legs burdened by the length of my dress. The beautiful silky fabric wrapped tightly like a noose, I remember when I first put it on... I felt so feminine, free, but it might just be the thing that drowns me along with my dark thoughts, my jagged ends.

*You'll never find her.*

*Crack.*

I break the surface once again, sucking in a desperate, ragged breath. Precious oxygen searing my lungs—only to be swallowed again as another wave crashes over me. I choke, sputtering, my body convulsing as salt water forces its way down my throat.

*You are nothing.*

*Crack.*

I try to clear my eyes despite the salty water pounding mercilessly at my face. I see a flash of white thrashing in the waves ahead of me. I know I have to get to her. Now. But she still feels so far out of reach as I see her go down... again.

*Just forget about me, like you always do.*

*Crack.*

My heart drops in my stomach. A surge of unrelenting dread hits me so much stronger than the storm around us. My limbs flail, but the ocean is stronger, colder, relentless in its grip. It doesn't care how hard I fight. It only wants to pull me deeper.

*You can't save her now.*

*You'll never reach her in time.*

*Crack.*

"NO!" I scream into the storm, my voice cracking and filling with water as the thunder matches my ferocity. Trying not to let that darkness take me, like so many times before, I dive under the turbulent waves, fighting tirelessly against the whirling current, searching around for her.

Desperate. Frantic. Helpless.

The salt water burns my eyes before I force them shut again. The current coils around me like unseen hands, dragging me toward the blue-black abyss below. The weight of the water presses against my chest, squeezing the air from my body. I have to get back up to the surface, which seems like an impossible task when every movement feels sluggish, useless. Just a little bit more. A thought slithers through my drowning mind.

Maybe this is what I deserve.

Maybe the sea is punishing me.

Maybe it's simply finishing what was always meant to happen.

*Crack.*

In what seems like eternity, kicking my frozen feet and burning thighs, my face is blasted with rain the second I get my head above water gulping precious air into my lungs. A mix of sweet relief and sharp pains hit just inside my ribs reminding me what endless fighting feels like. But I can't focus on that. Lightning flashes above as the thunder rolls.

The storm continues above, below, and within.

As my body jerks back and forth in the waves, my eyes search quickly, every movement stinging and screaming with how tired I am. Just as I look around, hoping to see where she might be, another wave crashes down, but this time it feels intentional, like a giant with a determined hand pushing me down with brute force. It wants me to stay down here forever.

Forever drowning.

*Forever in the dark.*

*Crack.*

I'm not sure how much more of this I can take. My chest hurts and feels tight with every push to the surface from the last. My eyes are clamped shut when I hear the muffled water moving around me. I can't decide for how long, but this time feels like the longest yet.

I let myself rest. Just for a second. Holding my body still while sinking further into the unknown. Down under the chaotic surface, where I am strangely cradled in the deep. I open my eyes to take in the darkness around me. It feels almost peaceful as I twist my head side to side in what feels like slow motion under the water.

I tip my head back to watch the stormy sea above, reeling with maddening tides.

My body sinks deeper, feeling the tightness grow with more pressure, but somehow it continues to feel lighter, slower. Conflicting thoughts seem to dissipate.

*Let go.*

My arms float in front of me, slowing down, taking in the stillness. I don't feel the cold anymore as I move my hands through the blue-black water. My dress seems to dance slowly to its own rhythm, floating freely around me... such a different world under the chaos of a raging sea.

*You're free.*

Time feels different here, watching the tiny bubbles glimmering in the blue depths as if they are the only light source...my eyes flutter in slow motion fighting to stay open, but I don't dare close them, anything can be lurking, waiting.

*Embrace me.*

Fatigue drags at me, heavier than the water itself. My limbs float eerily still despite the storm above, barely responding as I stare into the endless void below. The deep calls to me, vast and unknown. Its mysteries curl around my fading thoughts.

This is how I die.

Not in a warm bed. Not with whispered goodbyes or hands clasped in comfort. But here, swallowed by the sea, alone in the cold. Abandoned by my recklessness. Broken by my selfishness.

Never made whole.

*Crack.*

I will never have the chance to say goodbye to my family. Never take the risks I was too afraid to embrace. Never fully let myself love so fiercely it hurts. Even though I already feel like I do. Maybe love was worth it after all.

I wonder if this is what Ophelia felt like just before the fight seeped from her body. A slow descent into an abyss of her own making.

My body hurt before. Not so much now... the weight of that thought settles over me, a final realization sinking deep into my bones.

The darkness won.

Just like it did with her. Just like it consumed my mother.

I was cursed from the start.

Maybe I was always meant to follow my mother in death after all.

To slip beneath the surface in silence, like petals floating on still water—soft, unassuming, already surrendering. I could almost see her now, my mother, draped in grief like it was silk, her hands outstretched beneath the weight of everything she never said aloud. Maybe we were both made of the same fragile porcelain, passed down and cracked too many times to hold anything without leaking sorrow.

It was in my blood—the ache, the unraveling. The way even beauty could feel like a burden. In this fleeting moment, I didn't fight it. I let the shadows press in around me like water filling lungs.

Not drowning. Just... vanishing.

Like Ophelia.

Like her.

Like me.

# Chapter Thirty-Four

## "I've Got You"

Something white sways delicately straight ahead, pulling me out of a trance-like state. I focus on it as much as my eyes will let me. It feels close, yet so far away. It's her, there! She's not moving. My eyes widen, and I see the little girl in front of me, her dress floating around her. I make a hopeful last push with my legs and arms, desperately trying to propel forward. It feels as though I am moving through quicksand rather than water with every attempt.

There she is, I notice how pale her skin is— almost translucent as I draw closer. I reach out and wrap my arm around her waist. Heaviness surrounds us as I kick like hell toward the tortured surface, even though I feel like I have no oxygen left.

Like I have nothing left to give.

She feels so heavy and limp. I hope she's still alive. Please be alive.

I kick my legs again, and again, ignoring the pain or the hollow feeling in my stomach. How did I get so far down? My lungs squeeze, begging for air. What feels like an endless battle, I finally breach the surface of the tumultuous sea, taking a big gulp of air and water at the same time, and I feel the burn in my lungs like fire.

You are too late.

Crack.

"I've got you, hold on, I'm here," I say helplessly to the girl, pulling her along. I don't feel her breathing as I fight to get to shore. "Almost there, hold on," I whisper in her ear.

Her face is so pale that it has a purplish hue.

One arm in front of me, pulling the water to inch farther toward the shore, and my other arm clamped down on her waist, I will *NOT* let her go. I *will* get her body out of here.

*You won't.*

*Crack.*

"Almost... There... Just ahead." I trudge and kick, and pull at the water, and keep repeating until we finally make it to the shallows. The sky is as angry as ever, with its whorls and swirls of clouds and rain smacking my face, biting my skin. Thunder makes itself known; something feels terribly wrong. I searched the shore for anyone to help me. But there's no one.

*Alone.*

*Crack.*

I feel the weight of everything as I force my legs out of the water, dragging her lifeless little figure with me. "We made it. We're here, little one."

*She's dead.*

*Crack.*

*You failed.*

*Crack.*

How can I possibly help her? I can't even help myself!

I drag us further out of the water and onto the shore enough to lay her down, checking her for a pulse. "HELP!" I scream and plead, but my plea falls short with no one here to answer.

*Alone.*

*Crack.*

And now she will suffer for my negligence, my need for solitude. My punishment. The harsh result of my trauma screams in my face.

I touch her tiny face. Her lips are blue, void of life, the warmth stolen from her cheeks. She is still—too still. My hands shake as I press against her chest, pushing down with a frantic, desperate force.

*Breathe.* I seal my lips over hers, willing air into lungs that refuse to take it. Come back. My fingers tremble as I pump her chest again, harder, faster, but she doesn't stir. She doesn't gasp. She doesn't fight.

"No, this can't be happening. I'm sorry, so sorry." My words disappeared into the wind.

I can't save her.

*I can't save her.*

*Crack.*

A broken sob rips from my throat, raw and guttural, lost to the howling wind and crashing waves. I scan the beach, searching for a stranger, a traveler, anyone. Hot tears fall against my frozen cheeks, melting through the cracks. God, I'm so broken. I look down at her and scoop her into my lap. The storm seems to pause or settle and I look up—the eye of the storm.

She's gone. The realization crashes over me, heavier than the sea itself. My cries spill freely now, shaking, shattering, begging, though I already know the truth.

*Crack.*

"I've got you," I whisper-cry in her ear. "I'm here, it's alright. Shhhhh." I can't save her.

I've failed.

*Rest now.*

"I won't leave you, sweet girl." I rock us back and forth. My body trembles with shock wave after shock wave until I no longer desire to feel. I can't make my body move either.

Understanding settles over me as I continue to cradle the little girl.

I can't leave. I have to stay.

Everything fades to black.

*I'm so sorry.*

*Crack.*

"Dammit, Eve! Don't die on me! I need more time with you! I refuse to let you go. I can't. Can't you feel my racing heart? I love you. It's too soon. It's too soon. Please don't leave me, don't leave me." Adrian's voice is raw, cracking with desperation, a distant echo. He pleads for my life as if it's fading, as if every breath he takes is meant for me. His strong arms wrap around me, pulling me close, but the warmth feels faint, like I'm grasping at something just out of reach.

*Wait. Where's the girl? Save the girl, I want to scream at him.*

My heart feels so slow and yet so loud in my head, barely pulsating.

I try to hold on, to anchor myself to him, but the world tilts, soft and hazy—the edges blurring like a dream unraveling. I can't feel my body. Why can't I feel anything? He's calling my name, his voice thick with something I don't understand. I want to tell him not to cry.

"Stay with me, Eve. *Tesoro.*" I hear the pain in Adrian's voice, faint and far away, somewhere I can't reach him. *Wait. Don't leave me*, I echo the girls' words as if they were my own. I'm right here.

But the words won't come.

*Just breathe through me. Give me life. Tether me.* I want to stay, but I have no air left, no strength to say it out loud. There's that tightness in my chest again.

I just want more. More of his warmth. More of his touch. I try to move closer, but it's like wading through mist, slipping further away.

Flashes of shimmering light dance across my closed eyes as my mind races back to a time when I see Mom dancing in a white lace dress—happy and free, just me and her. Twirling me under her arm and holding my hand so tenderly. She doesn't have pain here, no darkness haunts her face. I smile at how peaceful the scene plays out before me, tears in my eyes, yet none fall in this dream.

I soak up this moment, the memory fading to black.

# Chapter Thirty-Five

## "Breathe"

Lights of white, purple, gold, and silver dance once again to a soundless melody until I am lying in yellow and purple flowers of a familiar field—Mama and Papa with me as a child squished in between them. They tickle me, making my face scrunch tight, embracing me. The sound of giggles sends a surge of rainbow light toward them until they are all glowing like the sun overhead. We look so happy and beautiful. One of my first memories, how have I forgotten?

The way Mom gazes at Dad, with so much love, that infectious warm light radiates between them. I feel it now, somehow in the middle and yet just on the outside. I close my eyes again.

*Darkness.*

I am running in an endless sea of darkness—barefoot and bruised—away from deep intimacy and relationships, uncertain on how to fully open myself to trust. In this pit, I am falling into the unknown, feeling the sharp edges of broken, jagged pieces cutting my body, leaving scars along my skin, continuing deeper than the surface.

The emptiness grows.

What have I done?

A final descent into an abyss I allowed to grow. A final destination.

I didn't get to say goodbye to my family and.... *Adrian. I will always carry you in what remains of my heart. Even as I slip beyond this moment, beyond time itself, I know I will never be truly alone. Your love lingers, woven into the very fabric of my soul, a part of me that even death cannot erase. I see that now. I feel it. My lighthouse.*

I'm sorry. Sorry that I wasn't strong enough, that I couldn't fight it this time. This life was not mine to keep, not with these broken pieces that have cut so deep.

*"How can I give you all of me, when I can only offer shattered and broken pieces?"*

My body grows heavy, burdened by the weight of all I was.

Once again, those dancing lights flicker in the darkness before revealing the moody beach, trapped in the eye of the storm—the girl I was trying to save is staring right back at me with those wide aquamarine eyes, with wounds she never should have carried. The girl who was in the club that night was haunting me in my dreams.

My eyes. *Familiar.* Carrying something vast and infinite.

I am her. She is me.

She is here, my younger self. I see her small frame and her wind-blown hair, just standing there, soaked. A shadow settles behind my ribs, but I don't look away. I can't. We stand face to face in the quiet. Our soft ivory dresses, somehow dry despite the storm, the soft wind kissing our chestnut hair. She tilts her head to the side, regarding me.

I take a hesitant step toward her, "Are you okay?" I question, hoping she feels safe.

The air is soft, dream-like, and every sound muted as though sealed behind stained glass. A strange tenderness rose inside me, steadying me against the harshness of the storm.

*"You have forgotten me,"* she states softly, her eyes now holding no fear.

My brow furrows as my mind spirals, sinking into itself. Shame slithers through me, its inky tendrils wrapping tight around my ribs, like a poison I can never purge. It festers, staining the deepest parts of me, a mark that can never be washed clean.

"I know. I'm so sorry." I look down at my bare feet in the sand. I dig my toes into the rough texture, but I feel no discomfort. "I couldn't save you." I breathe out, my heart weighing heavily in my chest. I bring my eyes back to hers. She acknowledges me with a slight tilt, but again, no resentment.

"I should have been able to protect you, and I failed," I held my arms tighter around my body. "I wish I could go back and try harder for you. To get to you sooner, to help you feel safe and warm." She just stands there, so still, eyes penetrating deeply into mine as if she can see everything past and present.

I kneel, reaching out, my fingers trembling as they brush against her cheek. She flinches at first, untrusting, but I do not pull away. "Is there...?" I pause. "Is there something—you need?" She smiles. A beautiful smile that reaches into the darkness and shines the brightest, most gorgeous, warm light, emotion unfurls deep within a forgotten depth.

*"A hug."*

I sob. I release...everything.

I cry out the burned memories of the past as I open my arms to this little girl I have neglected. The little girl in me. She was there the whole time, shrouded in a cloak of darkness, waiting to be loved and cared for. She kept quiet in the background until the pain became too much to bear.

Before it took her completely. Before she became a husk, void of life.

This darkness, this trauma fed on the wounds and scars I so easily left unguarded. Lost in the negative experiences and memories of my Dad's death—of Mom's depression—the cunning manipulator. And even then, I kept giving it more and more with each passing year until it became a haunting inner landscape.

I open my arms wide. She runs toward the invitation, and I wrap her in my arms, holding her close, letting her feel the rhythm of my heart.

"I'm here," I whisper, fragile and uneven. "I see you. I hear you. And I will never leave you again." She melts into me, small hands clutching my dress, and for the first time, I do not shrink from the weight of her pain. *Our pain.* I embrace it. I embrace *her. Us.* Her skin glows in my arms, changing her pale, sickly skin to a warm, flushed color.

"What can I do to make this right?" I ask, a weary breath leaving my chest.

*"You can breathe..."* she says, so simply.

"Breathe?"

*"Yes. Breathe, just like your name. Be open to let love in. And live your life."*

She moves her body to the side, exposing Adrian over my limp body on the sandy shore, breathing into my mouth and pumping my chest intermittently. I touch my lips, feeling his lips on mine, but still far away. My chest feels warm, but an unknown feeling is there too.

"Don't you dare leave me, Evolet, *il mio respiro.* I am not leaving you. Please come back to me." Adrian's hands work tirelessly between pumps and breaths. "You are my stunning light, you have become my whole life. There is no road I will not travel. *Ti portero.* I will carry you through whatever you need, *per favore,* come back, *Tesoro.*" His voice cracks, and my heart breaks all over again for Adrian and all that he's freely given me, and I was too scared to see.

To feel.

I plead with my younger self, *"Please..."* A choked sob escapes my lips.

"I'll do better. I want to do better." I try to negotiate. I'm hesitant to ask, but I make myself form the words. "Am I dead?"

*"No, but you are close. You still hold life in you."* She looks back at my lifeless body, coupled with Adrian's agony, and my heart feels so heavy. I just stare at him, my body motionless. Frozen in time.

"I don't deserve him. His light. His love. But gosh, do I want to soak up everything he has to offer. He's everything I have ever wanted. He's perfect. I am far from it, but I'd like to be. For him, I'd like to try."

She just stares at me. Regarding me again. Assessing.

I pull her close once again as I remember all those times of feeling unworthy and forgotten. All those moments of ignoring my own pain just made matters worse by not asking for help.

*I let it go.*

Taking on mom's pain as my own, so she didn't have to.

*I let it go.*

Masking my hurt with years of fake smiles to appease those with pitying eyes allowed me to live at a surface level, so I looked stronger than I actually felt on the inside.

*I let it go.*

This dark power was rooted in my mind and heart, distorting everything in its wake. This villainous manipulator knows no mercy. It preyed upon my vulnerability, and I let it. The scars are still there. They may always be. But they do not define me.

They do not define *us.*

With a finality I haven't felt since Dad died that fateful night, I took on my family's pain as my own. I proclaim, *"This ends with me,"* Squeezing the little girl tighter as a knitting sensation tugs into a comforting blanket that embraces us both.

*"Thank you,"* she sighs into the space between us. As the storm finally fades, a hush settles over the world—a quiet that feels sacred. The sun emerges from behind the dissolving clouds, not with blinding brilliance, but with a tender glow that kisses the earth in gold. Light spills across the broken fragments of who I once was, warming the pieces I believed too shattered to ever fit back together.

I take notice of this girl I left behind.

The version of me who once hid in shadows out of survival, who carried sorrow like it was stitched into her bones. She reaches out, the fear no longer etched into her face. I take her hand, fingers intertwining with my past, not to mourn it, but to honor it.

Together, we step forward.

The sky opens above us, ablaze with a sunset so beautiful I hope to paint it one day—lavenders and rose golds melting into amber, streaks of fire and grace painting the heavens like a masterpiece. Each step we take is a brushstroke, blending memory with a becoming.

A bright and colorful future. And at that moment, I understood. Healing doesn't erase the darkness—it transforms it. It weaves it into the light.

We walk toward the horizon not as two, but as one—whole, imperfect, and radiant. A living canvas touched by a chaotic storm blended with the rising sun.

# Chapter Thirty-Six

## "Alive & Healing"

The storm has passed.

The world is quiet now, the chaos washed away, leaving only the soft hush of waves lapping against the shore. The air is thick with salt and rain, but it carries a gentleness now, no longer howling with fury. The sky, once torn apart by lightning and darkness, begins to soften, streaks of pale gold and lavender bleeding through the heavy clouds.

I stir, my body aching, heavy—but warm. A presence surrounds me, strong arms wrapped around my trembling form, anchoring me to this moment, to *life*. My breath shudders as I blink against the lingering haze, my lashes damp with sea and sorrow, my mind slowly piecing itself back together.

And then I see him.

Adrian.

On his knees, soaked and shaking, his hands trembling as they hold me. His face was pale, lips parted as if he'd stopped breathing the moment I did. His face, inches from mine, is etched with exhaustion and fear. With something so deep and raw, it steals the faint breath I just fought to reclaim. His normal bright crystal blue eyes swirl with a storm of their own search mine—desperate, disbelieving, as if he's afraid I will slip away again.

"You're here," he whispers. His voice is rough. Breaking at the edges. "I thought I'd lost you forever, *Tesoro*." His fingers tighten, pressing into my skin as if to reassure himself that I am real.

That I am alive.

Tears burn behind my eyes as I lift a trembling hand to his face, tracing the salt-streaked lines of worry that do not belong there. "I'm here." I hate that he was worried about me. But he only leans into my touch, exhaling a shaky breath, pressing his forehead to mine.

"Evolet," he sighs heavily, voice raw, like it had been torn from somewhere deep. "You scared the hell out of me."

"You... pulled me out." My voice barely above a rasp.

"*Si.* Yes. I would've followed you to the bottom if I had to," he replies, a storm of emotion cracking through his words. "You hear me? I would've *drowned* with you if it meant being with you until the end." Tears gather in his eyes, and one after the other, they fall. "I can't—I *won't* lose you, Eve. I love you. *Ti amo.* I'm so in love with you. Not some convenient version of you, not just the beautiful parts—I love *all* of you. Even the broken pieces. Especially those," he chokes out, repeating them over and over again like a prayer. "What were you doing in the ocean, of all the days?" He asks, voice strained.

"I was trying to save a girl. Or...who I thought was a girl. It turned out to be something else. I've learned something, a deep misunderstanding that's been chasing me for years. But I don't want to talk about that right now." I reach up to cup his cheek, warm and wet beneath my frigid palm. He came for me. He saved me. I will spend the rest of my life showing him how grateful I am.

He showed up for me.

"I'm so glad you are okay," he says, as he wipes my hair out of my face.

"Me too." I whisper back, soaking up the warmth and love he gives.

The waves murmur in the distance, and the scent of rain lingers in the cool evening air. But none of it matters. Not the storm that nearly took me, not the darkness that almost won.

Only this.

Only him.

His heartbeat against mine, his breath mingling with my own, his love wrapping around me like the sun breaking through the clouds—steady, warm, and unwavering. I let my eyes linger on him for a long moment, breath shallow, eyes wide. And then, through the fear and salt and pain, a ghost of a smile curls at my lips.

"Easy there, *Romeo*," I chuckle, voice still shaking but lighter now, a flicker of warmth sparking and seeping into my soul.

Adrian let out a soft, choked laugh, the tension cracking just enough to let in his sweet tenderness. He leans down, pressing his forehead to mine, his hand finally settling over my heart as if to remind himself it's still beating.

"Only you would almost die and still manage to throw shade," he whispers, voice thick with love and disbelief.

"Only you," I whisper back, reaching up to brush his dripping hair away from his face, "would make me want to live again and again. If only to see your face one more time."

And even though this space feels fragile—between fear and laughter, between loss and love—we held on to each other, no longer running, no longer pretending. Just two souls ready to figure out this thing between us without all the other heaviness or noise of the past.

I finally reveal what's in my heart, not in fear of the future. But because I refuse to live another moment without declaring a future with him.

For my beating heart.

After what felt like the longest trek back to the car. Adrian snuggled me in the passenger seat with a blanket and the heat on full blast. Apparently, he had a tracking device on his car in case it was ever stolen. Luckily enough, he found me just in time.

"When I couldn't reach you on your phone, I stopped by the villa to see if you had left it behind when you left for Florence. I saw that your painting was still in the studio, but you were gone," he says, with a sadness that breaks my heart.

Adrian glanced from the corner of his eye, hands steady on the wheel, but I could feel his nervous energy. He let the silence stretch just long enough, then cleared his throat softly.

"So," he says, tone cautious, "I was thinking...next time you feel like nearly dying, maybe just send me a text instead? Something like, *Hey Adrian, feeling emotionally unstable, might go for a dramatic swim. BRB.*"

I let out a snort—a real, surprised laugh—and covered my mouth quickly, blinking as tears welled again, this time from the way Adrian softens even the hardest edges.

Adrian smiles, relief flickering across his face. "Too soon?"

I shake my head, wiping my eyes. "Only you would make jokes about drowning twenty minutes after pulling me out of the ocean."

"What can I say? I'm gifted. Tragic near-death experiences really bring out my best material." He risks a glance at me. "I just needed to hear your laugh again. Even if it's at my expense."

I looked at him then, really looked, and the emotion in his eyes nearly undid me.

I played nervously with the edge of the jacket sleeve. "Adrian..."

"I know." His mouth stills as understanding settles in. "You didn't turn it in."

The submission. My masterpiece.

The dream I'd poured everything into.

Gone.

I lower my gaze, voice barely above a whisper. "I missed the deadline."

"I figured," he says softly, occasionally, scanning my body to make sure I really am okay. "But you were busy...you know, almost dying and all." He smiles, but it doesn't quite reach his eyes. Tension still coiled in his shoulders.

He reaches across the console, his hand warm and sure as it curls around mine. "Eve, your life is worth more than any deadline. And your art—your *voice*— doesn't expire just because you missed one moment. There will be others. And I'll be here for every one of them. I mean, unless you keep jumping into oceans, then I may need to reconsider." I really did scare him. He's going to be even more insufferable now. I smile to myself. Thankful for his steady presence.

I let out another laugh, watery but real, gripping his hand tighter.

"You're ridiculous."

"And yet... strangely irresistible," he replies with a wink.

A beat of quiet settled between us, but this time it felt safe—like the kind of silence that heals instead of hurts. I leaned back into the seat, finally taking a full breath.

"I was scared. Stefan was in a climbing accident, and then I lost it. When I finally broke out of my haze, it was too late to make it to Florence. I knew then that I had lost the chance to submit it. As if on autopilot, I came here. To the beach. Gosh, I've messed up so bad." I barely finished before I let out a strangled cry. "Oh, Stefan. I hope he's okay. My sister could've nearly lost us both." I continue to cry, not holding back anything anymore.

The mask is gone.

Adrian squeezes my hand, his thumb brushing over my knuckles. "It's okay, Eve, we will figure this out together. You are not alone. Not anymore. I'm not letting you out of my sight now," he says with a little smirk on his worried face.

I looked over at him, and for once, I didn't imagine all the ways it could fall apart.

"Okay," I reply, my voice faint. It's a start. One I keep rolling over in my mind as we drive back in silence—not knowing still if my brother was alive, but understanding I didn't have to do it alone.

I had Adrian. And that was enough right now.

We arrived in Venice in record time, just barely past midnight. Adrian suggested we take the night to rest at the Villa, but I insisted we get on the road, anxious to see my sister and Stefan. I tried to call my sister after she left several of my text messages unread. They went straight to voicemail. I was a ball of chaotic energy, anxious to see my family.

We stepped into the lobby, my shoes squeaking on the clean marble floor, heart hammering hard enough I thought it might echo down the hallways. There was an ache in my chest that pressed heavily against my ribs, but I kept moving.

I spot Gi immediately. She's pacing beneath the harsh overhead lights, arms crossed, worry etched deep into her expression. Her phone clutched in one hand, the other anxiously tugging at the edge of her sleeve.

"Gianna," I call for her, voice trembling.

Gi's head whips around, eyes wide. "Eve?" A breath rushes out of her as she moves toward me. We collide in a tight, wordless hug, unspoken fears and childhood memories wrapped in a single desperate grip. Gi's shoulders trembled. This all felt so familiar—waiting on Stefan's birth the last time—while now it is in stark contrast.

"They still don't know," she whispers into my shoulder. "He's stable... but they won't tell me what's wrong yet. He's in and out. Head trauma, maybe? Internal injuries. I don't know, Eve. I don't *know.*"

I hold her tighter and whisper in her ear. "We're here now. We'll get through this. We always do."

"When I couldn't reach you, I was so worried, Eve. Why do you have a phone if you don't ever pick it up?" she mumbles into my hair, and I huff out a laugh.

"I was trying to call you after you left several of my texts unanswered! They must not have gone through. I may need a new phone." I growl, more at my phone than her.

Gi pulls back slightly, sniffling, her gaze flicking over my shoulder. Her brow furrows. "We? Wait... is that—?"

Adrian stands just a few steps behind me, respectfully giving us space, his dark curls tousled from the almost three-hour car ride, eyes filled with quiet concern. But steady.

Gi blinks several times, caught off guard, then glances at me with a slow smile forming. "You brought *Romeo* to Venice?"

I let out a shaky laugh, brushing my hair behind her ear. "He wouldn't let me come alone."

Josh appears around the corner, holding two coffees, looking at me and then at Adrian. "Oh, hey, you made it! And...Romeo?" he asks with an inquisitive smile on his face.

Adrian steps forward and offers Josh his hand. "Good to see you, but I prefer Adrian. Romeo is a nickname from my family, and I can't seem to shake it; also, the tourists love it." He winks at Gi, giving his hand to her next, and I melt all over again. He is so genuine and at ease with my family, it's refreshing.

"Nice to see you again, Adrian," Josh replies. Gi takes his hand warmly, her smile more relaxed now. "Likewise. Thank you for being here. Really."

"I care about Eve," Adrian says softly, his eyes never leaving mine. "I wouldn't be anywhere else."

Gi gives me a long, knowing look—the kind only a sister could give. "You look different," she says quietly. "Even with everything going on...you seem stronger. Lighter."

"I'm trying," I reply quietly. "I have something to tell you, but not right now. Later"

Before Gi could respond, a nurse in pale blue scrubs stepped out from behind the swinging doors. "Family of Stefan—Stefan Moretti?"

We all turned at once.

"That's us," Gi said, her voice tight. Josh wrapped his arms around her, knowing what she needs. He really is perfect for her. I know she's going to have the best life with him.

The nurse nodded. "He's awake. A bit disoriented, but asking for you."

Relief swept through me so fast my knees nearly gave. Adrian reached out, steadying me, his hand warm at the small of my back.

As we follow the nurse down the hallway, the hospital lights flickering softly above, I reach for my sister's hand. And with Adrian by my side, I feel—despite the fear and the unknown—that I'm not walking toward grief this time.

I was walking into a new era of hope and possibilities. One I could thrive in no matter the challenges. It's a long road of healing. But if my siblings could do it, so can I. I am letting the past stay in the past. I don't want to live in fear of living for my future anymore.

I can move forward, in all my fractured imperfections.

Slowly, but surely, gluing the pieces back together over time.

# Chapter Thirty-Seven

## "Hope"

The late afternoon sun bathed the villa in a golden hush, soft Tuscan light casting long shadows over the stone terrace. Beyond the olive groves and rolling hills, the horizon stretched the way only Italy could, tinged in a soft peach and rosy pinks. The storm had passed days ago, but its echoes still linger in my mind—in the pause between words—but so did something else.

Peace.

After a few days in the hospital, we were ready to leave. Especially Stefan. He was triggered by hospitals, a fact that coiled in my chest and a little guilt sat sour in my stomach. I wasn't the only one who lost something the day Dad died. Stefan never knew our father. Somehow, I want to show him what he was like, I needed to.

I sat cross-legged on a cushioned bench beneath the terrace archway, cradling a mug of tea, steam curling upward like a slow exhale. Stefan was across from me, legs stretched out and bandaged ribs carefully protected by a worn hoodie. He looked tired, a bit thinner, but alive—and for now, that was enough—a stark reminder of what could have been. But I'm trying hard not to think about that.

Gi leaned against the wrought-iron railing, sipping wine and watching the sun ease toward the western hills. Her face was flushed from the warmth, eyes soft with quiet affection.

We were safe. All of us. And we were together.

Silence stretched for a few minutes, but it wasn't uncomfortable. It was the kind of silence that comes only after surviving a storm together. I didn't want to sour the moment with what happened to me, but I knew I couldn't put it off any longer. The longer it stewed, the harder it would be to tell them.

"I, uh... almost didn't make it either," I say finally, my voice low but certain I needed to get it out. Stefan turned to me, eyebrows drawing together. Gi looked up from her glass.

I swallowed the heavy lump in my throat that had been building the last few days, waiting to tell them what happened to me. I didn't want to worry about me, but keeping it from them wouldn't be right either. "Just after I got the call about you, I was a mess. I fell apart and missed the deadline for my art submission. And before you say anything about it being your fault. It's not." I look at Stefan with my best stern face. "There was a deep pain already brewing inside me, and it just snapped. A troubled part of me I could no longer keep in or hidden. I had to face it. And I did."

Playing with the edge of the lukewarm cup, I pushed through the tension in my chest. "I drove to the beach to put some distance between me and the pain I was feeling. I was caught in a storm at the beach, thinking I saw someone in the ocean drowning, so I jumped in." I looked up at them, seeing their faces muted with shock. "The waves pulled me under. But luckily, Adrian saved me."

I left out the whole '*I was seeing myself from my childhood*' bit because that was just for me. And probably for my future therapist.

The words hung in the air, quiet but heavy.

"I didn't tell you before because I didn't want it to be about me. But... I think I needed to say it. To *admit* it. I've been pretending I'm fine for so long that I forgot what it felt like to break. And to be *found* again."

After many years of avoiding love, because of what it took from us, from my parents—I was learning that love wasn't the culprit of separation. It was avoidance. I avoided taking care of myself properly and getting the help I desperately needed. But no more. Talking about it instead of pushing uncomfortable conversations down, is the fresh start I need.

Gi walks over and kneels beside me, pressing her forehead gently against mine. "You're not alone," she whispers. "None of us is. We are never alone, as long as we have each other. You can lean on us, Eve. We can take it. Stop carrying everything."

Stefan lets out a long, slow breath. "Hell of a way for all of us to reset." He grins, and though it's lopsided and pained, it was real. "I mean, between cliff falls and ocean drownings, I think we've got the dramatic trauma market cornered."

We laugh, and the tightness in my chest finally loosens. I look at my brother and sister, tears brimming in my eyes. But this time they were soft, not heavy. For a moment, nothing else matters.

"We're kind of a mess," Gi says, settling next to Stefan and reaching for my hand.

"Yeah," Stefan adds. "But we're *our* mess. And we made it through."

"Well, I wouldn't have characterized my honeymoon as a mess; I'm doing pretty well compared to the two of you." Gi declares, as she often does with her optimism. We all laugh.

"Touché, sis, let's keep it that way." Stefan squeezes both our hands and brings us in for a hug, then immediately regrets it, crushing his bruised ribs. "Oof, didn't think that through."

We sat together, bruised, healing, whole in the ways that mattered as the sun dipped lower in the sky, painting the terrace in amber. Birds chirped in the nearby cypress trees, the warm breeze carrying the faint scent of lavender, earthy and content.

For the first time in years, I felt like I could breathe. Really breathe.

Not because the pain was gone—but because I knew now the past didn't have to define me. I was meant to live free this whole time, and I'm not going to waste any more time doing so.

And as the light slipped gently into the evening, we stayed like that. Not clinging to the past, but letting it go.

Together.

"My Romeo"

After saying goodnight to Gi and Stefan, I wandered into the Villa's studio to finally look at my painting. The studio door creaked open with the familiar groan of old hinges, as I stepped over the threshold, my feet bare.

It smelled of paint, linseed oil, and memories of late-night paint sessions coupled with moments of Adrian holding me up against the wall in passion and need. Early mornings were enriched with coffee and pastries while Adrian brushed his fingers along my skin just to see the line of bumps that followed. I smile into the space, almost feeling his hands on me now.

Everything was just as I'd left it. Brushes rinsed but not put away, my well-worn apron still draped over the chair, paint-streaked palettes lining the shelves.

But the easel stood empty.

The space where my painting had once lived—the one that nearly broke me and brought me back to life—was bare.

My breath caught in my throat.

I shuffled quickly across the room, my feet thudding against the cold tiled floor. I touched the edges of the easel, as if the painting might still be there, just invisible. My chest tightened.

No. No, no, no—Had someone taken it?

Had I somehow misplaced the only thing I poured everything into?

Panic rose in my throat like seawater, acidic and cold. My mind raced—*Did I leave the door unlocked? Did someone think it was discarded? What if—*

"Looking for this?"

I turn around at the sound of Adrian's voice, breath hitching.

He stood in the doorway, holding a small envelope. His eyes, warm and steady, locked on mine. My voice wavered. "Adrian—where's my painting?"

He takes a step closer, offering the envelope with both hands, almost reverently.

"I had it delivered," he says softly, eyes full of warmth. "Framed and packed properly. It's en route to Florence. One of my contacts at the Art Institute owed me a favor. I... may have pulled a few strings."

I blinked, completely still.

"What?" I whisper, my eyes darting back and forth.

He smiles, not smug, but proud—of *me*. "It deserved to be seen. You deserve to be seen. And I wasn't going to let it rot in silence just because life tried to drown you."

Tears welled in my eyes. "You did that... for *me*?"

His gaze softens, and he reaches out, brushing a curl from my cheek. "*Tesoro*, I'd do it a thousand times over. You have no idea how extraordinary you are. Watching you paint that... it was like watching someone stitch their soul back together."

Emotion crashes over me in waves—shock, disbelief, and deeper still. *Certainty.* I reach up, cupping his face with trembling hands, heart pounding as I search his eyes.

"I love you," I blurt out boldly, the truth falling from my lips, breathing life into those three little words. "*Ti amo, my Romeo.*"

There's a pause—heavy and raw.

Adrian releases a heavy breath, his smile growing slow and radiant, like dawn spreading across his face. "About damn time," he whispers, voice rough with emotion.

And when he kisses me, it's not out of urgency or fear—it was with reverence. Steady. A promise written in warmth and all the ways two people choose each other, even after the storm.

I fall deeper into that truth, his warmth, and into this moment of clarity.

After each storm, each chapter of uncertainty, it feels like the future stretches out before me—bold, bright, and finally *mine*.

*Ours.*

# Chapter Thirty-Eight

## "Trencadis"

"Broken Pieces"

*Three Months Later*

The afternoon sun spilled its golden light over the rolling hills, bathing the vineyard in the warm glow that only Tuscany could conjure. A long table was draped in soft linen beneath strings of lights that swayed gently in the breeze. Laughter floated in the air, mingling with the aroma of roasted garlic, fresh basil, and the sweet tang of crushed tomatoes simmering on the stove inside Nonna's kitchen.

After many weeks of planning and moving, I was finally living in Italy. A dream I didn't know I wanted, but I can't imagine my life anywhere else. This is where I want to be. And even though I turned down the opportunity to attend the Art Institute after I was accepted, I discovered that my heart was in a different place after all that happened. I wanted to open an Art Center for any artist going through pain or trauma. I wanted to help by creating a safe space to land and create, just like Arian did for me.

I stood at the far end of the back yard next to the elaborate gardens, barefoot in the grass—a wine glass in hand, my sundress swaying just slightly in the breeze. My cheeks were flushed from laughter and sun, my heart impossibly full. This is what happiness feels like without waiting for the metaphorical shoe to drop. Freedom is in letting go of control and living in the present moment.

*La dolce vita.* The sweet life.

Adrian's Nonna, small but sharp-eyed, waves a wooden spoon like a conductor's baton as she bosses Gi and Nikki around the kitchen, muttering in Italian and letting out the occasional exasperated *"Dio mio!"* when someone stirs too slowly.

I let go of a laugh, a smile gracing my face often these days. *Mom and Papa would have loved this.* I think to myself. I grab hold of their memory and remind myself of all the good they created instead of harboring the past in the shadows. I still get sad. My heart still aches at the thought of my inner child ever feeling abandoned. I've created the habit of physically hugging myself every time I think of *her.* The thought of her suffering tugs at my soul. I don't see her anymore, and that's okay. I know she's found peace within me.

I have found peace.

Out on the lawn, Arlo prowls through the herb garden, completely at home. He's spent the last few weeks making it known that he was no longer a city cat. He was a *vineyard cat* now—wild, proud, and absolutely spoiled. Nikki had joked that "The Cat" needed his own passport after the flight, no one could deny he's found his paradise. Matching my sentiments exactly.

Adrian bought his Nonna's house so we could stay in Tuscany. It grew on us all. Josh and Gianna told us they bought the Villa where they were married as a "Summer House," but I had a feeling that once they start growing their family, she will become a permanent resident. I would absolutely love that.

Stefan is already planning his next climbing adventure after being signed by one of the most prestigious brands. Not letting his accident keep him from doing what he loves most. Even though both Gi and I were initially nervous, we knew he was living his best life, and we did not want to stand in the way of that. He deserved to live his big dreams, too. We are proud of him and his tenacity.

In what feels like hours but really was adequate time, Nonna makes her way outside and lays out a feast with the help of Josh, Gi, and Nikki. Its colors stand out against the linen. Fresh-cut fruit in pottery bowls, meats and cheese on fine china, with fresh figs cut open. And Nonna's famous pasta dish, with enormous amounts of garlic and fresh basil —the main attraction —sits in the middle. Everyone stands nearby, ready to eat what smelled like heaven.

Josh takes a step back as Gi lifts her glass from the table, raising it high. "To family! The ones we're born with, and the ones we pick up along the way."

"To Tuscany!" Nikki added. "And to Arlo, who survived an eleven-hour flight without scratching me once. That's personal growth." She raises her glass while Arlo continues to roll around in the herb garden. Pretty sure Nonna put catnip in there. That cheeky woman.

Everyone laughs as Arlo saunters over and flops beneath Stefan's chair, stretching like a king who owns the estate. Adrian moves behind me, his hands gently finding my hips. "This," he whispers in my ear, "feels like something out of a dream."

I turn to him, my smile soft. "That's because it is." I give him a kiss and whisper against his ear. "I never thought I'd live this kind of joy. Not like this."

He returns my kiss, slow and deliberate, taking a measured breath. *"Il mio respiro.* My Breath. *Tesoro.* My treasure. *Dimmi che mi ami.* Tell me you love me." Adrian breathes while holding me in reverence. I will never get tired of him speaking in Italian. So romantic and endearing.

"I love you," I whisper back. Kissing him over my shoulder, our mouths dance in a slow dance only we know the music to. Our own rhythm ignites between us. He looks into my eyes a second before pulling away as a quiet hush falls over the table. Adrian steps forward, his hand finding mine without hesitation.

"I know everyone's been enjoying the wine," he says, his voice warm, light, "and probably thinking, don't *let the romantic Italian start a speech.* But... I need a brief moment of your time."

I blink, my heart skipping a beat. My siblings exchange wide-eyed glances. Nikki's jaw drops slightly. Adrian turns to face me fully, holding my hand in both of his now, his voice steady and quiet beneath the golden canopy.

"I almost lost you," he says. "And in those terrifying moments, the only thought I could hold on to was—*please, let me have more time. More time to love her.*" Tears burned my eyes as he knelt, sunlight catching in his dark hair, and a hush settled over the vineyard like the earth itself was listening. "Eve, you taught me that art is born from pain, but also from joy. That healing is messy and beautiful. That love isn't perfect—it's brave. And I want to be brave with you for the rest of my life. I know we barely know each other, but I know enough. I know that I want to spend the rest of my life getting to know you more deeply. Just more of you. *Vivi solo una vita.*"

He pulls out an elegant vintage ring—something understated, something *me.* A filigree band that reminds me of the lush gardens, and in the center, a simple solitaire cradled in a hexagonal halo. It's perfect. "Will you marry me?"

My other hand covers my mouth, and for a moment, I am speechless. I nod through the tears, my smile trembling. "Yes," I softly reply, then louder, laughing through my tears. "Yes!"

Cheers erupt around the table. Josh and Gi hug, and Stefan jumps to his feet, sending an alarmed Arlo back to the gardens, where it was safe. Nikki squeals. Even Nonna claps from the back door, muttering an approval in Italian as she wipes her hands on her apron.

Adrian stands, wrapping me in his arms as the lights flicker above like stars. The vineyard and everyone—all blur in the background as I press my forehead to his.

"I love you," I whisper, holding him as though nothing else mattered.

His lips find mine, capturing them slowly, softly, like the first stroke on a new canvas.

And in that moment, surrounded by the laughter of family, the scent of rosemary and wine, and the warmth of a setting sun, my heart bursts at the thought—*this was the masterpiece I'd been creating all along.*

These messy, fractured pieces created a beautiful Mosaic of light and shadow, of joy and heartache. All the pieces that make up my life are put together by the love of family and friends.

Together, we create a Mosaic of life.

No piece is the same, and none can be duplicated.

Messy and beautiful just the way we were.

*La fine.* The End.

# EPILOGUE

## "Trencadis"

*Tuscany, One Year Later*

The sun hovered low on the horizon, casting a rich, honeyed glow over the rolling hills of Tuscany in late September. Wild poppies dotted the fields like bursts of flame, stealing the last bits of Summer. Laughter spilled from the open doors of an old stone villa set on a hill with a panoramic view—now lovingly transformed into *La Casa dei Frammenti*, or *The House of Fragments*.

I stood in the open courtyard, hands dusted with flecks of grout and gold leaf. A mosaic shimmered on the curved wall behind me—an intricate swirl of broken glass, shattered teacups, chipped porcelain roses, and sun-bleached pottery. It wasn't perfect, but that was the point. Each piece, donated by someone in the community, had a story. A memory. A past.

And now—reborn—it serves a bigger purpose.

*"Trencadis"* carved at the base in Italian, which stands for *"broken pieces."*

Anyone who comes to this place can create what their heart desires in one of the many art rooms or the open, shared spaces filled with easels, paints, canvases, or simply visit the small gallery and bistro on the property. It's a dream come true for both Adrian and me. After getting married in a very small and intimate ceremony at the same Villa as Gi and Josh now own, we started right away searching for the perfect spot for our art center.

Here we are. *Finalmente.*

I shift my gaze slowly across the gathering crowd. Artists from Florence, local schoolchildren with paint on their cheeks, travelers who had heard whispers of our creative sanctuary tucked away in the hills. A smile forms easily on my face as I take in our community. Friends and families from near and far rallied with us to get this place completed.

All of a sudden, I feel a set of masculine arms come around me from behind, grounding as always. He sends hot kisses down my neck with labored breaths, accompanied by a deep chuckle on my sweaty skin. "*Tesoro.*"

"Mmmmm. Keep doing that." I slide my hands along his corded forearms, his white shirt rolled at the sleeves, smudged with charcoal—proof of a full day spent helping our visiting artists set up. His eyes sparkled as we looked out over the crowd.

"Think they'll come back tomorrow?" he teased, voice low.

A laugh bubbles out of me. "They haven't even left yet, *Romeo.*"

He held me tighter, kissing my temple. "They'll always come back. Because this—what we've made—it's been *needed.*"

"Definitely. I want it to be the start point for someone, anyone who ventures back to a starting line they didn't see coming or having to plan for." I say, thinking back on when I feared starting over and wanting a safe place to begin again.

"*Si vive una volta sola.* You only live once." Adrian reminds me of one of Italy's most precious sayings and mottoes to live by. "I'm the luckiest man to experience this life with you, Evolet."

I turn in Adrian's arms, wrapping my arms around his neck and say—surprising him, "*La dolce vita.*" The sweet life. After a healthy dose of newlywed bliss, a love I am quickly learning will never fade, no matter the length of time. We make our way near the back of the courtyard, where Nonna sits proudly in a chair she insisted on bringing from home, a cane resting at her side.

Even though age hit her hard over the last year, she was still her fiery self. She helped with the gardens and food, of course, and she's lived with us in her own little cottage on the property. She didn't want to bother us too much after we were married, but still wanted to care for her gardens—Arlo became her sidekick. I think it's because of the catnip, but I'm not complaining. We are all living our best lives.

Our sweet life.

I met Adrian's parents when they attended our wedding. But they are still a little estranged; they are simply settled in their life in Puglia. Maybe someday they will join us for a longer stay.

Josh and Gi chatted nearby, glasses of lemonade in one hand and a hand cradling her belly with the other. It's no surprise they are expecting; both wanted to start a family soon, and they found out the honeymoon went a lot better than they expected. Nikki—now officially an Inernational Event Coordinator—sat on the mosaic steps with one of the locals, a Negroni in hand, no doubt. She bounces back and forth between Boston and Tuscany until she finds her next big thing. I would be lost without her.

A bell chimed softly from inside the gallery, and the guests quieted as Adrian stepped forward, offering his hand. "You ready?"

I looked at the mosaic wall, my voice steady but reverent. "Yes."

I took a deep breath in and let it out before turning toward the gathering of like-minded creatives and artists. "Thank you all for coming today and sharing our creative space with us. This place was born from brokenness," I began. "Not just mine, but all of ours. The cracks we try to hide, the mistakes we carry, the losses that never leave us." I pause, letting my eyes sweep the crowd. "We built *La Casa dei Frammenti* to remind every artist, every soul—your broken parts don't make you unworthy. They make you art."

The crowd murmured with emotion.

Adrian stepped forward beside me, his hand brushing the edge of the mosaic.

"We invite anyone who enters these doors to take what's been broken and reimagine it," he said. "This is a space not just for painting or sculpting, but for *becoming*—whatever that means for you."

A small girl from the village raised her hand. "Even if I don't know how to draw?"

I smiled. "Especially then."

Laughter rippled through the group, warm and light.

Later, as the sun dipped behind the olive trees and the lights strung above the courtyard flickered on, Adrian and I stood beside each other, watching as the first guests began their own mosaics. They are bent over shards of sea glass and porcelain, arranging chaos into beauty.

"I didn't think this was possible," I whispered, leaning into his side. "A year ago, I was drowning."

Adrian kissed my hair. "And now you're teaching people to breathe again."

I let the breath go, steady and slow.

Together, we watched the evening bloom with shards of light, bursts of color, abundant joy—rising from the pieces once believed could never be whole again.

And in every shattered shard now shining in the walls around us, there was a quiet truth stitched into the mortar.

*We are not less because we are broken.*

*We are more because we survived.*

*"La vita va avanti"*

*Life goes on.*

# ACKNOWLEDGEMENTS

Oh my gosh, we did it!

Although this might not be the best work of fiction, it's mine, and no one can ever take that away from me. With that said, I never thought I would see the end to the never-ending tunnel of writing, edits, more edits, and even more edits. I wrote this book over the course of two and a half years, and in that time I learned the how-tos of writing, found my writing style, and developed a voice beneath it all. Imposter syndrome reared its ugly head at every turn during the biggest healing journey of my life. I've lived with chronic pain my whole life, but I didn't realize it could get worse as I aged. There were many dark days and even darker nights, crying and begging the universe to take away my pain.

Shadows lurked in the corners, physically and mentally. It was one of the hardest challenges to work through and heal. This story actually started as journal entries to help me through my darkest moments. I bled my heart into this beautiful character, *Evolet,* and she became my reminder to *breathe.* The hardest part about trauma is that it can come out of nowhere. I wanted to write about childhood trauma in this way, as well as depression. So, if it seems like Eve's darkness came out of nowhere, it's because it did the same for me. One of the funniest comments my editor made about Eve was, "Girl, your toxic trait is knowing all of your toxic traits." And that made me laugh out loud. Because I've felt that way a time or two when feeling helpless, but I still did nothing to help my healing journey. Whether it be that I was too exhausted from existing or I wasn't in a healthy place, sometimes I just wanted to wallow.

This is Eve's story, but it's also mine and anyone else's who's felt broken, lost, and overwhelmed by life. Our chaotic experiences, messy vulnerabilities, and uncomfortable emotions—our jagged ends are a collaboration of our crazy beautiful stories. Stories worth telling, sharing, and exploring. Only when we are willing to explore the darkness and let go can we truly embrace our messy, fractured pieces. To heal. To learn and appreciate what makes us human. Because without the darkness, we cannot discover the infinite power of our light. Our vulnerability does not make us weak... it ignites our most sacred desires and feeds our innermost passions. That passion propels us forward toward infinite possibilities.

You are a masterpiece, a beautiful Mosaic, made up of a collection of memories, experiences, good and bad, raw emotions, and choices that have led you to where you are now. This book is a reminder to go after your dreams even when they are scary or feel out of reach. You never know what is on the other side of your comfort zone! To my readers, thank you for taking a chance on my debut novel. I hope you enjoyed this book and you've found at least an ounce of your beauty in it. I'm so proud to share it with you. This book will forever be my heart book, and I hope to only grow from here with my future stories! Thank you so much for taking a chance on Eve's story. It means the world to me, more than I can ever say.

And of course, I could not have finished this book without a mighty support system behind me! First and foremost, my husband, Isaiah, who has stood by my side and felt every roller coaster of emotion, heard every rant, has held me through my darkest moments and endless tears. You are truly my rock! To those who thought that Adrian may be too good to be true, it's because I've had that type of love and devotion in my hubby. Blame him. Lol. I also have to acknowledge my two beautiful daughters! They have been my cheerleaders every week, every month, and through every insecurity. I've done an insane amount of healing, so they didn't have to carry my "baggage."

Yes, this book was about generational trauma as well as childhood trauma, and though I had my fair share, I wouldn't be who I am today if it weren't for my Mother's strength and fortitude to survive in harsh circumstances. Our life wasn't easy, but I am grateful for it. And that's all I want to say on the matter. I want to thank my sister, Alisha, who is my ride-or-die, best friend, and biggest supporter. Thank you for checking up on me frequently and encouraging me to write. I love you, sissy, always and forever. To the rest of my family and friends, thank you for being at the beginning of this journey with me and celebrating every milestone!

To my incredible Alpha readers, thank you for walking beside me through every messy draft, stubborn plot holes, and bearing with my horrible use or lack of commas. And here I thought I was an okay writer... You have to start somewhere. To my amazing and thoughtful Editor Laurynn, your encouragement turned edits into growth, and your belief in this story kept me believing it, too. I'm endlessly grateful for your time and the heart you poured into these pages. This book is better because of you. To my dear author friend Christina, thank you for being the steady voice that reminded me I could finish this, even when I wasn't so sure. Your encouragement and wisdom carried me through the hardest pages. I'm endlessly grateful for your friendship and for the way you believed in this story right alongside me. I couldn't have done this without you.

To my wonderful writers group, thank you for every sprint, every patient answer to my million new-author questions, and every moment you lifted me out of doubt. Your support turned this journey into something joyful and possible. I'm so thankful for the community we've built and for the way you showed up for me, again and again. This book exists because of you. And to my Barnes & Noble family, thank you for cheering me on through every shift, every "someday I'll finish this book," and every moment I doubted I could. Working beside fellow book lovers reminded me why stories matter, and your encouragement helped carry me from bookseller to author. I can't thank you enough for the support and laughter you gave me along the way.

I can't wait to share more stories with you! All my future books will be Romance books as well but I will be skipping around genres, with Dark Romance, Modern Fantasy, Romantasy, and even a High Fantasy trilogy! I have so many plans and I am breathing them into existence, even if it takes me the rest of my life to do it. Thank you again for your willingness to step into my stories. I look forward to being your next favorite Author!

With love,
*Melissa Carter*

## About the Author

Melissa is a hopeless romantic and longtime storyteller, using imagery as a photographer for over 13 years, until recently, when she trusted her own voice to write the emotional stories she's always wanted to write. Melissa loves to read Romance and Fantasy above all else, and is a big Indie Author supporter. When not writing, she loves hiking with her favorite companion, Amara, a Catahoula Leopard Dog full of love and personality. She lives in her hometown in Montana with her hubby and two daughters, but hopes to one day live in the PNW, where the other half of her soul lives with the ocean and forests. She's a Taurus after all, and cannot escape the deep, calming color Green that is her branding color. She's gone from photographer to bookseller, and now Author and hopes to one day be a bestselling author.